SHADOWS
OF **DOUBT**

ALSO BY MERISSA RACINE

Silent Gavel

SHADOWS OF DOUBT

A CRAWFORD MYSTERY

MERISSA RACINE

WIND DRIVEN PRESS

ISBN (print) 978-0-9993033-2-0
e-ISBN 978-0-9993033-3-7

Cover Design by Izabeladesign at fiverr.com
Book Design by Maureen Cutajar

For Gabby

Chapter One

" *I* am old, Mr. Phillips. Not senile." Margaret Archer squared her rounded shoulders as she glared at the attorney who had been questioning her since nine o'clock that morning.

"Mrs. Archer, no one is accusing you of being senile." The attorney gave the elderly woman a practiced polite smile.

Feisty old lady. Lauren Besoner smiled inwardly as she captured every word spoken on her stenograph machine.

"Oh, but I think you are, young man. I have sat in this uncomfortable chair …" Margaret looked at her attorney "… no offense, John. You have a nice conference room here, but really, these chairs are not meant for sitting in for such a long time."

John Whitmore, her lawyer, nodded. "Sorry about that. But be thankful we're not at the courthouse. At least mine are upholstered."

Lauren wanted to raise her hand in agreement. She'd sat in plenty of uncomfortable conference room chairs for depositions, but knew the hard oak chair used for witnesses in the courtroom was much worse.

Mrs. Archer returned her attention to the short, stocky lawyer sitting across from her. "I've been answering all your questions. Correctly, I might add. And now? Now you're asking me the same questions over again. Do you remember the first few questions out of your mouth this morning?"

"Mrs. Archer —"

"I do. 'State your name and address.' And I answered you. And 'How many times have you been married?' I even answered that question though only the Lord knows what that has to do with the reason why I'm here. And now here we are at," she looked at the watch on her bony wrist, "ten-thirty and you're asking me again where I live." She crossed her arms over her chest. "Either you're the one with the poor memory, or, more likely, you're trying to trip me up. And I refuse to sit here any longer and have you waste my precious time."

Margaret Archer's clear gray-blue eyes focused on her son Raymond Newell, who sat next to his attorney, Mr. Phillips. "I'll answer the question one last time. I live in Crawford, Wyoming. Always have. And today's date is still May tenth. And I'll save you the trouble by also saying a half hour from now it's still going to be May tenth."

"I've explained to you at the beginning of the deposition," said Mr. Phillips, his dark-framed glasses shielding the amused expression on his face, "I need to confirm a few —"

2

"Yes, yes, I heard what you said earlier but at this rate if you keep dragging this deposition out – is that what you call what we're doing here, John – my answer will have to be May eleventh."

Mr. Whitmore laid a reassuring hand on his client's thin forearm. "Let him ask another question, Margaret." He looked at Mr. Phillips. "I haven't objected to your redundant questions but my client is correct. If you have any other questions that haven't already been asked, please continue."

The woman brushed her lawyer's hand away. "John, I'm sorry but I have had quite enough of this. He's just having me answer questions he already knows I know the answers to." She snatched up the doctor's report that lay on the table between them, turned to the last page, and tapped a gnarled finger at the last sentence. "'Patient is oriented as to date, time and place.' What more proof do you need?"

"It's not my intent to upset you, Mrs. Archer. Your children are concerned," said Mr. Phillips. "As I explained earlier, they've hired me to make sure you can still manage your affairs."

"How? By asking how old I am over and over? It was embarrassing enough having to go to a doctor and answer all his questions. And now this? I feel like I'm on trial and my freedom is at stake."

"Your children only want what's best for you." Kevin Phillips spoke in a calm, cajoling tone, as if explaining something to a toddler. "They don't want anyone to take advantage of you. That is all this is about, I assure you."

Mrs. Archer ignored his explanation. "Less than an hour ago you asked me how old I was. I told you I was seventy-nine." Margaret gestured with her hand to Lauren. "I'm sure this nice young lady can confirm that for me. But if you keep repeating the same questions over and over, who knows, we might be here celebrating my eightieth birthday. And heaven forbid we are." She turned to her lawyer. "John, remember, I like chocolate cake." She cocked an eyebrow at her own comment, the sharpness in her eyes momentarily erasing the deep-set wrinkles in her face, revealing the attractive woman she had surely once been.

Lauren wrote on her machine, suppressing yet another smile. This lady definitely has all her faculties, she thought, but three of her four children wanted a court to declare her incompetent. Today's proceedings were meant to elicit whether Mrs. Archer was capable of taking care of herself. It was a serious matter, but the woman's uncensored remarks were refreshing amid the dry legal setting of a deposition.

"And as far as being taken advantage of, that's hogwash. I'm quite capable of fending for myself. What my children want – what you two want," Margaret turned to her son and daughter and shook the sheath of papers as she spoke, "is control of my money, control of my land. You're all tired of waiting for me to die. The only one I can count on is Millie. At least she's not part of this ... this ambush."

She fixed her gaze on her son and added, "And you, Raymond, you have no room to talk about being taken advantage of. If you only knew ..." Margaret's voice trailed off.

"We're getting a little sidetracked here," said Mr. Whitmore.

Raymond Newell, Crawford's chief of police spoke up. "Mother, how could you think —"

"And," Mrs. Archer's voice quivered as she turned her attention back to Mr. Phillips, "they've hired *you* to convince a court I'm incompetent and need a guardian when *all* of you know darned well I don't." Margaret pushed the sheaf of papers across the table, stood and started for the door.

Mr. Whitmore set his reading glasses on his legal pad, rose and followed his client. "This is a good time for a break." Over his shoulder he said, "Let's take about ten minutes, Counsel."

Lauren started to scroll through the transcript on her laptop, looking for proper names she needed the correct spellings of.

Mr. Phillips waited until Mr. Whitmore and Margaret were out of the room, then turned to his clients. "This is good. This is what we want to show a judge, that she's —" He stopped speaking and looked at the court reporter.

Lauren felt the silence and looked up.

"Would you mind?" Mr. Phillips nodded toward the door.

Well, you could all leave and talk somewhere else. "Of course not." Lauren understood attorneys needed to speak with their clients alone in order to maintain their attorney-client privilege, even if she weren't part of their conversation. She closed the lid of her laptop and left the conference room.

Chapter Two

*A*fter using the restroom Lauren walked into the reception area and over to the paralegal's desk.

"How are things going in there?" Emma tilted her head toward the conference room while keeping her focus on her computer screen and typing.

"It just got a little heated. That's the reason for the recess."

"There's a fresh pot of coffee in the break room. Can I get you some?"

"No thanks." When Lauren first started out as a court reporter, she quickly learned to decline offers of coffee during a deposition. Once questioning of a witness was underway, she had no time to drink it. By the time she had a chance to take a second sip, the coffee was always cold.

Emma and Lauren chatted for a few minutes until the phone rang and Lauren took it as her cue to leave Mr. Whitmore's paralegal to her work.

She returned to an empty conference room, sat and pulled her phone out of her messenger bag and checked her email. There were six new messages, none of them requesting her court reporting services. She dumped the phone back in the bag and slumped in the chair.

A moment later she straightened in the seat and began to scroll through the transcript on her laptop, jotting down proper names on the back of the Notice of Deposition that she needed the correct spellings of.

Margaret Archer entered the conference room with a fresh cup of coffee.

"Mrs. Archer, if I could get you to look these the names you testified about earlier, and give me the correct spellings." Lauren turned the sheet of paper toward the woman who picked up a pen and went about crossing through some of the names and replacing them with the correct spellings.

When Margaret finished, she turned the sheet around and slid it over to Lauren. "I'm sorry for my little outburst earlier." She smoothed her skirt and looked at Lauren. "Do you have children?"

Lauren shook her head. "No."

Mrs. Archer looked toward the open doorway. "They certainly can be a disappointment. If Ray's father were still alive he would be absolutely appalled at what he's trying to do."

Lauren didn't have a response so said nothing, sitting in the awkward silence.

Margaret cocked her head. "You look familiar. Have we met before?"

"I was thinking the same thing." Lauren had been thinking the same thing ever since the deposition started.

It suddenly dawned on her. "I've seen you at the animal shelter. I volunteer there."

"Yes, yes, that's where it must be. I'm a board member. Past board member. I was in charge of coming up with fundraising ideas." She smiled at Lauren. "You volunteer there. That's so generous of you. It's nice to meet a fellow animal lover."

"Same here." Lauren thought back to the few times she'd seen Margaret at the shelter and returned the smile. "You used to bring cookies from Dominick's Bakery, didn't you?"

"I did. I just love, love Dominick's. *So* much better than the grocery store bakeries. We're lucky to have him in our town."

"I agree. I go there all the time. We've probably seen each other there and didn't even realize it."

"I'm sure you're right. So you do this," Margaret pointed to Lauren's writer, "and also volunteer. How long have you been a … a stenographer, is that what you call what you do?"

Lauren nodded. "Yes, stenographer or court reporter. Going on nine years almost." *Where did the time go? Feels like I just graduated.*

"Does the schooling for it take long?"

"It varies. Once you learn the theory – the basics of how to write on the machine – the rest of the time you're working on building speed. That can take anywhere from a year to three."

"Such an interesting profession. You must hear all kinds of things."

"I do." That was the most common remark she heard during breaks when polite conversation was being made.

"I've lived to be almost eighty without ever having heard the word deposition, much less have to *give* a deposition." Margaret shook her head. "I could go another eighty years without ever doing this again."

Mrs. Archer was about to say more when Ray Newell and his half sister Vera Mann filed into the room, followed by Kevin Phillips, their attorney. Margaret visibly tensed, then pulled herself tall in the chair.

Everyone returned to their seats and the questioning resumed. Mr. Phillips's inquiry changed from Mrs. Archer's competency to questions about Newell Ranch.

"Do you run the day-to-day operations of the ranch yourself or do you have help?" asked Mr. Phillips.

"When Ray's father was alive we ran it together. After he passed away I hired a ranch manager."

"Who was that?"

"Dallas Black."

"Is he still employed by you?"

"Yes."

"How long has he been in your employ?"

"Objection, relevance," said Mr. Whitmore.

"You may answer," said Mr. Phillips.

Margaret raised an eyebrow at her attorney.

"Unless I tell you otherwise, you can answer his question. The judge will sort out all the objections at a later time."

Mrs. Archer nodded at his explanation, then turned to Mr. Phillips. "Too many years to count. Thirty or so, I believe. After I married Charles, Dallas left my employ. But I rehired him after Charles and I divorced."

"And I'm sorry if you told me previously, but was Mr. Babcock your second husband or third?"

Margaret let out an exaggerated puff of air. "Charles Babcock was my second husband. Harold Archer, Millie's father, was my third." She smiled at some distant memory before returning her focus on Mr. Phillips.

More questions were asked about the ranch. She explained how she and her first husband started Newell Ranch.

Lauren was impressed by the woman's memory for details as to exact years when adjoining land was acquired, from whom, and the amounts paid for each parcel of land. Mr. Whitmore sprinkled in objections in between Mr. Phillips's questions and Mrs. Archer's responses, but he let his client answer after he spoke up.

"And it's true you own the mineral rights under your land?" asked Mr. Phillips.

"Objection. That question has no relevance to the matter at hand." Mr. Whitmore leaned forward and spoke to Mr. Phillips. "We're here to establish my client's competency, Counsel. That question is totally irrelevant."

"Your objection is noted." Mr. Phillips gave a dismissive smile to Mr. Whitmore, and said to Mrs. Archer, "You may answer the question."

Mrs. Archer narrowed her eyes as she said, "Yes, I own the mineral rights."

"And you have an oil and gas lease agreement that allows Blackstone Oil to drill and extract that oil, do you not?"

"Don't answer that, Margaret," advised Mr. Whitmore.

"On what basis, Counsel? May I remind you this is a deposition and not a trial," said Mr. Phillips. "I have a wide latitude in the questions I ask."

"And may I remind *you* this is not a fishing expedition. Your questions should be directed to her competency and nothing else."

"I think this is relevant to her competency." Mr. Phillips turned to Mrs. Archer. "You have to answer my question."

"No, she doesn't." Mr. Whitmore tossed his pen on his legal pad. "You have been given great latitude in asking my client questions that have nothing to do with her competence. But that stops now. So if you don't have any more questions relating to her ability to make sound decisions, we are done."

Lauren, fingertips poised on her machine, waited for someone to speak.

Mr. Phillips scrolled through his laptop screen, brown eyes intent on whatever he was reading. After a moment he straightened. "Do you know a Nicholas Fisher?"

"Yes, I do."

"He owns the land adjacent to you, on the west side of your property?"

"Yes. He inherited it from Malcolm, his father."

"Has he offered to buy your ranch?"

"Objection. Don't answer, Margaret."

"I have a right to ask these questions. You can object but she has to answer," said Mr. Phillips.

"She doesn't have to answer if I instruct her not to, and that's what I'm doing," replied Mr. Whitmore. "If you don't like it, take it up with the judge."

"I will. I'll be filing a motion with Judge Jenkins to compel and we'll be back." Mr. Phillips added, "With you footing the bill for the second round."

"Only if you prevail," replied Mr. Whitmore, "which I doubt you will. But I look forward to seeing your motion. In the meantime, if you have other *relevant* questions, go right ahead and ask."

Mr. Phillips blew out an exaggerated breath. "No further questions. Until next time."

Mr. Whitmore looked at Lauren. "And we have no questions."

Lauren closed her realtime feed, turned off her machine and gathered the doctor's report which had been marked as an exhibit to the deposition.

Mr. Phillips powered down his laptop. "Ray, Vera, I'll meet you outside. I just need to use the restroom before heading back to Cheyenne."

"Margaret, let's talk in my office." Mr. Whitmore stood, tucking his legal pad under his arm.

Mrs. Archer reached out a weathered hand to Lauren and smiled, the creases around her eyes deepening. "It was nice to meet you, Lauren."

Lauren shook the woman's hand, surprised at its firm grip. "Nice meeting you as well."

Ray Newell hoisted his bulky frame out of the chair. Vera Mann remained seated, her red painted lips pinched together as she eyed her mother. There was little resemblance to her mother with her round puffy face and small brown eyes. Throughout the morning Lauren wondered if Ms. Mann were in the throes of menopause, as she sat next to her brother fanning herself with a copy of the doctor's report that was provided to everyone.

Mrs. Archer ignored her children and started to walk out with her attorney. She stopped just outside the doorway, turned and spoke to Ray and Vera. "You both disappoint me. I don't think I'll ever be able to forgive you for bringing this ridiculous lawsuit." She added, "And since your brother Lawrence isn't here, you can pass this along to him. You will get control of *nothing*. I'm going to see to that."

"Mother, don't be –" Ray began, but Mrs. Archer turned and walked out of the room.

Vera looked at her brother and huffed. "Didn't I tell you this wasn't going to be easy? She's going to fight with us every step of the way, the stubborn old –"

Ray Newell nudged his sister. "We'll talk about this later," he whispered.

Mrs. Archer's voice could be heard as she and her attorney walked down the hallway toward his office. "Yes, John. I have no doubt my decision was the right one, a new trust definitely ..."

The sound of Mr. Whitmore's office door closing swallowed up the rest of Margaret's words.

A new trust? Had Mrs. Archer beaten her children to the punch and already made arrangements for where her money, her land, her whole estate would go? She glanced at Ray and Vera. The siblings made eye contact with one another, then quickly turned their attention to Mr. Phillips. The look in their eyes made Lauren shiver inside.

Chapter Three

The old Coachman lumbered out of the drive, Aunt Kate smiling and waving goodbye. Lauren went to the Volvo and grabbed her overnight bag. She slammed the trunk shut and looked around, her gaze stopping at the unobstructed view of the snow-covered peaks of the Medicine Bow-Routt National Forest.

Maverik and Helga lay on the porch, back-to-back, mouths open, tongues dangling loose, panting in unison. Lauren smiled. "Finally met your match, haven't you, Maverik?" A soft slap of her dog's tail against the wooden planks answered her question.

After Mrs. Archer's deposition, Lauren came home and grabbed what she needed for the extended stay at Kate's ten-acre parcel out in the county. The request to take care of her aunt and uncle's alpacas, and Helga, their dog, while they took a little road trip, was perfect timing. Lauren hadn't disclosed to her aunt the recurring nightmares she'd been having. They left her drained of energy and irritable, even if there was no one around to be irritable at. So at least for the next few days she would get much-needed rest. She planned to use the time here to think what it would take to get her life back to normal. *I need normal again.*

"Maverik, come." Once inside, she trudged up the carpeted steps with her bag of essentials and several changes of clothes still on their hangers. The guest bedroom looked the same as it did when she spent time recuperating here seven months ago. She placed her things by the bed, sat on the mattress and bounced a few times, testing the firmness of the bed. It was as she remembered. Soft.

She walked to the window and peered out into the fading daylight. The view offered a direct line of sight to Detective Overstreet's property. Sam's long drive wound its way behind his house to his large shop, its doors open, lights on. His Dodge pickup sat parked next to the police-issued Ford Explorer, his new patrol vehicle he got to take home when he wasn't on duty at the City of Crawford Police Department.

"Maybe we'll drop by later, say hi. Or have him over for dinner? What do you think?" Maverik spun around a couple of times, his tail touching his nose. "Okay, okay. But I said *maybe.*"

Lauren leaned against her aunt's kitchen sink rubbing her cheek while the coffee pot gurgled, and thought about the nightmare. Maverik had jumped on the bed nudging her in the side until she woke. It took a long moment to realize she was in Aunt Kate's and Uncle Jack's guest room, not in her basement, smoke and flames engulfing her. Only then did her beating heart slow its frenzied pace.

Her mind foggy from lack of sleep, she went through the routine of pouring a cup of coffee and taking a sip. Sleeping in a new location hadn't squelched the nightmare's return. She closed her eyes and let the steam from the coffee reach her cheeks.

Maverik trotted into the kitchen, sat by her side and looked up at her expectantly. "Claude was right. I need to see someone." When Lauren confided in her best friend about the recurring nightmare, her response had been quick: "You need professional help." She had stated it as a fact, without sarcasm.

Lauren set the coffee cup in the sink, went upstairs and dressed. She stuffed her pajamas and toiletries in the overnight bag. Since her plan for a few nights rest was now history there was no point in sleeping here.

Helga and Maverik chased each other while Lauren checked on the alpacas, making sure they had fresh hay and water. She patted Helga. "Maverik and I will see you later. You two will have plenty of time to play together." She stood by the barn door, pulled her hoodie tight and looked out toward the horizon at the sapphire sky awaiting the sun's arrival.

❋ ❋ ❋

At home she showered, put on a long-sleeve T-shirt and sweats, and went into the kitchen for something to eat. She pulled a blueberry yogurt from the refrigerator, topped it with a handful of Lucky Charms, then went upstairs and powered up her laptop. She opened the file with Mrs. Archer's deposition and began the process of editing the transcript. Thinking of the woman, Lauren smiled to herself. Margaret Archer had held her own with Mr. Phillips. He tried to trip her up, tried to prove she was easily confused. All his attempts failed. There was something to be said about being old and saying whatever you wanted, no longer constrained by politeness.

After an hour of editing, Lauren took a break and checked her email. There was one from Mr. Phillips's paralegal. She opened it assuming it was a request to provide the transcript ASAP. "Of course, you want it as soon as possible." She shook her head. "You attorneys always do." She opened the email.

Ms. Besoner: Mr. Phillips no longer needs the deposition transcript of Mrs. Archer. Please bill us for an appearance fee for yesterday's deposition.

She turned from the computer screen and stared out the window not focusing on anything. No transcript needed. She turned and looked at the small table next to her desk. On it was a printer and an inbox with unpaid bills. Seven months ago she was an official reporter, with a salary. Now a freelance reporter, her income went up and down like mood swings. Unpredictable.

Her phone rang, and she backed away from the mini pity party she was about to enter.

"Hello, this is Lauren Besoner."

"Hi Lauren. It's Emma. Have you heard from Mr. Phillips's office today?"

"Yes, I just got an email. They don't want the depo transcribed." Lauren tried to keep the disappointment out of her voice.

17

"Did the email say why?"

"No."

Emma lowered her voice even though Lauren imagined she was alone in the reception area if she was talking with her. "Mrs. Archer was found dead last night."

"Dead? Oh, my gosh! What happened? Did she have a heart attack or something?"

"No. John told me Dallas Black, her ranch assistant, found her last night. John said she'd been killed. Attacked in her home."

"Attacked? How?"

"I don't know any details."

"Attacked," repeated Lauren. "That's awful. Did you know her well?"

"No. She'd been a client of John's since before I started working here. She didn't come in much. Well, not until recently. She'd been in more frequently since the start of the involuntary guardianship proceedings. She was a sweet old lady."

Emma and Lauren spoke for a few more minutes about the death of Mrs. Archer. Emma only knew she'd been found in her kitchen, blood all around her.

"I've got another call coming."

"Thanks for letting me know what happened, Emma."

"Of course." Emma lowered her voice again. "I wouldn't be surprised if that family starts fighting over the woman's will. But you didn't hear that from me."

"From what I heard yesterday you're probably right."

"But if there is another lawsuit, you'll be number one on my list to call if we need a court reporter."

"Thanks, Emma. I appreciate that." Lauren ended the

call and stared at her computer screen thinking of Margaret Archer. Before yesterday she had forgotten that she knew the woman with the silver hair, and the deeply lined face, no doubt acquired through years of ranching in Wyoming's brutal climate. But by the end of the day, she felt like they had a connection, their mutual love for four-legged friends. She liked her. And now the woman was dead.

Chapter Four

The deposition transcript was still open on the computer monitor. Lauren closed the file and swiveled in her chair. "Great. I don't have any transcripts to work on. That's not good, Maverik. Not good at all." Hearing his name, her dog got up from under the desk and nudged his muzzle into her lap. She pressed her face against his, grateful for his presence, then ruffled his fur.

Downstairs, Lauren opened the kitchen door. Maverik bounded onto the back porch, sniffing at the brisk morning air. Something caught his attention, a bird or rabbit. Or maybe the wind rustling the cotoneaster bushes with their new budding leaves. Whatever it was, he would be content to run around for a while.

With the morning no longer filled with work, Lauren stepped into her garage and flipped the switch for the overhead fluorescent light above the mini workbench she built with her father's help. Or more like her helping him. She was grateful for his expertise, making the bench small enough to where she had room to pull her car all the way in and still be able to work on small projects.

She opened the playlist on her phone, scrolled to Chris Stapleton's "I Was Wrong," docked the phone on the speaker above the bench and listened to the voice, deep and rich, as he sang about how sorry he was for his thoughtless words.

While Chris lamented about the mistake he'd made, Lauren turned to her latest attempt of breathing new life into a beetle-killed pine tree. The small bookcase would be getting its third and final coat of polyurethane. Lauren opened the can of varnish, waved away the strong fumes before dipping a clean paintbrush into the milky substance. She started on the top with long steady strokes over the faint blue hue of the pine. Each pass of the brush removed a layer of stress. Stress of not enough work. Stress of hearing about the passing of a nice old lady. By the time she started on the bottom shelf, the morning's events had dulled, leaving her only with thoughts of how a tiny beetle could fell a pine and change the mountainous landscape around southeastern Wyoming forever.

She took a step back from the bookcase, checking for any thick streaks of varnish. Satisfied there weren't any, she went inside, cleaned her brush in the sink with soap and water, and set it upside down in a glass to dry. With Maverik inside, she went upstairs, changed into jeans and a clean T-shirt, then shoved her arms into a brown hoodie with the University of Wyoming bucking bronco logo stamped in gold on the front. "I'll be right back. Be a good boy."

The drive into downtown Crawford took ten minutes exactly, something she knew from her five-days-a-week drive to the courthouse when she was Judge Brubaker and Judge Murphy's court stenographer.

It was after one o'clock when she opened the door to Dominick's Bakery. She raised her eyebrows at the sight inside. One table was occupied. All the rest were littered with dirty plates, crumpled napkins and used silverware. *That's not like Dominick.* She walked up to the glass case which at this hour usually still held a few muffins and pastries but today was bare except for a lone danish.

Dominick, the owner, came out from the back, wiping his hands on a towel. He didn't acknowledge she was there.

"Hi, Dominick."

"Oh, hi. I'm about to close up. What can I get you?"

No, 'How's my favorite customa this morning'? The ever-present smile was absent from his round face and he had dark circles under his eyes. "I'll take that last danish and a pistachio latte."

The last of the lunch customers, two women in business attire, stood to leave. Dominick didn't give his usual, "*You ladies enjoy the rest of your day*" parting comments.

He placed a white sack with the danish inside on the counter and turned to make her drink order.

Lauren tried for small talk. "Looks like you've had a busy day."

Hector, the baker's assistant, appeared carrying a large gray plastic tub. He nodded hello to Lauren, before walking over to the closest dirty table to begin the cleanup process.

Dominick turned back to her, handed her the drink, then looked out at the sea of dirty tables. He shook his head. "I've been gone most of the morning. It's been too much for Hector to take care of by himself."

His words surprised her. She'd never known Dominick to be absent from the bakery.

"You haven't heard, have you?"

Lauren shook her head. "Heard what?"

"Danny's been arrested. For the murder of Margaret Archer."

"Arrested? Holy – that's terrible, Dominick. Why do they think Danny killed her?"

"I don't know. He's a pizza delivery driver. Works nights." He shrugged. "That's where I've been, down at the sheriff's office. I was trying to explain they musta made a mistake, that they got the wrong guy. My nephew is no killer."

"I know the woman you're talking about. I just took her deposition yesterday." *I still can't believe she's dead. And they've already arrested someone. They arrested Dominick's nephew.*

"She's a regular here. Sweet as can be."

"She did seem nice."

He slapped his hand on the display case. "Damnit. They won't let me talk to him, Lauren." Dominick paced behind the counter, tossing the bar towel from hand to hand as he went.

Lauren pulled out her credit card and the baker stopped his pacing long enough to run her card through the machine. "Do you think there's anything you can do? I mean, I thought since you're involved with the court system and all..."

Me? "I – I don't think there's anything I can do. Being a court reporter doesn't really carry extra weight, or any weight when it comes to the police. I'm so sorry." She was at a loss as to how to help her friend. "I could ask Sam, Sam Overstreet. He's a friend of mine. Maybe he can tell me what's going on. Since he works for the Crawford Police Department he probably knows someone at the Albany County Sheriff's Department, someone that might be willing to share information." It was the police chief's mother that was killed, thought Lauren. The detective on her case would keep Chief Newell updated. Maybe he'd share that with his detective. "Are you sure he's been arrested? That they're not just questioning him?"

"I'm sure. First-degree murder. That's all Sheriff Wolfenden would say. I'm going back there as soon as we close up."

Lauren nodded. "Maybe by then they'll let you talk to him. Or maybe they'll have found out some more about the situation and change their minds about charging him." *Why did I say that? There's no way that will happen.* It hurt to see one of the nicest guys she knew in such pain. With her drink and danish in hand, she walked toward the door. Hector looked up as she passed. They made eye contact. He shrugged, as if he too couldn't offer any comfort.

Chapter Five

"Well, look who's here," said Gunner. The deputy's solemn face broke into a wide grin when he spotted Lauren in the queue to go through the security checkpoint before being allowed to go further into the historic courthouse.

Lauren felt herself relax a little at his remark. *This gig will be okay.*

"What are you doing here?" he said. "Oh, wait, I know. You must be filling in for Zoe in the murder trial, right?"

"Yes, I am." Lauren set her steno writer on the mini conveyor belt, followed by her messenger bag containing her laptop, and then the small dolly she used to carry them with. She passed through the metal detector and set the

25

alarm off. She stopped, raised her arms out to her side and let herself be wanded.

Gunner approached her and whispered, "I have to do this with all visitors. Sorry."

"No need to apologize. You're just doing your job." Lauren knew she was nothing more than another visitor to the courthouse, no longer an employee, a part of the judicial staff. She gathered her equipment off the conveyor belt.

"How long do we have you for?"

Lauren hit the up button on the lone elevator. "Zoe will be out for about six weeks."

"It'll feel like old times seeing you here." He gave her a thumbs-up.

"Yeah, old times." Seeing Gunner Hart would be the upside of old times. She enjoyed their playful banter when she used to work here. It was one of the things she missed.

The elevator let out a soft ping, stopped, and its doors opened to the second floor. As Lauren walked past the media room, she saw a young man setting up his camera equipment. He wore a jacket with the logo of a Cheyenne news station on the back. Daniel Throgmorton being on trial for the murder of Mrs. Archer was big news for Crawford. She wondered if he knew he would not be able to film the jury selection process. Maybe he was just practicing so when he was filming, it would be a smooth process.

Lauren inhaled, then exhaled slowly, shaking off the nervousness which returned on the short elevator ride, opened the door and entered the familiar office space.

Susan Mumford, the judge's judicial assistant, looked up from her desk. "Oh, Lauren, how nice to see you."

"Hi, Susan."

"It's been *so* long." Susan spoke as if they were old chums from high school who hadn't seen each other in years, when, in fact, it had been ten months since Lauren left her position here as official court reporter.

"We'll have to have lunch while you're here. You can tell me what's been going on in your little world." Susan's voice sounded chipper but the deep creases around her eyes and mouth told a different story. The roots of her hair showed a half inch of gray. Lauren wondered if it was by design to let her hair go natural or if she was too busy to keep on top of her personal appearance.

"That – that sounds good." Lauren shifted the bag on her shoulder. "Do you have the file? I need to take a look at the witness list."

"Of course, of course, but first …" The judge's judicial assistant pulled out a clipboard, along with a key attached to a large metal keychain. If it had a chunk of wood on the end of it it would look like the ones Lauren remembered from childhood, when her father would take her and her sister Stacy on road trips and they stopped at a gas station to use the restroom.

"Just sign here." She handed Lauren the clipboard. "We have to sign the key in and out. New security rules. You understand."

"Sure." *I am, after all, just a visitor.* Though she wondered how many people, if any, used the key to access the courtroom from chambers and the court reporter's office.

"The key is just until I get you a temporary badge ordered from IT. You should have it this afternoon. I was going to do that last week, but it has been so hectic around here I just didn't have time."

Just like you didn't have time to send me any information about the case. Same old Susan.

The judicial assistant stood. "Now, where is that file?" She made a big production of scanning her desk and the credenza behind her. "Oh, right. I have to get it off of Judge Jenkins's desk." She waddled down the hall to the judge's office in her too-tight skirt.

Lauren waited at Susan's desk for a minute. When she didn't return, Lauren called out, "I'm going to get set up in the courtroom and I'll come back for the file."

Lauren entered the courtroom, stood for a moment, and surveyed the cavernous space. It looked the same as when she was employed here. *It's a courtroom. Of course it's the same. What did you expect?*

She sat, fired up her laptop and pulled the stenograph machine out of its case and set it on its tripod. Her – or rather Zoe's chair was the same one she used to use. She pulled the stenograph writer close to her. The court reporter's chair was adjusted to Zoe's height. Lauren pulled the handle on the side and lowered the seat as far as it would go. Better.

An old adage suddenly came to her. *You can't go home again.* Did that also apply to returning to a job that you never expected to leave?

She shook her head to escape the melancholy that crept into her thoughts and stroked the date on her machine to get the realtime feed going on her software. She then turned toward the bench, stood on her tiptoes to log into Tony's computer using the password he taped in plain sight next to his microphone. With the court reporting software open on his laptop, up popped the date she had written. The hookup was a success. Her jaw muscles relaxed.

For the briefest of moments she expected her old judge, Judge Brubaker, to walk in. Funny, she thought, not Judge Murphy, the judge she worked for last. Lauren told herself it was because Jane Murphy hadn't been a judge very long before she was killed.

Satisfied everything was hooked up and working like it should, she returned to the judge's chambers to retrieve the court file from Susan.

"I don't know why that young man just didn't plead guilty." Susan handed Lauren the thick red file folder. "We have to waste all this time and money when I know he's going to be found guilty."

Innocent until proven guilty. Or have you forgotten how the law works, Susan? "Well, that's for the jury to decide."

"And our docket is so busy. For the next few weeks we have to squeeze other short matters in over the lunch hour. You're going to be one busy bee."

"Thanks for the warning. Is Tony in yet?"

"Yes. But don't forget," Susan said, her voice singsong, "it's Judge Anthony Jenkins now."

Lauren gripped the file tight. *Of course it is.* "Judge. I'll try to remember that." She made her way to what once was her office. She had called Tony many things over the years. After their divorce and learning what he'd done, some not very nice things. *Judge* would be just one more name to add to the list.

Lauren stowed the leather messenger bag under Zoe's desk and looked around. She moved the many *Congratulations on your new bundle of joy* greeting cards from the desk and set them on top of the filing cabinet.

Other than the view outside – which used to be her view she thought – and the desk and filing cabinet, it didn't resemble the space she once laid claim to. Zoe had taken the time to decorate with knickknacks and photos of her husband and their young family. The new coat of paint in a soft blush of pink was not something she herself would have ever thought of, but it worked in this space, making the office inviting.

In the courtroom, with the caption, jury and witness list in hand, Lauren set about entering names and words unique to the trial into her job dictionary. Her old habit of coming in early and preparing for the trial served her well today.

Since she was no longer the official court reporter, she had no access to the court's electronic filing system. An email to Susan sent last week asking for the juror list, witness lists and exhibit lists went unanswered. The judicial assistant's reply came only after Lauren emailed her again. Susan said she would send all the information by Thursday morning. Friday morning arrived and there still was no email from her. Susan's work ethics hadn't changed. Too busy avoiding work to get any work done. Why Tony kept her on as his assistant when he took the bench was a mystery Lauren didn't have time to ponder. With the trial starting in less than an hour, she had to hurry and finish her prep work. It was a reminder that not having to work with Susan every day was a positive thing in her life.

"Good morning, Lauren." The defense attorney laid his briefcase on the table, snapped it open and pulled out a small laptop.

"Hey, Eli. I didn't hear you come in."

He held his hands out, wriggled his fingers. "Quiet, like a mouse I am. Or is it a snake?" He grinned. "If you're here, that means Zoe must have had her baby. It's good to see you. It's been a while."

"It has been, hasn't it? I'm looking forward to hearing your amazing, spot-on objections."

"You know me. Never at a loss for words."

"Do they teach you that in law school, to never be at a loss for words?"

"If you mean being able to answer any question a judge asks you, then yes."

"And did I ever tell you how much I appreciate that you don't spew them out at three hundred words a minute?"

"I don't think you ever have. That sounds *really* fast. Is it?"

"Uh, yeah. Too fast. Thankfully most people speak slower than that."

He smiled at her. "I'll have to try and keep up the good work then. Wouldn't want to disappoint a former client of mine."

"Thanks. It's very much appreciated." Lauren met Eli Dresser when she hired him to represent her in her divorce three years ago. Tony offered to prepare and file all the necessary paperwork for their parting of ways and make it as painless as possible. He wanted out of the marriage. She assumed it was his way of making himself feel better. She would have taken him up on his offer except Aunt Kate insisted she at least talk to a lawyer first before agreeing to let Tony handle everything.

With Eli's help she avoided paying more than her fair share of credit card debt the two had accumulated during their relatively short marriage. And with his help made sure she received her half of the refund from their tax return. After her divorce she moved to Denver, then returned to Crawford a year later, where they ran into each other at the courthouse. He told her about his recent breakup. They met for coffee to commiserate about ex-spouses and became friends. She learned he had been a year behind her ex in law school at the University of Wyoming.

He looked at his watch. "Why are you here so early?" He pulled a file from his briefcase, then glanced at her. "We don't start for another hour."

"Because –"

"Oh, I know why. You couldn't wait to see me."

"Yep, that's what I was going to say. Nothing gets past you." She looked at her laptop. "Plus, I needed to get set up."

He nodded understanding.

"And what about you? You're here pretty early yourself."

"I'm going back to talk to my client." He gestured with his head to the hallway leading to the secure holding area. "They should be bringing him over from the jail any minute." Eli approached her desk. "What are you writing? We're not even on the record yet."

"Just adding names to my dictionary. Your client's name is Daniel Throgmorton. Daniel is in my dictionary, but Throgmorton isn't because I never had that name come up. I'm adding it, at least for this job, so that way it will come up correctly when Tony – I mean when the Honorable Judge Jenkins – reads his realtime screen."

"Makes sense. Sort of." Eli came to the side of the desk, leaned in and watched as she wrote on her machine.

She motioned with her head for him to watch her laptop. THROG MORE TON appeared on her screen. From her steno machine Lauren tapped on some keys, and soon the name Throgmorton appeared in their place.

He watched again as the untranslated word THROPLT came up on the laptop screen, and after two keystrokes from her writer it also turned into Throgmorton.

Lauren looked up at him. "See? So easy even an attorney could do it." She laughed at her own joke.

He raised one shoulder. "I think I get it. But I'll leave that little magic machine to you." Eli straightened. "So tell me, what's it like working with your ex?"

She shrugged. "Today will be the first time I've worked with him since he came on the bench. Ask me when the trial's over." Lauren breathed in the just-showered scent Eli gave off and now surrounded her workspace.

"I will. We'll have to get together for coffee."

"Sounds good. Assuming Tony hasn't driven me crazy before then. In which case I might need something stronger than coffee."

"Well, we are *drinking* buddies. Who's to say it can't be a beer?" Eli raised a shoulder and walked back to the defense table, his black hair iridescent as a raven's feathers

33

under the fluorescent lights. Over his shoulder he said, "It'll feel like old times seeing you here."

"You're the second person who's told me that today." She smiled to herself, then spread the list of jurors' names in front of her. She looked at him. "I'm looking forward to working with you."

The door to the judge's bench opened and Judge Anthony Jenkins walked in. The next keys Lauren hit on her steno writer didn't translate into any actual words. She reminded herself this was just another job, just another judge. No reason to be nervous. If she let her emotions get in the way she risked writing like crap. Crap her ex-husband would read on his computer screen.

"Good morning, Your Honor," said Eli.

"Good morning, Mr. Dresser. How are you today?"

"I'm well, thank you. I was just going to check and see if the deputies have brought my client over from the jail." Mr. Dresser retreated through the door leading to the holding block, looking like a tall, gangly adolescent who'd outgrown his going-to-church suit, with too much cuff and wrist exposed.

"Lauren, it's good to see you. Thank you for being available to help us out," said Tony, his tone all business.

"Happy to," she swallowed hard, "Your Honor. I'm glad it worked out." What could she say? The truth? Work had been so slow she was desperate enough to accept a job knowing it meant working daily with her ex?

"We're going to keep you very busy for the next few weeks."

"Susan warned me." Lauren turned her attention to writing on her machine, continuing to add names to her dictionary, hoping Tony would take the hint that she still had work to do before the trial started.

"There shouldn't be any late nights involved, but I plan on using some of our lunch breaks to hear any motions that the parties need to make out of the presence of the jury. I hope that won't be a problem for you."

"Susan gave me a heads up so no, no problem."

"And there might be one or two half-hour motion hearings in other cases that we might have to do during the noon hour, but I'll make sure you have time to eat something."

Lauren nodded. "Thanks. I'm here to cover whatever you have on your docket."

Tony leaned over the bench and spoke as if there were someone in the room who could overhear. "This will be my first murder trial. I am stoked." He grinned. "And it should be an easy win for the prosecution."

"The realtime is going, we're all set."

"Good, good. I've come to rely on the realtime Zoe provides me. She's such an awesome court reporter. Now I'll get a chance to see who writes better, won't I?" Tony wriggled his eyebrows, then looked at his monitor, missing the look of annoyance in Lauren's eyes.

She gritted her teeth. *We've been together less than five minutes and I'm already regretting taking this assignment.* The accolades bestowed on Zoe shouldn't have bothered her, yet they did. Lauren knew herself to be a good reporter, but Tony had never witnessed firsthand her realtime capabilities. In less than an hour from now he would.

You had your chance to work for him. Her ex-husband had offered her the position when he was selected as the new judge, though she suspected he only offered it to her know-ing she would say no. His cheating behind her back had been a huge blow to her self-esteem and made it impossible to ac-cept his offer. The loss of a steady paycheck was the price she paid, something she was reminded of at the end of each month when bills assailed her mailbox and inbox.

And now she had the uneasy feeling she would be com-peting with the awesome Zoe. Lauren didn't like the path her mind was on. Self-doubt. Nervousness. Irritation at her ex-husband. She lassoed in any further negative thoughts and continued prepping for the trial.

"Excuse me! I don't know who's speaking," Lauren called out. Seventy-five prospective jurors sat in the gallery. She spoke her annoyance to the special prosecuting attorney. The process of selecting a jury was underway. Within fif-teen minutes this was Lauren's third interruption because Ms. Martindale didn't identify the juror by name after they had raised their hand. Instead, she jumped right in asking questions leaving Lauren struggling to know who spoke. *I am NOT a mind reader.*

Jennifer Martindale stood at the podium, running a chubby finger down the list of names in front of her. "That was Juror Melenkovich. My apologies, Madam Reporter." The prosecutor did an actual head shake, her dyed blonde hair brushing her shoulders as she did so, as if literally brushing off Lauren's interruption.

Despite the head shake, the prosecutor from that point forward announced the name of any juror she was about to speak to, with an occasional raising of an eyebrow toward Lauren, as if to ask, *Satisfied?*

"Ladies and gentlemen, the state must show the how, the where and the when Mrs. Archer was killed. But we're not required to answer a big question everyone has. The why. Why she was killed. Why did the killer do it. Raise your hand if you need the state to answer the why, if you need that answered before you can convict the defendant." Ms. Martindale searched for any raised hands in the jury pool but found none.

"Like I said, we're not required to answer the why, but in this case you will hear the why. You'll hear evidence that it was to obtain drugs for this defendant's habit. Drugs Mrs. Archer had in her home."

Lauren watched the jurors' expressions, some raising their eyebrows, others turning to look in the direction of defense counsel table where Mr. Throgmorton sat.

The judge had not put a time limit on either the state or the defense for how long they could question the potential jurors, so it came as no surprise to Lauren that Ms. Martindale was still at the podium, conversing with the jury panel at noon when everyone was excused for lunch.

Chapter Six

$\mathcal{L}$auren exited the courthouse, strode down the court-house steps as fast as her high-heeled clad feet would allow. She took in several deep breaths to calm herself. With the prosecutor talking fast and some jurors not wanting to speak up, the morning's proceedings had been difficult to report. Lauren walked the two blocks to Dominick's to pick up her lunch. When she rounded the corner she saw all the umbrellaed tables at Dominick's were occupied, customers taking advantage of eating outside in the perfect fall day. Inside, the sounds of conversation and the clinking of cutlery on plates mingled together.

Lauren stood in line and looked around the shop. Dominick spotted her and held up a white sack containing her online lunch order, motioning with his hand to come ahead of the others in line. He met her at the end of the counter opposite the cash register.

She held out her credit card but he waved his hand, dismissing her offer to pay. "I got this one, young lady."

"That's not necessary, Dominick."

"Hey, it's my store, I can do what I want. Am I right?"

"Yes, you're right. And thank you. But you really shouldn't."

He rested his toned forearms on the high counter and lowered his voice. "How's the trial going?"

Lauren stopped at the bakery last Thursday, and while picking up a scone mentioned she would be covering the trial. "It's moving along, but it's a big case. I don't know if we'll have a jury picked by the end of the day. The state is still questioning the jurors."

"How's the state's attorney doing so far?"

"I'm personally not thrilled with Ms. Martindale but it has nothing to do with the case. I'm having a hard time taking down what she says. She's a mumbler. I hate mumblers. I like people to speak clearly. I'm sure they don't teach that in law school, public speaking. It's like she's afraid of the microphone." Lauren looked at Dominick. "I'm sorry. That's not what you want to know. As far as how the case is going, it's way too early to say. I'll have a better feel for how she's doing once she gives her opening statement and starts questioning her witnesses."

"How's Danny holding up?"

"He seems okay." She didn't want to tell him her focus had not been on his nephew at all. Her attention was funneled to the members of the jury and whoever was speaking at the moment.

"I want to be there for him. I just can't get away from the store. I can't leave Hector alone. We're just too busy."

"I'm sure he understands. And it's early. You don't need to be there for the voir dire."

"For the *what?*"

"The jury selection process. That's what it's called."

"Then speak a little plain English here, would ya, please." He raised an eyebrow, and for a split-second Lauren caught a glimpse of the easygoing Dominick.

"What do you think of his lawyer, Eli Dresser?"

"He's a good attorney." She had no sense of Eli's skills when it came to a homicide case, but in the weeks to come she would soon find out. Lauren hoped the words she said to Dominick would turn out to be true.

"I told my sista I'd be there to support Danny. I ain't gonna let her down. Plus, I want him to know he's got someone in this town on his side. He didn't do this. No matter what the cops say, I know my nephew, and he's no killer. He did not kill the police chief's mother."

Lauren nodded. She wanted to tell him about what she'd learned from the deposition she took several months ago of Mrs. Archer, that her and her children were in the middle of a contested guardianship, her children drawing lines and taking sides, and it wasn't pretty. Lauren considered there might be motive tucked away amongst the weeds and was tempted to say as much but being a professional she knew she should not be giving out information in a case or be giving the baker false hope that someone in Mrs. Archer's family may have somehow been involved in her death, especially with nothing to back the idea up with.

If she did divulge any information about the Archer/Newell discord, it might innocently leak out, spread like wildfire through town, and land on Chief Ray

Newell's doorstep. Lauren had no doubt he would connect her to the information going public. He might be the type to harass her about it, or worse, tell his attorney. It could cost her future work.

It made her wonder who benefitted from Mrs. Archer's death the most. Or if there would be a fight amongst her children regarding her estate. Lauren had not been hired to cover any more depositions in the matter since Margaret's death. Maybe the family was waiting for the trial to be over to start litigation. She knew the woman's demise would likely heighten the bickering amongst the siblings. She'd seen it in lawsuits before. If anything, there would be one more reason to fight. They could now fight over her will. Or maybe everyone got what they wanted and were happy with their mother's division of her property.

"I can talk to my friend Claude," Lauren said. "She works in the county attorney's office. Maybe she has some information that might be helpful."

"Thanks." Dominick cocked his head at the full-to-capacity seating area. "I better go give Hector a hand."

Lauren looked over her shoulder at the growing line of customers. She gestured to the white sack. "Thanks again."

"For my favorite customa, any time."

Back in the judge's chambers, Lauren stored half of the turkey, bacon and avocado sandwich in the break room refrigerator, saving it for the afternoon recess, along with half of a lemon blueberry scone she didn't order but yet somehow made its way inside the bag.

On her way into the courtroom she told herself she would do what she could, look through any police reports that were put into evidence. Maybe, just maybe, there would be something inside them to help Daniel Throgmorton.

Chapter Seven

"All rise," the bailiff called out. It was five fifteen. Lauren stood by her writer and watched the jury exit the courtroom. She rolled her shoulders, moved her head left and right, releasing the tension's tight hold on her neck. Once the jury pool was escorted from the courtroom, she closed out the file on the stenograph writer, gathered the jury list and seating chart and paperclipped them together. The sound of the double doors opening made her look up.

Sam Overstreet came to the low wooden gate and stopped.

Lauren took in his attire, open-collared gray button-down shirt stretched across his chest, black slacks and broken in cowboy boots. "Hey Sam. What's up?"

"Thought I'd come up, see how the trial was going"

"It's been okay. I'll be glad when voir dire is done. It's always the hardest part of a trial. For me anyway."

"Are you covering the whole trial?"

"Yes."

He watched her as she continued to tidy up her work area.

She looked over at him. "Did that shelf work for you? I haven't seen you since you bought it ."

"I found the perfect spot for it in my hallway. And thanks again for the great price."

"I wasn't sure what to charge. It's my first time selling anything like that." On Labor Day weekend Crawford's downtown retail district hosted a Before the Snow Flies Fair. Both ends of Main Street were closed off, and shop owners put their merchandise outside on folding tables. Artisans and crafters set up tents in the parking lot across from the train station at the far end of Main Street. Lauren brought a few pieces of her beetle-killed pine collection to sell out of her aunt's alpaca wool booth.

Sam bought the last piece left, a small shelf. He said he needed it but Lauren thought he was just being kind. With nothing left to sell they went in search of food and drink, stopping at a local food truck, ordering pulled pork sandwiches, his piled with coleslaw, hers plain.

"That was some seriously good food they had." He patted his stomach.

"I was thinking the very same thing. The owner should open a restaurant, never mind a food truck. I bet they'd do great."

"How's work? You been busy?"

She cocked her head at her steno machine. "I left for Lander right after Labor Day. Had a few days of depos there. You know my motto, have writer, will travel."

"So I've heard you say." He nodded toward the jury box. "Got a jury yet?"

"No. I'm thinking they'll have one seated by the end of the day tomorrow. Which is a good thing. The jury pool is dwindling."

"What do you mean? Are you going to run out of jurors?"

"No, no. We started with more than normal so we're good. I was just joking." Lauren backed up the day's trial to the cloud. "Chief Newell is on the witness list. I wish I knew what day they were going to call him."

"Why?"

"I was planning on calling in sick that day."

"I know. You're just joking." Sam shook his head. "He hasn't talked about the case. But I can tell he's anxious. He hasn't been his usual self."

"Is he someone new and improved?"

Sam raised an eyebrow at her.

"Sorry. That wasn't very nice of me. His mother was murdered and here I am badmouthing the man." Lauren flashed the detective an insincere smile. "I'll save my comments for after the trial." Last year Chief Newell had been pushing Sam to arrest Lauren for the murder of Judge Murphy. It was a sore spot for her and knew it would take a long time to get over, if she ever did.

"Good idea."

Lauren glanced around her workspace, checking to see if anything needed to be taken to Zoe's office where it would be more secure. She tapped a key on her computer, confirming it was turned off, and placed the jury list face down on the closed laptop.

The bailiff walked over to them. "If you don't need anything from me Lauren, I'll be leaving."

She smiled at him. "I'm good. Thanks, Charlie. See you in the morning."

"You want to grab a bite to eat? My treat." Sam asked.

"I don't know. Maverik has been home alone all day. Unless I want to clean up more of my shredded dirty socks and other … things, I better go home."

Sam gave her a questioning look.

"He can be a little naughty sometimes. Maybe another time?"

"Sure." The word was laced with disappointment.

"Why don't you come over to my place?"

"No, that's okay. You do look like you've had a rough day."

"I have, but I still have to eat. Might as well eat together. And I can tell you what kind of citizens we have in this town, and what some will say to get out of jury duty."

"Oh, I can imagine. They're like the people I used to pull over for speeding back in my patrol days. You wouldn't believe some of the excuses they had for going so fast. But if you're sure about me coming over."

"I'm sure. I'll warn you though, it won't be anything as tasty as those pork sandwiches we had."

"I'm sure whatever you fix will be fine."

She offered him a sly grin. "My only promise is to not feed you anything moldy and unrecognizable."

"Thank you for that. How about I come by about seven? That give you enough time?"

"Perfect. See you in a little while." She watched him leave, then went to the jury box and adjusted the fourteen swivel chairs so they all faced the same direction. She suddenly felt reenergized and began thinking what she could possibly make for dinner.

Chapter Eight

"Door's open," Lauren called out.

Sam entered the living room and walked through to her kitchen, a six-pack of Budweiser swinging at this side. "You should never – and I mean never – say that when someone knocks on your door, Lauren."

She stopped slicing the celery stalk and turned to look at him. The expression on his face said he was serious.

"We did agree on seven." She pointed, knife in hand, at the clock on the stove. "I thought it would be a safe assumption."

"Well, it's not. You can never be too safe. That's all I'm saying. I know everyone thinks Crawford being a small town, it's safe to leave your door open. But it's not."

"I unlocked it a couple of minutes ago. And Maverik's here. He'd alert me if a stranger tried to come in." Lauren looked at her dog, who had come over to Sam, licking the six-pack container. "I guess you have a point."

She motioned with her head for Sam to take a seat at the small round kitchen table. She pulled plates, napkins and glasses out of the cupboards and set them all on the counter, then chopped the rest of the celery and added it to a bowl of tuna. "I didn't ask you earlier, how was your day?"

"Just another day in the trenches." He twisted off the cap on one of the beer bottles, offered it to Lauren.

She shook her head. "Maybe later."

He stretched out his legs under the table and took a long drink.

"Any interesting cases you can talk about?" She set two plates with tuna salad sandwiches on the table, grabbed a bag of chips from the cupboard, and sat opposite Sam.

"Doing follow-up work. I'm investigating a vandalism at the quarry."

"What kind of vandalism can someone do at a quarry?"

"Destroy machinery. Break windows."

"Oh."

"But they didn't. In this case someone broke into the main office and smashed computers, printers. Upturned a couple of desks. Spray painted a few colorful words on the walls."

"Some neighbor who didn't like the idea of a new quarry in their backyard, you think?"

"Can't say, ma'am. It's still under investigation." He grinned. "But considering what the graffiti was, that's most likely who did it."

"Or," Lauren picked up the line of thought, "it could be some disgruntled ex-employee trying to make you think it was one of the surrounding landowners."

"Did I ever tell you I like the way your mind works?"

Lauren pretended to study the ceiling. "No, I don't think you have."

"Well, I do."

"What else do you like about me?" *Did I just ask that?* "Don't answer that. I was just kidding." She took a swallow of iced tea. "Anyone on your radar for the break-in?"

"Too early. But I'll be out there tomorrow interviewing several of the neighbors whose backyards abut the quarry's. And I'm also working on two late-night robberies recently."

"I heard about them. So scary for the clerks."

"Yes. From the security footage it looks like the same person robbed both truck stops. Hope we catch him before he strikes again."

"You think he will? Or she will?"

"From the footage we're pretty sure it's a male. And yes, they got away with it twice which means they're most likely feeling confident right about now."

They'd finished their sandwiches and Lauren put the dishes in the sink.

Sam took another beer out of the fridge and offered it to her. "Ready for one now?"

"Sure." Her taste buds weren't in the mood for a beer but since he'd brought it over, she wanted to be polite.

He followed her into the living room. Lauren switched on a lamp on the end table and sank into the sofa.

Sam dropped his muscular frame into the opposite end. They sat quiet for a few moments.

"I have to say, you were right." Lauren nodded at him as she took a sip of beer.

"Of course I was." He arched an eyebrow. "But you'll

have to remind me, what was I right about?"

"About going to see Patricia Holland, the chief's wife." Lauren tucked her legs under her.

He looked at her, a blank expression on his face.

"You don't remember. You said if I was having trouble dealing with the aftereffects of what happened to me last year, it might help to talk to someone. And if I did decide to go see a counselor, I should give her a try."

"Oh, right. Patricia – Trish. I remember now. So you took my advice and it's been working out?"

"Yes. You put it a little nicer. Claude just said I need professional help. It took me a little while to feel comfortable opening up to her. It would have been a hard thing to do with anyone, but especially her. When you first suggested I go see Chief Newell's wife, I thought, dang, what the heck have you been smoking?"

"Why? What do you mean?"

"Come on. We both know he doesn't like me. Why would I go see his wife?"

Sam didn't argue. "How long have you been seeing her? If you don't mind my asking."

"About two months. She helped me connect the nightmares I was having with Amanda trying to kill me. That part is obvious. Setting my basement on fire and ..." Lauren's words trailed off. Even after all this time it was still hard to think about what almost happened that night when a crazed Amanda Capshaw showed up at her front door. "Patricia is helping me deal with what happened. I didn't think I needed anyone's help, thought I could handle it on my own, that all I needed was time, and the memory would fade. Turns out I was wrong."

51

He set his beer on the steamer trunk Lauren repurposed as a coffee table and looked at her. "I didn't realize you were having nightmares." His dark eyes offered warmth and compassion, even understanding.

"I really thought they'd go away after a while." She raised a shoulder. "Anyway, Patricia's helped me so much I'm hoping not to need therapy much longer."

"That's great. Sometimes we can all use a little help."

She rubbed the smooth opal that hung on a chain around her neck. "I wasn't sure at first it was a good idea."

"You mean opening up to a complete stranger? Embarrassed that you need help to work things out?"

"Yeah, exactly. How did you know?"

"I'm a detective."

"Well, you're good at what you do, Detective."

"That's why I get paid the big bucks, ma'am."

Lauren giggled. "I'm sure it is. And it helps that she has lunch hour appointments. Saturdays too. I'll be able to continue seeing her while the trial's going on."

"I thought she'd be a good choice. You know she's running for congress, right?"

She nodded. "I've seen her signs around town. No one could miss them, not unless you were driving around town with your eyes closed."

"I don't recommend it."

The corners of her mouth suppressed a smile. Maverik ambled up to the sofa. Lauren patted the cushion and the dog jumped up and lay his head on her thigh. "At our last session Patricia mentioned she's going to close her practice temporarily to focus on her run for office."

"Did you know I put up almost all of the signs you see around town?"

"I didn't know that. So you're helping her with her campaign?"

"No, no, no. That's not my thing. But I like her running platform so I offered to do that much for her." He rested his ankle on his thigh, the heel of his cowboy boot worn down, showing its age.

"I wonder how much it costs to run for office." Lauren wriggled and set her feet on the trunk. Maverik raised his head and looked at her as if to say, *Hey, don't move. Can't you see I'm comfortable?* He lay his head back down.

"I don't know but I did overhear her and the chief talking one day. His mother donated money to get her campaign started. That must have ended when she died."

"I took Mrs. Archer's deposition the day before she was killed. They never talked exact numbers, but she had to be worth a *lot* of money. I'm thinking millions."

Sam nodded. "But I didn't think about Trish's practice. Makes sense that she'd have to close shop eventually, focus all her energy on the campaign." He rested his arm on the back of the sofa. "I admire that she wants to try to help the people of Wyoming. I myself could never go into politics." He waited a beat. "Too much politics."

"Very funny. But I'm with you on that one. Not something I could ever do."

"She wants to make a difference. Maybe she will."

"Or maybe she's running so she won't have to be around her husband so much. How much time does a congressman … congresswoman have to spend in Washington D.C.?"

Sam shook his head but said nothing.

"She already helps people, just on a smaller scale. And thanks to your suggestion that I try her, and me getting help, if I do decide to leave," Lauren looked around the living room, "it won't be because of what happened."

"Leave? You mean sell your house?"

"Yes. And move away." Lauren did a slow head nod at the possibility.

"You're thinking of leaving Crawford? What, the town not big enough for you?" He raised an eyebrow.

Even though his voice was light, Lauren heard the surprise in his question. "Crawford's plenty big for me. Except when it comes to freelancing. There's just not enough work for me here. I still have to travel to make ends meet. I don't mind driving to Cheyenne to cover a job since it's only an hour away. Except in the winter and the highway sucks." She looked at Sam. "So, yeah, sell the house. Move. Fresh start. Maybe move to Casper. I wouldn't have to travel as much if I lived there. I would *never* go back to Denver. Definitely too big for me."

Lauren made circles in Maverik's soft fur with her fingers. "I haven't been in the house long enough to have any real equity, but I hear it's a seller's market. If I don't make a profit, I'll at least break even."

"Why Casper?"

"That's where I grew up. My dad's still there, and my sister Stacy. I know there would be plenty of work for me in either place. I told my aunt I was thinking about moving."

"What does she think about the idea?"

"She told me if I moved, I'd just be running away from my problems, my issues, as she put it." Lauren blew out a breath. "I didn't even mention the nightmares. She worries about me too much as it is."

Lauren hadn't yet told her aunt about seeing a therapist. She wasn't sure why she was confiding in Sam, but her feelings, now given a voice, began to flow, at first like water seeping into cracks in a dam, then bursting through the concrete.

"Maybe Aunt Kate is right. Even without the attempt on my life, I do have issues. She is convinced everything wrong in my life, every bad choice I've made," *mostly about men,* "goes back to when my mom left me – uh, left us."

"Oh, wow. I'm sorry, I didn't know.

"No, don't be sorry. It was a long time ago." Lauren took a deep breath and exhaled slowly. "She dropped me and Stacy at Aunt Kate's house one afternoon, said she was going to the store and would be right back." Lauren leaned over, cupped Maverik's head in her hands, scratching behind his ears. "Only she never returned."

"That had to be tough on you. And on your father."

"It was. He never remarried."

"So he raised you by himself?"

"Yes. He had a lot of help from his sister. Aunt Kate was like a mom to me and Stacy. My dad never talks about it. *Never.* To this day if I try to bring up my mother or that time, he acts like he didn't hear me and changes the subject. It's been years since I even tried."

Sam leaned over Maverik, reaching his hand out, letting his fingertips graze Lauren's forearm.

Goosebumps rose on her skin.

He pulled his hand back and cleared his throat. "That was a good dinner. It hit the spot."

"Dinner? You call that dinner? It doesn't take much to please you, does it? That was just a sandwich. A tuna fish sandwich."

"With celery and lettuce. And don't forget the bag of potato chips." Sam patted his stomach.

"Thanks. But I still won't be quitting my day job any time soon to become a chef." She was happy to change the subject about her past, about her feelings of abandonment. She turned, gazed out the living room window, at the sky turning a deep blue in the twilight.

"How does it feel being back in the courthouse again?"

"Kind of feels like I never left. It's all so familiar. Except for the judge, of course." She reached for her beer and took a sip. "I mean he's familiar but in a whole different way."

"How's he been to work with?"

"So far it's been okay, but it has only been one day."

"I hear you."

"Ask me again in a week or two."

"Do you miss working in court? Being ... what do you call it?"

"An official." She thought about the question. "Yes and no. By the end of a long week – and I know this will be a long one – I'll be leaning toward no. I'll be telling you it's too much work and I'll be happy to go back to freelancing."

"Right now the trial is all anyone around the department can talk about. When the chief's not around that is."

"And I'm sure everyone is convinced Daniel Throgmorton did it, right?"

"Pretty much. Don't you think so?"

"No, I don't. He used to volunteer at the animal shelter. I saw him there a few times."

"I didn't know you volunteer there."

Lauren nodded. "He was awesome with the new arrivals, especially the cats. He just gave off a calming vibe."

"So what are you saying? If he's kind to animals he can't be a killer?"

"Yes. Well, no, but I think he was just convenient. Last one to see her alive sort of thing. Doesn't mean he killed her." She shifted on the sofa. "I didn't know him very well because he quit coming to the shelter. They lost a good volunteer."

"Did he ever tell you why he quit?"

"No. he just stopped coming." Lauren cocked her head to the side. "As you know I was on the receiving end of being suspected of killing Judge Murphy– not arrested, but still ..." She let the words hang in the air as if to say, happened before, can happen again.

"It all worked out, didn't it? You were never arrested. Amanda Capshaw was brought to justice." Sam gave her a half smile. "No harm, no foul, right?"

"Easy for you to say." An unexpected twinge of anger rose inside her. She suppressed the feeling. She didn't want to start an argument over something in the past. Besides, she and Sam would never have become friends if she weren't first a suspect.

"You know what I mean, Lauren. I came to the right conclusion in the end. Remember, I didn't know anything about you when I got the case."

"I know, I know." She sighed. "And I finally realized you weren't the total ass unreasonable detective I thought you were."

"See? We both learned something."

"Yes, we did. And now, to change the subject, I saw Dominick today. Did you know he's Daniel Throgmorton's uncle?"

"The guy that owns Dominick's Bakery, right?"

She nodded.

"Yes, I knew."

"Dominick is also convinced his nephew is innocent."

"Family never wants to admit to themselves that their son or daughter ... or nephew is capable of murder."

Lauren shrugged. "I'm sure you're right, but there weren't any eyewitnesses, so all the evidence is circumstantial."

"And it's all pointing to him."

"But that's only because he was there. There must be other people who had motive. Maybe the sheriff's department quit looking."

"I'm sure they've got a strong case against him or they wouldn't be going to trial." Sam tipped his beer back and swallowed the last drop. "Dinner's on me next time."

"Okay. But I'll be expecting something equally yummy. Do you think you can top a tuna sandwich?"

"I'm sure I could. And I know just the thing. Steak. Elk steak to be exact."

"I've *heard* about your steaks."

"You have? And is that a good or bad thing?"

"Oh, they're legendary, didn't you know?" She laughed. "In a good way. Aunt Kate's told me how amazing they are. Said they're better than Uncle Jack's." Lauren leaned across Maverik and fake whispered to Sam. "She did tell me that when Jack was out of earshot."

"She's just being kind. Though it is one of the few things I can cook."

"A little more involved than opening a can of tuna, I'm sure."

"Not really. It's all about the rub, the spice rub that is. And the flame. Other than that, pretty darn simple." He gave her an emphatic head nod.

She leaned back into the soft-cushioned sofa, looking at the ceiling. "I haven't had elk steak in ages. My dad would hunt every fall when we were growing up. He filled our freezer with elk, antelope, almost every wild game Wyoming has to offer." She smiled to herself. "But I'll tell you, when spring finally arrived, I was *so* ready for a cheeseburger from Wendy's."

"I get it. Does your father still hunt?"

Lauren had to think about the question a moment. "I think he does, but now it's more social, catching up with old friends than it is about filling his freezer. Back then I know the hunting was more a necessity, helped a lot with the grocery bill."

"Well, next time I fire up the grill I'll invite you over."

"I'll be there."

"Unless you'd rather I take you out to Wendy's."

"Hmm." She held her hands out, palms up, pretending to weigh the choices. "I don't know. Such a hard decision."

He placed his hands on his thighs. "Think about it."

"I will."

Maverik jumped off the couch and ran to the kitchen.

"He needs to go out. I'll be right back." She padded out of the room, opened the back door, let Maverik out and waited for him to return. When he didn't come right back, she closed the door and went into the living room.

Sam stood by her front door, ballcap on his head, hand on the doorknob. "It's getting late."

She glanced at her fitness band. "Oh, I didn't realize the time."

"I have an early morning, and I know you do too."

Lauren nodded her agreement.

"Good night." He closed the door. Lauren threw the deadbolt and jiggled the knob to make sure it too was locked. From the partially open living room curtains she watched him get into his pickup. She gathered the beer bottles, emptied hers in the sink, opened the door to the garage and added them in the recycle bin. Maverik scratched at the back door. She let him in and he trotted straight into the living room, circled the sofa, then went to the front door, bushy tail swiping at the air. He turned to look at Lauren as if to ask, *Where did Sam go?* She answered the look on his face. "He's gone."

Maverik sat, head cocked to the left, tail still.

"Don't look at me like that. I don't know what happened. One minute we're visiting, getting along, opening up to each other, and the next minute, eight-thirty is late."

Chapter Nine

The bailiff banged the gavel. "All rise. District court is now in session, the Honorable Judge Jenkins presiding."

"Thank you. Everyone, please be seated," said the judge. Well into the fourth day of trial, all the jurors knew the routine and sat before he did. In that span of time several people had been called to testify: Dallas Black, two of Mrs. Archer's children – Millie Archer and Lawrence Newell, a first responder and a few others.

"I note for the record the presence of the jury panel. Is the state ready to call its next witness?" asked Judge Jenkins.

Ms. Martindale stood, straightened her shoulders and lifted her chin. "Your Honor, the state calls Dr. Amelia Grant."

Lauren watched a petite woman, somewhere in her early forties, enter the courtroom and approach the bailiff whose right hand was raised awaiting the doctor's arrival. Dr. Grant mirrored the movement, listened to the oath and replied, "I do." Once seated she bent the microphone down toward her and waited for the first question.

Ms. Martindale started with the basics, the doctor's business address, where she worked, which Lauren already knew from her online search of the doctor. She always tried to find out about an expert's background before they testified. It made her job easier knowing in advance where a physician attended medical school and where they practiced medicine.

Dr. Grant was employed with a hospital in Denver, Colorado. She had been a pathologist for the past ten years. The prosecutor asked about her educational background, where she went to medical school, where she did her residency, and what states she was licensed to practice medicine in, all the routine questions to establish the doctor competent to testify on the subjects she was about to embark upon.

Then she moved on to asking her what a pathologist does. Dr. Grant explained how she more or less dissects a body to determine the cause of death, ending that it's not as exciting as the old CSI TV shows make it out to be.

Next came questions about the autopsy performed on Mrs. Archer, the when and the where it took place.

"May I approach the witness, Judge?" Ms. Martindale asked.

"Yes. To save time, you need not ask each time you wish to hand something to the witness," said Judge Jenkins. "You may simply approach."

"Thank you." Ms. Martindale walked up to the witness.

"Doctor, I'm handing you exhibit thirty-seven. Do you recognize this document?"

The pathologist slid a pair of reading glasses on and looked at the document. "Yes. It's my report I prepared from the autopsy."

Lauren enjoyed listening to the doctor explain things in a technical, clinically detached manner, a mere stating of facts. For her the telling was better than the showing, the showing of the crime scene and the victim in eight-by-ten color photographs. Photos always had a way of getting stored in her memory, resurfacing whenever they felt like it.

"Doctor, where in the autopsy report does it say what the manner of death is?" Ms. Martindale flipped through her copy of the exhibit, then looked at the witness. "I'm having trouble finding it."

"Would you clarify your question?" Dr. Grant asked.

"Yes. Where in your report do you say Mrs. Archer was murdered?"

Lauren's fingers were poised on the keys for an answer at the same time inwardly groaning. She knew Tony would be doing the same. At least she hoped her groan was inward. In court she tried to keep a neutral expression. Depending on what came out of a witness's mouth, it was harder to maintain than other times. The rumors about Ms. Martindale's ability, or more accurately, her lack of ability, to try a case effectively were becoming more and more apparent as each witness took the stand.

"As I've explained before, I don't determine manner of death. You won't find the word murder in my report. I determine cause of death. What caused the woman to stop breathing."

"Well, was Ms. Archer murdered?"

The tips of the doctor's sleek silver bob moved, grazing her square chin, the only evidence that the woman shook her head at the question. Dr. Grant cleared her throat. "As stated in my report, the cause of death was the result of an internal brain bleed. A blow to the back of the head, causing a skull fracture, causing internal as well as external bleeding, hence the loss of blood. I do not determine whether a death is a homicide. I believe it's your job to connect those dots, so to speak."

Ms. Martindale looked at her open laptop perched on the podium. Maybe she was staring at it for some divine intervention, some magical question to nail the defendant as the killer beyond a reasonable doubt, and then she could slap her hands together like she were dusting flour from them and say, "It was all in a day's work." Then she could continue the charade of being a competent lawyer who knew how to ask a proper question.

"No further questions, Your Honor." Ms. Martindale returned to her seat at the prosecution table.

Out of the corner of her eye Lauren watched Robert Jessup, Ms. Martindale's second chair, kick the prosecutor's ankle, then tap his legal pad.

Ms. Martindale sprang out of her chair. "Excuse me, Your Honor, I misspoke. A few more questions, with the court's indulgence."

"Yes. But before you continue, this is a good stopping point for our midmorning break. Court will be in recess for fifteen minutes." Judge Jenkins rose.

"All rise," called the bailiff, and everyone did. The jurors laid their three-ring binders, the ones given to them for notetaking, on their chairs before being escorted out of the courtroom.

*   *   *

Lauren took the opportunity to use the restroom, get a drink of water, and grab half a donut out of the break room.

"How's it going in there, Lauren?" Susan asked.

"Well, if you ask me –"

Tony interrupted her. "Our special prosecuting attorney is an idiot. How the hell she ever get chosen to try this case is beyond me. Seriously."

"Maybe she slept with her boss." The words popped out of Lauren's mouth like they had a mind of their own.

Susan tsked-tsked. "Lauren, what a terrible thing to say. That's how rumors get started."

"I was just joking."

Tony shook his head. "She doesn't even know what to ask her own witness. This case has been practically handed to her on a silver platter. I just hope to hell she doesn't jack it up. I don't want there to be a mistrial in my first murder case."

"Why don't you tell us how you really feel, Tony," said Lauren. The words, *Your Honor*, stuck in her throat. Much easier to call him by his first name. He didn't seem to notice or maybe he just didn't care, but Susan did. Lauren caught the look of disapproval on the woman's face.

Tony paced in front of Susan's desk. "I had real doubts when I heard Martindale was selected to try the case. We were in law school together. Not the brightest."

"Where does she practice?" asked Susan.

"She's with the district attorney's office in Casper." Tony shook his head. "I've been trying to give her the benefit of the doubt. But now?" He pulled his fingers through his sandy blond hair. "There's no doubt in my mind, if this is how she tries a case I hope the people in Natrona County lock their doors at night because there's probably a lot of unsavory characters running around free."

He took a gulp of coffee. "I'm going to have to give Randall hell for having a heart attack, leaving the decision to choose a special prosecutor to Bob, his second-in-command's hands."

"I always wondered how they picked a special prosecutor," said Lauren. "I assumed they'd have to have one on this case because the victim was related to the police chief. But I didn't know Randall Graham, as *the* county attorney, would have a say in who they bring in to try a case."

Tony nodded. "Up to a point. It's too bad in this case because Graham is a great prosecutor and could have easily tried this himself."

"Someone else would have ended up trying the case anyway since he had a heart attack." Lauren took a long drink from her water bottle.

"True." He scratched the top of his head. "But anyone upstairs could do a better job than Martindale."

"You might want to do something about that." Lauren gestured to Tony's hair and laughed. "Unless you're going for the mad scientist look."

Tony ran a hand over his hair. "Better?"

"Much." Lauren bit into the maple-glazed donut.

"Wouldn't want the jury wondering what the heck I'm doing during our breaks." Tony grinned.

"How is Graham doing?" asked Lauren.

"He'll be out for eight more weeks. Though if he hears how Martindale's handling this case it might give him another heart attack." He placed his coffee cup on Susan's desk and turned to Lauren. "Are you ready to go back in?"

Lauren nodded.

Chapter Ten

$\mathcal{W}$ith court once again in session and the jury seated, Ms. Martindale rose from her chair. "If I may approach the witness?"

"You may," Judge Jenkins said.

She handed the doctor photographs taken during the autopsy and proceeded to go through them one by one, having the doctor explain each of them. The doctor described them but did not show them to the jury. When she came to the last photo in her hand, of the scalp pulled back and the actual skull exposed, Lauren glanced at the jurors. The face of a young juror in the front row paled at the pathologist's detailed description. *What are you going to do when you see the actual photographs?*

"I move for the admission of exhibits one through twenty, the autopsy photographs, Your Honor."

Daniel's attorney rose. "Objection, Your Honor. These

photographs do nothing except overly prejudice my client. The witness has already thoroughly described the autopsy. There's absolutely no need to fan the flames."

The two lawyers fought for their position, their words their weapons. The state said the photographs were necessary for the jury to understand what happened. In the end Judge Jenkins admitted six of the thirty-six exhibits, which were displayed one by one on a large monitor facing the jury. Some jurors wrote in their notebooks rather than look at the pictures. Others stared, transfixed at the images on the large screen.

After every photograph admitted was shown, Ms. Martindale said, "No further questions of this witness –"

Mr. Jessup waved his hand at his partner, catching her attention.

"One moment, Your Honor." The prosecutor stepped away from the podium and leaned over the table. Her co-counsel whispered in her ear. Red blotchy patches appeared on her neck and crept up her chin where they faded under the thick layer of makeup she wore.

She turned to the judge. "Your Honor, I'd like to admit the autopsy report into evidence, exhibit thirty-seven."

"Objection?"

Mr. Dresser spoke from his seat. "No objection, Your Honor."

Ms. Martindale glanced at her co-counsel, who gave an ever so slight nod. "No further questions," the prosecutor said.

"Mr. Dresser, questions for the witness?" asked Judge Jenkins.

"Yes, Your Honor." Eli approached the podium, pulled

on the microphone, positioning it as high as it would go, which still wasn't far enough. He bent forward to speak into it and began by asking the pathologist questions the prosecutor had already asked and received the same answers. Lauren knew a lot of attorneys that did that, and often wondered if it annoyed the jurors as much as it annoyed her. *After this trial is over, I'm going to ask Eli why attorneys do that.*

"And, Doctor, can you state the exact time of death of Ms. Archer?" asked Mr. Dresser.

"Not an exact time of death, no. I can tell you –"

"You've answered my question. Thank you." Mr. Dresser held up the autopsy report. "What was used to cause the trauma to Mrs. Archer's skull?"

"I don't know. Something with a large, flat surface."

"A baseball bat? Or something similar?"

"No, it would have been larger than that, and round."

"Dr. Grant, is there anything in your report, anything at all, that links Daniel Throgmorton to the death of Ms. Archer?"

The doctor gave the question some thought. "Not directly. In other words, my report involved the examination of the deceased to determine what happened to her that caused her to cease breathing, and therefore, living." She cleared her throat. "I am not the person in charge of testing DNA found at the scene."

"So you did not look at the results of the DNA testing?"

"That is not what I was charged to do, so, no, I did not."

"So you don't know if my client's DNA was on or near Ms. Archer?"

"That's correct, I don't know."

"What about fingerprints of my client's?"

"What about them?"

"You don't know if my client's fingerprints were found at the scene or on the body of Ms. Archer?"

"I do not test for fingerprints as they do not remain on the skin very long. So, no, I do not know if his prints were found at the scene."

"And do you know whose fingerprints were found at the scene?"

"No. Again, my focus was on conducting an autopsy, not doing a crime scene investigation."

Toward the end of his questioning Mr. Dresser peppered the pathologist with a lot of "what if" questions, trying to poke holes in the doctor's testimony, but her answers could not be pierced by his examination. He also questioned whether she did everything according to proper procedure. She had.

As Dr. Grant left the courtroom Lauren thought Eli hadn't scored any big points for the defense with the witness. She knew it was hard to argue with science.

Ms. Martindale spoke over her shoulder as she walked toward the courtroom doors. "My co-counsel will be examining our next witness, Your Honor."

Mr. Jessup walked to the podium. "Your Honor, the state calls Raymond Newell to the stand." While waiting for the witness to arrive Robert Jessup pulled at the cuffs of his black suit, straightened his tie, and ran a hand over his thinning brown hair. He adjusted his wire-rimmed glasses, then gripped the podium as if to keep his hands still.

Crawford's chief of police entered the courtroom and approached the witness stand, his hand in the air before Bailiff Johnson could raise his own. He wore his police uniform. His stomach pressed against the buttons of his blue shirt exposing bits of crescent-shaped white T-shirt underneath.

He sat in the witness box and turned his attention on Mr. Jessup, but not before shooting a look of hate at Daniel Throgmorton.

Lauren wondered if he would take revenge right here, right now in front of everybody. What if Chief Newell somehow had gotten a weapon through security? Heck, he was the chief of police. They wouldn't ask him to leave his firearm downstairs. What if he pulled his gun out, shot at Daniel, creating mayhem? She could get caught in the line of fire.

She stole her own glance at the defendant who focused his attention on the legal pad in front of him. A deputy sat a few yards to the right of him, and at the rear of the courtroom, close to the doors, sat a second deputy, both men there in the unlikely event he tried to get up and simply walk out. They wouldn't be able to prevent a stray bullet though. She shook the thought free from her mind, telling herself to quit being dramatic and get ready to pay attention. Besides, this man was a certified peace officer. Surely he would let the justice system run its course.

"Tell the jury about your mother, what she was like," said Mr. Jessup.

When Ray Newell didn't hesitate before speaking, Lauren knew this portion of the testimony had been gone over previously, rehearsed, and everyone in the room was going to be in for a mini biography of not only Margaret Archer's life but her impact on the chief's life, and possibly on the community.

He spoke of his childhood and how when he came home from school there would be fresh baked cookies waiting or a slice of homemade apple pie and a glass of milk. His mother was patient, kind, independent, intelligent. Lauren watched at least ten adjectives scroll across the laptop screen to describe the deceased woman. He made it sound like his mother popped out of some long-ago black-and-white sitcom.

Ray Newell spoke about his mother's homemade pizza. How when he was growing up she used to make the dough from scratch. He said when he moved back to Crawford and would visit her, he noticed how arthritic her hands had become. She no longer could knead dough and resorted to ordering in pizza from Sol's Pizza.

Lauren's fingers pressed the keys on her writer in a routine, no-need-to-think-about-it manner. Her mind wandered to the day she took Mrs. Archer's deposition. The air in the conference room had been filled with tension and animosity emanating from both sides of the table. And through Margaret Archer's testimony Lauren knew her and her son's relationship had been ... strained, to say the least. Strained to the point of there being no relationship at all. The jury, however, would never know this information. In fact, the man gave such praise to the woman, it was as if he were pleading his case before the pope that his mother should achieve sainthood.

"It was so very hard for me to leave Crawford and move to Casper," the chief was saying. "I visited my mother as often as I could over the years. Spent every Christmas and Thanksgiving with her. I spent all my vacation days here with her to help her on our ranch."

"*Our ranch?*"

Ray Newell cleared his throat. "I jumped at the chance to move back here when I was offered a position with the Crawford Police Department. It meant leaving Casper, but it also meant being close," he waited a beat, "to Mom."

Mr. Jessup handed Chief Newell a handful of photographs and had him identify each one of them. They were pictures of a medicine cabinet. One photo focused on an empty middle shelf.

"That's where Mom kept all of her prescription medicine, all of her painkillers."

"Do you know the names of some of the prescriptions she took?"

"Oxycodone, fentanyl. She struggled every day with severe arthritis and unrelenting back pain."

"The state moves to admit these photos into evidence," said Mr. Jessup.

"Objections, Mr. Dresser?" asked the judge.

Mr. Dresser stood. "Yes, Your Honor. There has been no foundation laid that Mr. Newell had any knowledge of what prescription medicine should have been there the day these pictures were taken. This shelf could have been bare for weeks."

"Objection overruled. Exhibits twenty-one through thirty-one are received," said Judge Jenkins.

Mr. Jessup, a few inches taller than the podium, squinted at the screen's laptop which sat perched on top of it before asking another question. The remainder of the chief's testimony centered on the big hole he had in his heart since his mother's death, how family get-togethers were not the same. "Life just seems to have less meaning now without her." He lowered his head.

Give the man an Oscar. Lauren wanted to take her hands off her writer and clap. Instead she looked at the faces of the jurors to gauge their reactions, see if anyone had been moved by his words. Two female jurors, somewhere in their late sixties, were nodding their heads sympathetically.

Lauren mentally shook hers.

"No further questions," said Mr. Jessup.

Mr. Dresser strode to the podium and cleared his throat. "Hello, Mr. Newell."

Chief Newell did not reply. He merely stared at Mr. Dresser, a blank expression on his face.

"Let me start out by saying how sorry I am for your loss." The defense attorney asked question after question, getting little more than one-word answers from the chief.

"You were at your mother's residence that evening. Was that a planned visit on your part?"

"No. I was still at the office and heard it on the scanner."

"So you immediately went to the scene?"

"Yes, of course. I did go inside briefly but one of the sheriff's deputies told me I had to wait outside."

"I see." Mr. Dresser approached the court reporter table, gathering the photographs Mr. Jessup used in his examination and placed them on the witness stand next to the microphone. "You testified these pictures depict your mother's bathroom cabinet."

"Yes."

"And the last time you looked in there, there were several bottles containing your mother's painkillers, is that right?"

"Yes, including the fentanyl patches prescribed to her."

"And when was the last time you had an opportunity to look inside the cabinet?"

The chief picked the photographs up, flipping through them.

"I'm sorry, I didn't hear your answer," said Mr. Dresser.

"I was thinking." He put the photos down. "I don't remember. I'm guessing maybe four weeks before she passed."

"So it had been four weeks since you visited your mother before her death?"

The chief's jaw clenched. "I didn't say that. I said I hadn't been in her bathroom in that long."

"Excuse me. Then when was the last time you visited your mother before her death?"

"I don't remember."

"Was it the day before?"

"No."

"Two days before?"

"No."

"Three days before?"

"No."

When Daniel's attorney reached fourteen days, he had made his point. Chief Newell hadn't been out to see his mother in at least two weeks.

Mr. Dresser appeared to be looking at his notes for a few moments. "So it's possible your mother decided to change where she stored her medication and you wouldn't know where, would you?"

"It's possible, but if she had stored it somewhere else —"

"Thank you. You've answered my question. Did you know all the medications your mother was taking?"

"I don't know if I knew everything she was taking, but I did know of several of them."

"Why is that?"

"What do you mean? I don't understand."

"Did you and she talk about what she was taking? Did you pick up her prescriptions from the pharmacy for her? How was it you knew what she was taking?"

"I — It was mostly from seeing them in her medicine cabinet."

"When would you have opportunity to see them in her medicine chest?"

Raymond Newell snorted like he had just heard the dumbest question ever. "When I used the bathroom."

"And so when you used the bathroom did you make it a habit to look inside your mother's cabinet to see what medication she had?"

"Not a habit. Just checking to make sure she — Yes, something like that." Chief Newell shifted in the witness stand.

"So you knew she was prescribed painkillers?"

"Yes. She had been for years."

"I see." Mr. Dresser flipped through more pages of his legal pad. "And did you ever take any of your mother's prescription medications? Ever take —"

"Never." The chief folded his arms across his chest, cocked his head to the side as if daring Mr. Dresser to accuse him of stealing.

"Please let me get the whole question out before you answer. Did you ever take any of your mother's oxycodone or fentanyl?"

"No."

"You never removed any prescription medicine from her home for your later use?"

"I sure as hell did not. What the – I don't like the sound of what you're implying. Are you –"

Mr. Jessup stood. "Objection, Your Honor."

"Are you suggesting *I* removed the medicine?" Color rose in the chief's face.

"Mr. Jessup, what's your objection?" asked the judge.

Chief Newell started to rise from the witness chair. "Are you saying I stole from my own mother?"

"Mr. Newell, please remain seated. And you need to wait and not talk while I deal with the objection," Judge Jenkins said.

"Sorry, Your Honor." The chief glared at Mr. Dresser before settling in the seat.

Mr. Jessup spoke, "Mr. Dresser is badgering this witness, a peace officer no less. There's no evidence Chief Newell knew precisely the contents of the cabinet. And it's irrelevant."

"Objection overruled," Judge Jenkins said. "You brought up the medicine and the medicine cabinet in your direct examination. The witness may answer. Mr. Dresser, repeat your question so we have a clear record."

"Thank you, Your Honor." He adjusted his tie. "I want to know if you ever took any of her prescription medications. By 'took' I mean removed from her home. Or let me ask that question. Did you ever take her medication?

Maybe you weren't feeling well and thought, 'I'll just take one. It's not a big deal.' Did you ever do that?"

Crawford's police chief stared at the defense attorney.

The courtroom fell quiet waiting for the chief's answer. Mr. Dresser placed his hands on both sides of the podium and leaned in. "Do you need me to repeat the question?"

"No. I know what the question is." Ray Newell's face now matched the color of the bailiff's red tie. Whether the flushed face came from anger or embarrassment at having been called out on the missing pills, everyone in the courtroom was about to find out.

"The answer is no. I never removed any medication from her medicine cabinet. Never took one single pill."

"Did you have access to her home? Did you have a key to let yourself in?"

"Yes, I did. Others did too though. Not just me."

Eli looked up from his notes. "Who else had access to your mother's home?"

"My half sisters, Vera Mann and Millie Archer. I'm not sure about my brother Larry. He may have had a key also."

"Anyone else you can think of?"

"Dallas Black, her … her helper, I guess you could say. He probably had a key."

"So there were numerous people who had access to the painkillers and could have removed them from the home; isn't that correct?"

Chief Newell's jaw tightened. "Yes, I suppose so."

Mr. Dresser flipped back the pages on the yellow legal pad until he reached the beginning. He looked at the angry man on the witness stand. "Just a few more questions. How were you notified of your mother's death?"

"As I already stated, I heard it on the police scanner."

"Where were you at the time?"

"Home."

"You hadn't been to your mother's house earlier in the day?"

"No, I hadn't."

"After you heard what happened, did you immediately go to your mother's home?"

"Yes, of course. I drove over there immediately."

"And what is your wife's name?"

"Trish. Patricia Holland."

Lauren could see the chief trying to decide if he should volunteer information.

"Trish ... Patricia was already established as a successful therapist in town when we married. We decided it was a good idea to keep her previous name."

"Mr. Newell, are you currently involved in a lawsuit with your half siblings over your mother's estate?"

Mr. Jessup rose. "Objection, Your Honor. Relevance. That is a civil matter and has absolutely nothing to do with why we're here."

"Sustained. Move to another subject, Mr. Dresser," said Judge Jenkins.

"No further questions, Your Honor," said Mr. Dresser.

"Redirect for this witness?" asked Judge Jenkins.

Mr. Jessup looked at his notes, whispered to Ms. Martindale, then said, "No, Your Honor."

"There being no further questions, you are excused. Since your testimony is complete you may stay in the courtroom if you'd like," said the judge.

Chief Newell stepped down from the witness stand

carrying the photographs with him.

"You need to leave the exhibits with the court reporter," said the judge.

"Sorry, Your Honor."

"That's all right. Just put them on her table."

Chief Newell placed the exhibits on the table as instructed, his back to the jury. He gave Lauren a look of disdain, then replaced it with the look of a grief-stricken son as he turned and strode toward the gallery.

What's wrong with you? Lauren wondered why Ray Newell looked at her that way but she dropped that train of thought and turned her full attention to the next witness entering the courtroom.

Chapter Eleven

As the last witness of the day exited the courtroom, Judge Jenkins announced, "Ladies and gentlemen, we'll be in recess until nine o'clock tomorrow morning."

Everyone rose. Lauren glanced around the room and saw Dominick sitting a few rows behind Daniel. Directly across the aisle sat Chief Newell, arms folded across his burly chest. When the jury was gone, the attorneys on both sides, along with members of the public, made their way to the exit.

Two sheriff's deputies approached Daniel. He knew the routine. He stood, let himself be handcuffed and walked toward the alcove that led inmates out of the courtroom and into a secured area where they would be taken to their cells. Before turning the corner, Daniel saw his uncle. With his hands shackled together he gave a little wave and a half smile.

When his nephew was gone, Dominick made his way to the center aisle. Lauren watched as Chief Newell approached the baker and stood, blocking his path.

"Chief Newell, I'm so sorry for your loss," said Dominick. "Margaret was a regular at my bakery. She always had a smile on her face. Her favorite thing to order —"

"Save it. When this trial is over and your nephew is put away for life, you might want to think about closing your little shop and relocating elsewhere."

Dominick cocked his head at Ray Newell. "I don't have plans of leaving Crawford. It's my home. Has been for many years."

"You may want to reconsider that thought. People have a way of remembering. I'm sure whenever they think of Dominick's Bakery they'll remember what happened to my mother."

It looked as if Dominick was about to say something more, but the bailiff walked over to the two men and said, "If you're done here, I'll be locking up."

Ray flashed a perfunctory smile. "Sure thing, Bailiff." He walked toward the exit and turned his head. "Think about what I said." Then he was gone.

Lauren spoke up, "Dominick, maybe you should wait a minute or two before leaving. Just in case."

"Nah, I'll be fine. He don't worry me. I'm going to see Danny before I go home. You have yourself a good evening, young lady." He turned and pushed through the double doors of the courtroom.

Lauren stared after him. As she gathered the exhibits, she noticed her hands were shaking. She took a deep breath, exhaled to steady herself, then began putting the documents in numerical order. She cross-referenced them to the exhibit list Susan had given her.

As she started to leave the courtroom, she noticed Eli's briefcase under the defense counsel table. The building would be locked up for the night, his briefcase safe until the morning. She clutched the exhibits and took them to Zoe's office for safekeeping.

What if Eli needs something and it's in his briefcase? In the next few minutes he'll be locked out with no access. She hurried into the courtroom and retrieved it. His office was directly across the street from the rear of the courthouse. She would just drop it off on her way home.

With her messenger bag slung over her shoulder and Eli's leather satchel in hand, Lauren went down the courthouse steps and headed in the direction of Mr. Dresser's office. She spotted Chief Newell speaking to one of his police officers. For a moment she thought about approaching him, asking him what the heck his problem was, giving her that look in the courtroom and talking to Dominick like that, but being too tired to argue won out. Plus, if she was being honest with herself, she did not want to confront a man who intimidated her.

She changed her mind about walking to Eli's office and instead went to her Volvo. The car keys slipped out of her hand and into the bottom of her bag. "Crap." She rummaged inside for the keys, cursing her clumsiness. She had an odd sensation that if she turned around right now she would see the police chief watching her.

Chapter Twelve

She drove across the street, parked at the curb and trotted up the steps of a nineteen twenties bungalow-style home-turned-office that sat on a corner lot. Over the years many homes surrounding the courthouse succumbed to being sold, demolished and replaced with squat, utilitarian office buildings, that is until a group of citizens banded together and convinced the city council to create what was now called the Hartford Historic District. For two blocks in all directions the remaining houses running north, south, east and west of the courthouse maintained their original charm and unique character.

Most of the homes were now businesses of one kind or another with the exception for one or two holdouts. Nestled between Eli's office and Gentle Breeze Counseling, her therapist's office, sat a used bookstore and a tattoo parlor. To the south of the Gentle Breeze was an artist co-op where her aunt consigned her alpaca wool creations.

Lauren turned the knob only to find the door locked. She pressed the doorbell and waited. She pressed it again. Still no answer. She was about to leave when Eli opened the door. The hinges on the heavy door squeaked, the sound a plea for them to be greased.

"I guess you don't have to worry about anyone sneaking up on you." Lauren gestured toward the door.

"I don't know about that. I almost didn't hear the doorbell." Eli nodded up the staircase where classical music came floating down. "Sean has a brief due. He always plays music when he's stressed by a deadline. I don't mind though. Beethoven's 'Moonlight Sonata' sort of grows on you. Who knew that was possible?"

He raised an ink-black eyebrow at Lauren. "We've just spent the whole day together and here you are on my doorstep. What, you can't get enough of this?" He tilted his head down, looking at himself.

"Yes, exactly." Lauren held out the briefcase.

He smacked his forehead. "Thanks for bringing it by, but you didn't have to do that."

"I know. I saw it and thought I'd drop it off on my way home."

"I appreciate it." He walked into the parlor-turned-office and placed the battered case in a chair in front of his desk.

Lauren looked around the room, its history preserved in the original oak flooring, wide ornate crown molding running around the ceiling, and the pair of windows, their glass etched from age.

"I know I've said it before, but I love your offices."

"So do I. All the architectural details are why we decided to buy the house. That and you can't beat the location. Takes me a whole minute to walk over to the courthouse."

Lauren nodded.

"It's a great place. Except in the winter. Not the best at keeping the heat in. But we're working on it little by little." He walked over to his desk.

"After you left court, Ray Newell got in Dominick's face."

"What happened?"

Lauren explained the brief exchange.

After listening to Lauren, he shook his head. "Thanks for telling me. Not anything I can really do, but I'll talk to Daniel. See if his uncle has said anything about the chief."

"I'll see you tomorrow. I can let myself out." Lauren turned into the entryway and came face-to-face with a man in his mid-thirties, a few years older than herself, his intense green eyes startling her. She moved to the left to let him pass as he went to his right. She was about to laugh but the expression of annoyance on his face silenced her.

He brushed past her, knocking her off balance. "Well, excuse you," she said, though she shouldn't have bothered. He took the stairs two steps at a time up to Sean Abram's office, not hearing her comment.

Lauren brushed off her shoulder, as if wiping off the man's bad manners. She stuck her head back in Eli's office. "Who was that, do you know?"

"His name is Nicholas Fisher. A client of Sean's. Always rushes in. Pretty important guy." The corners of Eli's mouth twitched with a smile. "Or so he thinks."

Where have I heard that name before?

Chapter Thirteen

On Saturday morning Lauren dragged herself out of bed. She wanted to sleep in after the long week in court. She told herself she would not make another weekend appointment, though she knew she would feel different once inside and sharing her feelings. Knowing it would be helpful in the long run.

Outside Gentle Breeze Counseling was a *Patricia Holland for Congress* campaign sign secured into the tiny patch of lawn with metal stakes.

Lauren thought about the name used. Patricia Holland, not Newell, and remembered what the police chief said on the witness stand about his wife keeping her name.

She glanced at her fitness watch. Nine fifty. Arriving early for everything must be in her DNA. It meant waiting around. Not being a fan of waiting, she tried not to show up early for appointments, but the plan always failed.

Inside the home-turned-office she read the sheet of paper taped on Ms. Holland's office door. *Quiet please. Counseling session in progress.*

Next to Patricia's office was another room with its door open. Lauren stood in the doorway and looked around. A sleek, glass-topped desk sat close to a draped window with a laptop, and two client or guest chairs sat opposite the desk.

"Good morning."

Lauren whirled around, coming face-to-face with a man somewhere in his late forties. His dark brown hair graying at the temples gave him a distinguished look. She took a step back.

"I'm sorry. I didn't mean to startle you." He stuck out his hand. "Alden Bates. You must be Allison James."

She shook the outstretched hand. "No. I'm ..." She looked him up and down. His attire looked handcrafted-casual, until she saw his shoes. Black shiny toe, a gray herringbone center and matte navy blue at the heel. Like it couldn't decide what fashion statement it was trying to make.

He tapped his toe from side to side.

Lauren looked up into his amused face.

"Christian Louboutin. It's the first thing people seem to notice."

"They look like they would go with everything."

He let out a small laugh. "They certainly do."

"I'm Lauren. Lauren Besoner. I'm waiting for Ms. Holland."

"My apologies. I'm expecting a new client. But nice to meet you, Lauren."

"Same here."

He released her hand, pushed his black-framed glasses up on his nose and walked past her. He placed his to-go coffee cup and cell phone next to his laptop.

Alden Bates. The name and the face were familiar. But from where? She felt like she'd been caught eavesdropping rather than just standing in his doorway. "I'm a little early for my appointment. I was just looking around while I waited."

"Of course. No problem."

On all her previous visits Lauren remembered the door had been closed. "Have you been in this building long?"

His gaze went to the ceiling as he thought about the question. "A few months now."

It came to her where she'd seen him before, which explained the recent office sharing with her therapist. Mr. Bates had a disciplinary hearing before the Wyoming Board of Certified Public Accountants a few months ago, and she reported the proceedings. He didn't seem to recognize her. She knew from experience once a hearing got underway, the court reporter faded into the fluorescent-lit surroundings. Just the way she liked it.

"Do you like being in a solo practice? You were with … it was Lerner and Associates before, wasn't it?"

Alden Bates tilted his head to the side. "How did you know I –"

Patricia Holland's office door opened, and a petite young woman emerged, eyes puffy and red, clutching a wad of tissue. Ms. Holland escorted her through to the front door and held it open for her. "I'll see you next week then." She returned and placed her hand on Mr. Bates's arm and with a Cheshire cat smile asked, "You're not trying to steal my client are you, Alden?"

"Only if she's looking for an accountant. Just a bit of mistaken identity on my part. I thought this young woman was my new client. I was explaining to Ms. Besoner we share office space."

"Yes. Cuts down on expenses," added Patricia. "Lauren, would you like some tea or coffee?"

"No thanks."

"I need a cup of coffee. I'll be right back."

As Patricia walked down a narrow hallway toward the small kitchen, the front door opened and a woman hurried in carrying a large manila envelope.

Alden straightened his glasses. "This must be my client." He walked over and introduced himself. "My office is right through there." He gestured to the open doorway. "I'll be right in." He walked partway down the hall toward the kitchen. "If you're free this afternoon we should talk Trish … Ms. Holland."

"Yes." Patricia emerged from the kitchen, walked past him and raised her coffee cup in Lauren's direction. "I'm free after this appointment."

The two women moved into the therapist's office. "Have a seat, Lauren." Patricia Holland motioned to one of two overstuffed chairs. A low glass table was busy with various items, a notepad, pen, tissue box, eyeglasses, and two small glazed bowls filled with potpourri. Lauren sank into the faux suede upholstery, taking a closer look at the bowls.

Patricia dressed in casual business attire, gray slacks and a twinset sweater. She crossed her long legs and opened her laptop. "My daughter made those for me when she was in high school."

"They're so pretty. I always wanted to try my hand at pottery."

"Andrea is very artistic." She pointed to a grouping of three photographs on the wall behind them.

Lauren turned to look at the photos. The one on the right looked to be an impromptu family photo of Patricia, her husband, daughter and mother-in-law. The middle photo, larger than the other two, was of Patricia and her daughter, heads together, mischievous grins on their faces as if they were keeping a secret from the person taking the picture. The photo on the left showed the therapist in a sleek black suit, holding a plaque in one hand and shaking the mayor's hand with the other. Her hair was swept into an Audrey Hepburn 'do, diamond earrings winking in the sunlight, the same ones she wore today.

"Wow. Your daughter looks just like you."

"I get that a lot. She's studying in New York. Cornell University." The therapist smiled as she tapped on the keys of her laptop. "If I win this election, I'll have the opportunity to see her more often."

"That'll be nice."

"It certainly will. I miss her." Patricia put on a pair of reading glasses and looked at something on the laptop, talking as she did so. "Tell me how things are going, Lauren."

"Things are good."

The therapist kept her eyes on the screen. "Uh-huh. I see we worked on biofeedback the last couple of visits. Have you been trying it at home?"

"Yes."

"And how is it working out?"

"I'm getting the hang of it. And it's helping."

Patricia looked away from her laptop, picked up the notebook, which looked more like a journal, and asked, "Have you been keeping up with some of the suggestions I gave you?"

Lauren nodded. "I've been trying to meditate. It's just hard for me to slow my mind down."

"That's a hard thing for everyone to do." She smiled, making the laugh lines around her eyes deep. "Especially with all of us having such fast-paced lives these days. Takes time and practice. What else have you tried?"

"I've been doing yoga regularly."

Patricia made a note, then looked up. "Do you find it helpful?"

Lauren nodded. "I think combined it's all been helpful. It's been a while since I had a nightmare."

"Good to hear. How is work? Any unusual stressors there?"

"Not really." *Should I mention her husband? How he openly dislikes me?* "I don't know if you know, I'm covering the murder trial." Lauren didn't have to elaborate. Everyone in town knew about Daniel Throgmorton being on trial for the murder of Margaret Archer.

Patricia dropped her pen. It rolled under the table and she bent to recover it, exposing gray roots beyond the ash blonde highlights.

"You're covering that trial?"

"Yes. The official court reporter is on maternity leave."

Patricia's face paled.

"Is something wrong? You don't look so good."

"I'm fine. It's just every time I think of that … that low-life, no good drug addict in my mother-in-law's home … killing her, it makes me so incredibly angry."

Lauren's eyes widened. She had never witnessed her therapist express much emotion – any emotion now that she thought about it.

"I'm sorry." The therapist exhaled and tucked a stray hair behind her ear.

"Don't be. It's understandable."

"No, no. My comments weren't very professional." She crossed her legs. "So you said you're in a good place work-wise. How long will the other recorder be on maternity leave?"

"Reporter."

"Hmm?"

"We're court reporters. You said recorder."

"Oh. Excuse me. *Reporter.*"

"Zoe will be gone five more weeks." Perfect timing, Lauren thought sarcastically to herself. It would be late October and she'd be doing freelance work again, traveling on snow-packed icy highways, treacherous driving conditions. *I'll be having a grand old time.* She pushed any further negative thoughts away.

There still was a half hour left in the session but Lauren suddenly wanted to leave and be outdoors. To be doing something active. She'd sat in court all week and she'd have to do it all again next week. She had a sudden urge to just get up and leave but dismissed the notion knowing she'd be charged for the full hour, not to mention it would be a rude thing to do.

"Have you decided if you're going to close your office so you can concentrate on your campaign? You mentioned that the last time we met."

"Yes. I won't be scheduling any more appointments after the end of the month. I need to visit all the towns and cities, make my presence known to people outside of Crawford. Meet with the citizens of Wyoming face-to-face. Share my ideas. I don't know if you watch much television –"

"A little. I stream most of the things I watch."

"I've run a few ads on TV, and on different social media sites but I think it's important to go door-to-door, let people in other parts of Wyoming get a chance to know me."

Lauren nodded. "Makes sense."

"But don't worry, I won't leave you stranded. There's a couple of therapists right here in town that I think would be a good match for you. And I can also refer you elsewhere, Cheyenne or even Fort Collins. Though I like to stay local when possible."

"Sure." Lauren had been thinking she'd gotten all she could out of therapy, hoping Patricia thought the same thing. Apparently she did not. She tried to think of something else to talk about and remembered yesterday's testimony. "You were there right after it happened, weren't you? At Mrs. Archer's house, I mean."

"Yes, I was. But we were asked to leave."

"I remember that. One of the deputies threatened to arrest your husband if he didn't leave."

Patricia's expression changed but Lauren couldn't make out what emotion lay behind her brown eyes.

"Ray was extremely upset. He didn't want to leave, of course. His mother was lying there and he wanted to stay and help. But I could understand the deputy's point of view. He explained the crime happened in the county, not within city limits, for one thing. Ray knew this, of course, but still …" Patricia picked a speck of lint off her pink cardigan. "And you couldn't very well investigate your own mother's death. I tried to get him to leave with me." The therapist gave her head a slow shake. "When I left he was still arguing with the deputy. I should have stayed, tried to calm him down but I was upset myself, and he can be very … let's just say the whole event was extremely stressful, and my husband was on the verge of losing it."

Patricia closed her eyes as if to block out the memory, then opened them and took a deep breath. "He eventually took the deputy's advice because he arrived home within minutes of me getting home."

"So you and your husband didn't go together to see your mother-in-law?"

"No. I was on my way there to return a … I don't remember now what I was returning. I think a pan or baking dish. She often made casseroles or baked something and would send some home with Ray. She was such a good cook." Patricia had a faraway look in her eyes. "Anyway, whatever it was was in my car. It was my intent to drop it off on my way home from work. Seeing all the police there, and Ray, I knew something terrible must have happened."

"What happened to Mrs. Archer was awful. I can't imagine what it must have been like, seeing her … like that." Lauren gave an apologetic look. "They've admitted a lot of photos during the trial. I assume you saw her lying there …"

"Of course. They hadn't taken her away yet."

"I'm sorry, I didn't mean to bring up such a bad memory.

Sometimes I get the testimony stuck in my head, and I end up replaying it over and over."

"That's all right. It helps to talk things through." Patricia gathered her hair, spun it around her hand and let it fall over the front of her shoulder. "If it's something you struggle with, if testimony is difficult to let go of, it could help if we talked about what was said. Maybe there's something your subconscious needs to explore. Or maybe one of the officers said something during their testimony and it has you questioning it, trying to make sense of a particular piece of evidence."

Lauren twisted her hands in her lap. Ray's behavior when he left the witness stand had left its mark on her. So did some of the things he said on the stand, but this was his wife. *Should I mention how he looked at me? Nah. How awkward would that be?*

"No, it's something I always do. No matter what kind of trial it is. Except if an economist is testifying. Then I'm just trying to stay awake. I know money, financial stuff, is important but as soon as someone starts talking about actuary tables or computing future lost wages, I sort of check out." Lauren gave a little laugh. "Ironically, that is the exact type of testimony I have to pay closer attention to. Make sure I get the numbers down right, don't transpose them."

"I think I understand."

"The testimony so far has been the typical things you'd expect to hear in a murder trial, if there is such a thing as typical. The pathologist was on the stand a long time. That stuff is very technical but it's also fascinating. To me anyway."

"Like what?" Patricia reached for her coffee mug.

Like what? You want details?

"I've never read an autopsy report."

"Oh, just the chemical analysis they run, the attention to every detail. All the things they look for and examine." What an odd question, thought Lauren. If the deceased were someone close to me, I wouldn't be asking about specific details.

"Ray hasn't shared much of what's gone on during the trial with me. Of course, he was devastated when it happened. We both were. And we were both so relieved the killer was caught so quickly."

Lauren nodded.

"I understand that everyone has a right to plead not guilty. But having to relive everything has been hard on my husband. He was especially upset after his testimony."

"I don't know him personally but he did seem a little upset." Lauren wanted to sound sympathetic but couldn't quite pull it off. If he hasn't shared much with his wife, he probably didn't tell her how Eli's cross-examination of him went, how Eli more or less accused him of taking his mother's prescription painkillers. If he was guilty of doing that, she could see why he would not want to bring it up, but rather keep it to himself.

"He'll open up to me eventually, but he has to be the one to bring up the subject." Patricia looked at her note-pad, then at Lauren. "Let's turn our attention back to you, shall we? If we keep up this conversation, I'll have to give you a refund for today's time."

They both laughed.

Lauren shared her feelings about a few more things before Ms. Holland checked the time on her computer.

"Let's see what I have open for ... we've been doing Saturdays the last couple of sessions." After checking her online calendar, they agreed on a time for Lauren's next appointment.

Patricia opened her door and escorted Lauren to the lobby. Alden Bates's office door stood open. He unclasped his hands from behind his head and dropped his Louboutin-clad feet off his desk as Lauren stood in the hallway saying goodbye to Patricia.

Lauren slid into the warm interior of her car. Seeing Alden Bates had been a little bit of a surprise. A therapist and an accountant sharing an office seemed like an odd combination, but it probably had to do with rental availability and nothing to do with professions. She started the Volvo and lowered the driver's window.

As she pulled away from the curb, she remembered another reason why his name sounded familiar, and it had nothing to do with his administrative hearing. Alden Bates had been Mrs. Archer's longtime accountant.

Chapter Fourteen

*A*pparently, lots of people today were ignoring the carbs-are-bad-for-you advice. Lauren stepped into Dominick's Bakery. The line of customers reached the door. For Lauren it meant summoning up extra willpower to buy only what she had come for. As she stood in the queue she mumbled, "It's been a long week. *I deserve* this." She glanced behind her. A mother, juggling a toddler on one hip, looked at Lauren and took a step back, busying herself with unzipping her son's light jacket.

The sunny, windless day beckoned Lauren to take her pistachio latte and white bakery bag containing two cheese danish – evidence of her loss of willpower whenever she stepped into Dominick's store – outside. She sat at one of three empty metal tables lining the windows of the bakery, umbrellas tied shut, waiting to be opened when the sun shone higher in the sky.

She sipped the drink and watched as people disappeared inside local shops, then reappeared with shopping bags in tow. She slid one of the delicate pastries out of the bag and bit into it. The cheese mingled with the sugar glaze and did a tiny tango on her tongue. She closed her eyes, and for the briefest of moments, the long week, filled with many hours of intense and sad testimony, took a back seat in her mind. She savored the moment. Willing it to last. Knowing it wouldn't.

The door shut with a loud bang. "I gotta get that fixed," said Dominick. He cocked his head at the empty chair next to Lauren.

"Of course. Sit."

"Hector will be okay for a few minutes. I saw you leave. Thought I wouldn't get a chance to talk to you."

"No, I just want to enjoy being outside while I can. I forgot how hard it is to be inside all day, every day. Even with all the windows in the courtroom, it's not the same as breathing in fresh air. I didn't realize how quickly I got spoiled in the freelance world."

"What do you mean?"

"Freelancing is not as hard as working in court every day. There are weeks where I only have one or two jobs."

"Sounds like a good gig."

"It is." Lauren paused. "Except when it comes to paying the bills."

Dominick rubbed his thumb over his middle and index fingers. "*Non abbastanza soldi.*"

Lauren raised an eyebrow.

"Not enough money."

She nodded.

"How's the trial going?"

Lauren looked at the baker who she thought of as a friend. Worry burrowed deep behind his espresso-colored eyes. *Should I tell him about Chief Newell's testimony?* "It's moving along pretty fast. We've had a lot of witnesses on the stand." *I know that's not what he wants to hear.* "Eli is doing a really good job. It might go to the jury soon. Depends if the defendant – it depends if Daniel takes the stand."

"Is he going to, do ya think?"

"I don't know. That's between him and Eli. But if he has a criminal background and gets on the stand, the prosecution will bring that up."

The baker's shoulders sagged under Lauren's comment.

"I go visit Danny as often as I can. He won't talk about the trial. Just asks how I'm doing, how his mom is holding up. And how sorry he is for upsetting her."

Dominick's serious expression disappeared. He smiled as two older women approached the bakery. He stood and opened the door. "Hello, ladies."

After they stepped inside he continued. "Is it looking as bad for Danny as the newspaper says?"

No one could know what a jury was thinking. She had been wrong before about a verdict. Heck, she'd been wrong several times, thinking a jury would do one thing and did the opposite.

"I haven't read the paper, but don't believe everything you read. They're just excited to have something sensational to put on the front page for a change. The fact it's a local trial is a bonus for them."

The just-right flavors of the latte made her smack her lips. "You outdid yourself. No one makes a better latte than you do. Not to mention, the danish is amazing. As usual."

"You're gonna have to thank Hector for the danish. He's taken over a lot of the pastry making. I've been concentrating on the bread. He's talked me into experimenting with gluten-free cookies, and even vegan brownies." Dominick gave a little shake of his head. "I'm not so sure about that though. We're gonna be rolling them out – get it? – in a couple of weeks."

Lauren smiled. "I get it. Has the trial had any effect on your business?"

He shrugged. "Doesn't seem to. There's been a few new faces. Don't know if they're in town for the trial, but they've been in a few times this last week or so." He looked up and down the street before he continued. "I did have the health department show up. Twice now. Last month and again yesterday. I can't prove it, but I think a certain someone had something to do with them showing up." He lowered his voice. "Has to be the police chief."

Lauren's eyes widened. "Really?"

"Yeah. Got a citation both times. Small stuff too. My walk-in cooler was off by one degree than what it's supposed to be. That was the first time. Second time the exit sign light, one of the bulbs was burned out. I mean, come on, give me a break."

"What makes you think it was the chief?"

"He never came into my shop before. Not on his own anyway. But he's been in a couple times since the murder happened. Didn't buy anything except a black coffee."

The baker settled his elbows on his knees, cradling his head in his hands. He spoke between splayed fingers. "I'm not worried about the bakery. I just know if I hadn't fired Danny, he never woulda gotten into this mess. I promised my sista I'd look after him. Some job I did with that."

"You can't blame yourself. You must have had a good reason to let him go."

Dominick exhaled loudly. "He showed up to work high a few times. He had been acting kinda funny, but I didn't know that's what it was it until Hector said something. He didn't want to tell me, but he said I needed to know. He was afraid the cops would show up at the bakery one day and they'd find drugs in the back room, and with Hector's past, he'd be the first one they'd suspect."

Lauren remembered Hector's words when she ran into him last fall outside the bakery. He had killed his number, did his full ten-year sentence behind bars. "Hector's right. Being a convicted felon has a way of following you for the rest of your life."

"Hector didn't want nothing to do with that life no more, and I couldn't blame him. And he said it would hurt business no matter where the drugs came from. He woulda been right about that too. Hell, they mighta thought the drugs were mine. I'll tell you though," he chuckled, "anybody looking for a laced brownie around here knows all they have to do is head south of the border. I'm sure they can get their fill in Colorado."

Lauren smiled. "You're right about that."

Dominick straightened in the chair. "I told Danny, no more. You come to work high again, you're outta here. He swore he wouldn't do it again, but I had a bad feeling.

Sure enough, it wasn't even a week later he showed up for work high on something. I could tell." He lowered his voice. "And I think he might have stole some money out of the register."

He gave a small shake of his head. "But he's family. I shoulda gave him another chance. I shoulda found a way to help him."

"I saw a lot of people with drug and alcohol addictions come in front of the judge. The one thing I learned from hearing them is you can't help someone if they're not ready to quit. They have to want to be done with that life-style. And even when they do, it's really hard to stop. Really, really hard. You shouldn't feel bad. None of this is your fault."

"Still, I told Theresa I'd watch over him."

Lauren stayed silent, knowing any words she spoke would not lift the weight of the misplaced guilt Dominick carried.

He rose, walked over to the next table and opened its umbrella. "Hey, I'm sorry to be bothering you with all this. It's the weekend, and work, I'm sure, is the last thing you want to be thinking about. I'm gonna quit before I scare off my favorite customa."

"With all your delicious pastries? Scare me off? *Never.* I know it's a tough situation. You can talk to me any time about it. I mean that." Lauren stood as he unfurled the next umbrella. "Besides, that's what friends are for, right?"

He gave a small nod. "Thanks. Now you go enjoy the rest of this fine day."

As Lauren walked down the sidewalk her thoughts were on the conversation with Dominick. It made her want to do something to help prove Daniel's innocence, but she wasn't sure what she could do to help. Without the murder weapon, the evidence so far was all circumstantial. From her memory of Mrs. Archer's deposition, there was enough animosity that maybe one of her children decided to get rid of her.

She thought about calling Emma, John Whitmore's paralegal, to see if there was anything she could share. She tossed that idea away. Even though they were friends, it didn't extend to talking about clients. *When the state puts the detective's report into evidence, I can at least look at that.*

Maybe it came down to Daniel Throgmorton getting on the stand and testifying. But if he did, would the jury believe him?

Chapter Fifteen

The second week of the trial was filled with a variety of witnesses, most of them evidence custodians and state crime lab technicians, people essential to showing proper chain of custody before evidence could get admitted.

By the time Friday came, the list of witnesses Lauren kept spilled over onto a second legal-size sheet of paper. It seemed everyone in town knew Mrs. Archer, and Ms. Martindale felt some need to have them all testify.

Lauren sat in Zoe's office during the final afternoon break for the week, scrolling through her phone, checking her emails. She stopped on the one from Emma Pearl, John Whitmore's secretary.

Lauren: I know this is super short notice but I forgot to contact a court reporter. Is there any chance you are available to cover depositions for us tomorrow? I know, it's a Saturday.

It starts at nine o'clock and is expected to last most of the day. Do you charge extra for weekend work?

She swiveled in the chair, trying to decide whether to take the job or not. This trial would be coming to an end in the next week or two. Her calendar, with its many pristine blank spaces, didn't bode well for her bank account. There would be more work covering court for Zoe, but a lot of the hearings did not turn into transcripts, which was where she made the bulk of her money.

If the jury found Daniel guilty, the appeal process wouldn't begin until after his sentencing, which wouldn't happen for at least two to three months. She wouldn't see any money from the appeal transcript for at least five months.

She thought of another reason to say yes. The depositions would take place in town, a definite plus. She could edit the transcripts after work when she got home. She tapped out her response. *Yes, I can cover. No, I don't charge extra for weekends.*

The deposition work would mean a boost for her bank account. And it would also help Emma out of a bind. A win-win. As she scrolled through the rest of her emails a new one popped up from Mr. Whitmore's paralegal.

Lauren, thank you soooo much!! You're the best! Oh, and one more thing. John said the parties are going to need the depositions expedited. Again, thanks. I owe you!

The win-win suddenly turned to a whine-whine. There went any time to relax on Sunday. She tapped out a response. *Now you tell me. And, yes, you do owe me. Big time! When do you need the transcripts?*

Before she could hit send Tony stuck his head in the doorway. "Are you ready or do you need another minute?"

"One minute. I'll be right there." Instead of sending the email, Lauren stood and texted one of the scopists she hired occasionally when she needed a fast turnaround on a deposition, checking on her availability to edit Saturday's depositions for her. As she strode down the hallway toward the courtroom, she remembered she had a therapy session scheduled for the same morning as the deposition. She made a mental note to make sure when court recessed for the day to contact Patricia Holland and cancel the appointment.

"Your Honor, said Ms. Martindale, "I know it's almost five o'clock, but rather than have the witness return Monday morning, with the court's permission I'd like to finish the questioning now."

Say no, say no, say no. The last hour and a half of the workday had already felt like three, and all Lauren wanted to do was go home. Go home now.

"If it's not much longer than five o'clock, permission granted," said the judge.

Lauren wanted to groan out loud to let him know how she felt, but instead kept her mask of indifference plastered on her face.

At five thirty the judge pronounced, "Court is in recess." To Lauren, those words were like a salve on sore muscles.

When the bailiff closed the door behind the last juror, Tony leaned over the bench. "Lauren, if you have a minute, stop by my office before you leave, please."

"Sure. Just give me a couple minutes, okay?"

Tony nodded and disappeared out the rear door.

Lauren gathered the ever-growing stack of exhibits, carried them to Zoe's office and plopped them down on the desk. She'd re-organize them first thing Monday before taking them back into the courtroom. She turned off the light, closed the door and made her way down the hall. "You wanted to see me?"

"Have a seat."

Tony typed on his keyboard, then turned his attention to her. She looked into his blue eyes. They were as intoxicating today as they were when the two first met.

"I just wanted to say how much I've enjoyed working with you."

"I've kinda enjoyed working with you too." Her words surprised her, but they were the truth. If she took their past relationship out of the equation, working for her ex-husband hadn't been as painful as she imagined it would be.

Tony leaned back in his soft leather chair. "That Martindale is some piece of work, isn't she?"

"Yes. Did you notice that Jessup nudges her with his foot to get her attention?"

"No. Really? I can't see his feet from where I'm sitting." He shook his head. "I was excited when this case started. Presiding over my first murder trial. But that was before I got a taste of how Martindale tries a case. I was expecting her to be a sharp attorney."

"Hey, it's my job to complain about the attorneys." Lauren smirked. "But Eli has been doing a good job."

Tony nodded. "He has, especially with what he has to work with, which isn't much. It should have been an easy case for the state, but Martindale is not doing a great job."

"I personally think the state's theory on motive is weak. The defendant killed Mrs. Archer so he could search her house for prescription drugs? And the state hasn't put on any evidence that they found her drugs in Daniel's possession."

Tony shrugged.

"That's what the prosecution was implying when they brought up the empty medicine cabinet. But it doesn't go anywhere after that."

"Dresser did do a decent job with that."

"He did," agreed Lauren. "But how would Daniel even know she was on any painkillers he could use to get high on?"

"Maybe he noticed how arthritic her hands were. Or how slow she moved. He could have seen them on her kitchen counter on one of his previous deliveries. And he probably didn't mean to kill her."

"That's all speculation. Besides, he had a job. He was working. He probably made decent tips."

Tony swiveled in his chair. "If he was into drugs, whatever he made plus his tips wouldn't come close to covering the costs of a drug habit."

Knowing it was true, Lauren didn't argue.

The two talked for more than an hour, discussing the case and the attorneys, and even the jury, observing that some constantly took notes and others never picked up their pens.

"So how do you like being a judge?" Lauren ran her fingers through her bangs, pushing them away from her face. "Doesn't look like it's gone to your head. Yet."

He raised one blond eyebrow. "Thanks for the observation. I'm loving it so far. The only downside is not having anyone to go out and have a drink with, talk about work."

"What do you mean?"

"Think about it. I'm a judge now. How would it look if I'm socializing with an attorney one night and they're in front of me in court the next day?"

"I hadn't thought about that."

"If we lived in a big city, it wouldn't matter as much. Until I came on the bench I didn't realize all my friends were lawyers."

"So that's, what, three people?" Lauren laughed at her own joke.

"Have I told you how much I've missed that sense of humor of yours?" He tapped his pen on his desk. "I unfriended so many people on Facebook, I'm thinking of just closing my account."

"You'll just have to make new friends."

Tony saw her look at her fitness watch. "It's getting late. I should let you get going." He cleared his throat. "If you don't have any plans, want to go get a drink, or grab a bite to eat?"

Lauren was starved. She almost caught herself saying yes, but the words Sam Overstreet spoke to her not quite a year ago in that small interrogation room were always right below the surface in her memory. *Your ex-husband had been having an affair with another woman, while you were still married.* And the kicker? The woman was Jane Murphy, the judge Lauren worked for. Tony never told her about his cheating. The only thing he said was, "I'm sorry", and that was after

112

she confronted him. Sam's words were the antidote to Tony's charm. With them she would never let Tony anywhere near her heart again. "No. I need to go home. I have to get ready for tomorrow."

"What exciting plans do you have for tomorrow?"

His tone came across as light but Lauren sensed something else in the way he asked the question.

"I'm working. I have depos starting at nine."

"You're working? On a Saturday? Haven't I kept you busy enough up here?"

"Yes, I'm working on a Saturday. And, yes, you have kept me busy up here. But this trial is about to wind down. I need to take the jobs while I can get them." She saw no need to tell him about her lack of a social life, or that she could use the money. What she did no longer concerned him.

"Maybe some other time."

"Maybe some other time," she echoed, knowing once Zoe returned, her and Tony's paths would rarely cross. She was okay with that.

"Let me at least walk you out to your car."

"Uh –"

"Lauren, it's dark out. I just want to make sure you get to your car safely."

*　*　*

They stood by her Volvo. Lauren tugged the collar of her jacket thinking if this were another time, another man, the moment would be romantic, the two of them standing side by side in the cool evening air, stars dotting the inky black sky, half expecting a goodnight kiss. But this was Tony. She almost thrust her hand out for a handshake, making it clear to him how she felt. Instead, she unlocked her car door, said a quick good night, and backed out of the parking spot.

A glance in her rearview mirror showed Tony standing under the lamplight, hands shoved in his pockets, watching her leave.

Chapter Sixteen

"Wore you out, didn't I, boy?" Maverik's tongue moved up and down rhythmically as he panted. "That should hold you over until I get back." Lauren poured kibble in his bowl, then went upstairs and took a shower. The run in the park turned out to be a good idea on two fronts, she thought, as she pulled a black suit out of her closet and tossed it on the bed. She felt energized and Maverik got in some good exercise.

She dressed and went downstairs in search of a quick breakfast. While her frozen breakfast burrito spun around on the microwave carousel, she went to her office and opened the email with the attachment Emma sent late yesterday afternoon. She printed out the information for the depositions scheduled for today, went downstairs, grabbed the hot burrito, placed it on a plate and looked over the first Notice of Deposition. "This might be an interesting day, Maverik."

He got up from his dog bed and trotted over to her, pressing against her thigh. "I'm sorry, that didn't mean treat time." Her eyes widened as she read the document she'd printed out.

Raymond Newell, Lawrence Newell, Jr., and Vera Mann, Plaintiffs vs. the Estate of Margaret Archer, and Mildred Archer, as personal representative, Defendants.

Lauren read the names of the people whose depositions were to be taken. *So the fight is on. Brothers and half sister on one side, the estate and the other half sister, Mildred on the other. Money trumps family again.* She sighed and put the paperwork in her bag.

✳   ✳   ✳

She pulled to the curb next to a one-hour-only parking sign. Another perk, though a tiny one, for working on a Saturday. No meter readers today. She stepped out of the car, collected her equipment from the back seat, and used her hip to close the rear driver's side door.

She tugged on the front door of Whitmore and Diamond Law Offices. It was locked. A glance at her fitness watch told her the depositions wouldn't start until another twenty minutes. She knocked on the glass door, then tried to peer inside, wondering if the depositions had been canceled and Emma had forgotten to let her know. It wouldn't be the first time that happened.

The idea of not working today began to appeal to her, even if it meant having driven here for nothing. As she waited to see if Mr. Whitmore would come to the door she thought about all the things she could accomplish. Finish the new pine beetle project she started. Do some deep housecleaning. Stop at Dominick's Bakery. Text Claude, maybe even meet up with her. Start that book she'd checked out from the library. The possibilities seemed endless.

Court finished late yesterday evening, tapping her out energy-wise. Her talk with Tony lasted into the evening. By the time she dropped her bag on the kitchen counter last night, the time on the microwave read nine o'clock.

* * *

Mr. Whitmore unlocked the door and held it open for Lauren, breaking into her would-be plans.

"Sorry for keeping you waiting. I'm running a little late this morning."

She noticed the attorney's wavy gray hair was damp. "No problem. I'm a little early."

"I was just getting a pot of coffee started. Would you like a cup?"

"No thanks."

"I'll let you get set up then."

He went into his break room and Lauren went into his conference room and picked her usual spot, the head of the table at the far end so no one had to pass – or trip – over her power cords and went about setting up her equipment.

* * *

At eight-fifty-five Dallas Black appeared at the conference room entrance.

"Come in, Mr. Black. Have a seat by the court reporter." Mr. Whitmore gestured toward the empty chair reserved for him.

Ray Newell, his brother Lawrence and Mr. Phillips scooted closer to the table so the tall wiry man could pass. He sat down, removed his cowboy hat and ran a hand through sparse gray hair. He gave a collective nod to everyone.

"Can I offer you coffee or water?" asked John.

"Yes, coffee. Black."

While Mr. Whitmore went to retrieve the coffeepot, Lauren looked around. The large room now seemed small with everyone crowded around the table. Brothers Lawrence and Raymond sat side by side, Mr. Phillips, their attorney next to Lawrence. Their half-sister Vera Mann now had her own attorney, Cora Trujillo, representing her interests. They sat opposite Mr. Phillips and Lawrence. Vera's interests were no longer in total alignment with her brothers, but they all shared a common goal: break the trust their mother had set up and redivide her estate.

Lauren scooted her chair, angling it slightly, facing Mr. Black more directly. Mr. Whitmore reached across the table, handed the witness a cup of coffee, then sat to Lauren's right, with his client, Millie Archer, next to him.

After the ranch manager took a sip of coffee and placed his mug down, Lauren said, "Mr. Black, would you raise your right hand, please."

Mr. Whitmore scheduled the deposition and so he took the lead in questioning Mr. Black. Dallas, in his checkered button-down shirt and bolo tie, kept his large and weathered hands clasped in front of him on the conference table, answering where he lived, how old he was, his education and experience. When asked what he did for a living, he faltered. "I work for Nicholas Fisher."

"When did you begin working for him?"

"I was hired by Nicholas Fisher on May twenty-first."

The answer surprised Lauren. Surprised that he was still working at all. He was old enough to retire but instead went looking for other employment. And surprised that in less than two weeks from the time she died he'd started working for Margaret's neighbor.

After more than an hour's worth of questions, Lauren and everyone in the room learned Mr. Black was Mrs. Archer's right-hand man. She depended on him for the day-to-day ranching activities, including handling the leases to rent out pastureland for cattle. And she even consulted him regarding the oil and gas leases she had entered into with Blackstone Oil.

At ten o'clock, Mr. Whitmore tapped his pen on the yellow legal pad in front of him. "Let's take a brief recess."

The room emptied. Lauren jotted down a few notes on the back of the Notice of Deposition. She thought back to Mrs. Archer's testimony months ago. According to her she relied on Mr. Black but not to the extent he made it sound. Whatever he said now, there was no one to dispute it. But there would be no reason for him to lie, would there?

Lauren observed that Mr. Black appeared comfortable answering all of Mr. Whitmore's questions, unlike when he testified during Daniel Throgmorton's trial, when he tripped over his words, kept tugging at his shirt collar, and spent most of his time on the witness stand talking into his lap, having to be reminded to speak into the microphone.

She didn't know why the change but was grateful that he spoke loud and clear. With everyone out of the room, she removed her phone from her bag, swiped the screen and checked for any texts. There were none.

Before she had a chance to put the phone away Mr. Whitmore walked in followed by Millie Archer. All the others filed in after Millie.

"I have no further questions," said Mr. Whitmore. "Mr. Phillips or Ms. Trujillo will now have the opportunity to ask questions."

Mr. Phillips opened his laptop and appeared to be scrolling through some notes. "I have just a few follow-up questions, Mr. Black."

Five minutes into his questions, the witness's posture changed.

"Are you a named beneficiary in Margaret Archer's will?"

"Yes."

Since the siblings were contesting Mrs. Archer's will, Mr. Phillips knew what was in the will and already knew what the answer to his question would be.

"And how old are you, Mr. Black?"

"Sixty-eight."

Lauren saw Mr. Phillips's eyebrows raise ever so slightly. *So, he's eleven years younger than Mrs. Archer. So what?*

"Did you and Margaret Archer socialize outside of work?"

"What do you mean?"

"Were you invited to her house for dinner? Did you ever go out for drinks?"

"I worked for her many years. So, yes to both questions."

"Did you and Mrs. Archer ever have more than a business relationship?"

Mr. Whitmore objected to relevance. Since John didn't represent Mr. Black, he couldn't tell him not to answer, and so Dallas, whose face turned scarlet, answered the question.

"Margaret and I were once in a relationship."

"When did this *relationship* start? And how long did it last?"

Mr. Black shrugged, then said, "It was a long, long time ago. I don't remember. It was after her divorce from Vera's dad, Charlie Babcock." His eyes darted to Vera and back to Mr. Phillips. "I was recently divorced myself. It – it just happened."

"And who ended the relationship?"

Mr. Black cleared his throat. "She did."

Lauren's fingers were poised on the keys ready to stroke the next question even before Mr. Phillips had the chance to ask.

"How did that make you feel?"

Dallas didn't answer immediately. "I was upset at the time. But like I said, that was years ago."

"And did you ever get back together?"

"No. She started dating Harold Archer and then they got married."

"But yet you continued working for her?"

"Yes. It was a good-paying job."

"Did you and Mrs. Archer ever disagree about how to run the ranch?"

Mr. Black hesitated before answering. "Everyone has disagreements. Nothing we didn't eventually work out."

Ray Newell, who sat next to Mr. Phillips, tapped the notepad in front of him with his pen. His attorney glanced at what the chief had written.

"Did Mrs. Archer ever threaten to fire you?"

"No, she did not. But the minute Margaret died, this one here," he gestured to Ray Newell with his chin, "fired me. I don't think he had the right to do that but I wasn't going to fight with him. Besides, I wouldn't have wanted to work for him."

"Why is that?"

Mr. Black shrugged. "We never did see eye to eye when Margaret was alive and running things. He never wanted anything to do with the ranch, you know, the day-to-day operations. I had no desire stay on and watch him run Margaret's hard work, her life's work into the ground."

Mr. Phillips sat silent, looking at his laptop screen. Then he said, "Let's take five minutes. I might be done."

Everyone left the room except Lauren and Mr. Black.

Mr. Black stood, placed his hands on his lower back and stretched. He looked at Lauren's writer. "You were in court when I testified, weren't you?"

"Yes." Lauren was about to say it's been an interesting case but stopped herself. This is the man who found his employer lying dead on the floor.

"I was pretty nervous. I never testified before." His expression grew dark. "That was a horrible, horrible sight. I'll never forget what happened that night."

"I can't even imagine. And it sounded like Ray Newell was pretty upset with you."

"Yes. The man never did like me so that was no surprise."

Lauren decided to ask a question that hadn't been brought out in the testimony so far. "How soon did he get there after you called the police?"

Mr. Black thought about the question. "Within minutes. I wasn't paying any attention to time. He arrived before they did." He looked around the conference room. "Is this what you do every day?"

"Not every day but, yes, this is what my day is like when I do work."

"I could never do what you do, sitting typing on that machine all day. It would drive me crazy if I couldn't be working outside. And even crazier if I had to deal with lawyers every day."

"And I couldn't do what you do." She left out that without lawsuits and lawyers she wouldn't be able to earn a living. That thought was not quite true. Her skills could be used for live captioning, to help the hard-of-hearing community. But she had started out on the legal side of court reporting and enjoyed the work.

He looked toward the door. "Seems to me that Mr. Phillips got to ask an awful lot of personal questions, don't you think? Is that normal?"

Lauren gave a noncommittal shrug. It would not be professional of her to comment on how any attorney questioned a witness. What Mr. Black said held some truth. Lawyers often asked questions that didn't seem relevant to why they were there, but unless their inquiry went totally off the grid, they were allowed to ask. And occasionally the personal questions led to important information about the case. "Every attorney is different. It's not unusual."

"Well, I don't like it. How is my relationship with –"
He stopped midsentence when the parties and their counsel entered the room.

"No further questions," said Mr. Phillips.

Cora Trujillo looked at her client with a raised eyebrow. Vera Mann shook her head.

"We have no questions," said Ms. Trujillo.

"So am I done here?" asked Mr. Black.

"Yes. Thank you for coming in on a Saturday. Let me walk you out." Mr. Whitmore glanced up at the clock on the wall. "Our next witness is scheduled at eleven so we have a few minutes."

* * *

Carissa Carlson raised her hand, displaying well-manicured fingernails.

The deposition began with Mr. Whitmore asking preliminary questions of the certified public accountant, then more specific questions related to why they were all crammed into a conference room on a Saturday morning.

"I understand you were hired to go over the books of Newell Ranch?" asked Mr. Whitmore.

"Yes," said Ms. Carlson.

"Who contacted you?"

"I was contacted by Raymond Newell – or I should say his attorney, Kevin Phillips," said Ms. Carlson.

"And what were you requested to do?"

"To do a complete accounting of the ranch."

"Were you told why the Newells wanted that audit done?"

"No."

A large stack of paper sat on the table in front of Mr. Whitmore. He showed the documents to Ms. Carlson one by one and had her explain what each was.

At eleven-thirty Mr. Whitmore said, "Let's take a brief recess, say about five minutes or so? I think I'm almost done." The room emptied. John took Millie Archer into his office, closing the door behind them.

Lauren stood and stretched, then went to the window and looked out. Ms. Carlson stood in the parking lot next to a blue four-door sedan. She reached inside her bag, pulled out a pack of cigarettes and lit one. She took a hefty drag, tilted her head toward the sun and did a slow exhale.

The desire for a cigarette hit Lauren hard, so hard she came dangerously close to running outside and yanking the cigarette right out of Ms. Carlson's fingers. *Get a grip.* She turned away from the window and the temptation. *Will I ever get over the desire to smoke again?* It had been almost a year since she had a cigarette. She blamed her ex-husband for falling off the nicotine wagon, but knew the elapse was on her .

She busied herself by sorting through the voluminous documents marked as exhibits, rearranging them and making sure they were all accounted for.

There were tax returns for the business dating back ten years. There were spreadsheets showing parcels of land Newell Ranch leased to various individuals, how long each lease was for, and when it began. There was also a separate spreadsheet listing oil and gas leases the ranch had with Blackstone Oil.

When everyone was again seated, Mr. Whitmore said, "Let's go back on the record."

As the accountant explained how the economy affected the late Mrs. Archer's estate, Lauren's mind drifted to what she should eat for lunch, and that she needed to pick up milk on the way home. Was there anything else she needed at the grocery store?

"Will you please mark this as the next exhibit?" Mr. Whitmore set a spreadsheet next to Lauren. She blinked away the boredom, grabbed the exhibit labels and placed one on the sheet. It was testimony like this that she glossed over when explaining to someone how interesting her profession was and how she heard so many interesting facts. As a rule she tried not to lie to people.

Alden Bates, the accountant who prepared tax returns for the ranch and Mrs. Archer for the last five years, was scheduled to testify in the afternoon. *I'll need an intravenous drip of caffeine to stay awake after lunch.* She remembered from Mrs. Archer's deposition he had been her accountant for many years. Lauren wondered if he was also Ms. Holland's accountant. Or even the chief's accountant.

"Did you come to any conclusions after your review of all the documents?" asked Mr. Whitmore.

"Yes."

"Please explain."

"After going over all the documents – more than once I might add – there are discrepancies between what assets are in the accounts and what the profit and loss statements say should be in the Newell Ranch account."

"So what are you saying?" asked Mr. Whitmore.

"I'm saying the accounts do not balance and there are

some serious omissions of important data that should have been included." Ms. Carlson added, "There is no reason why they shouldn't have been part of the profit and loss statements, unless ..."

"Unless what?" prompted Mr. Whitmore.

"Unless someone was deliberately not accounting for it, leaving it out on purpose."

"Can you give me an example?"

"The numbers themselves are basic math, simple accounting. The oil and gas leases Mrs. Archer had with Blackstone Oil call for her to receive a hundred percent of the royalties of gas drilled on her property. I've reviewed the paperwork, all the audits provided by Blackstone to Newell Ranch as to what it was owed each year, minus the expenses associated with the cost of drilling. There are two drilling rigs on the ranch so two different leases. One has been in effect for seven years and one for five. According to Blackstone's paperwork they provide as a part of their monthly and annual reports to shareholders, they paid Newell Ranch a total of five hundred thousand dollars for the second lease, the one that's been in existence for five years. But according to the profit and loss statement created by her accountant, it reflects Newell Ranch received one hundred thousand dollars total for that lease."

"Do you have an explanation for the discrepancy?"

Ms. Carlson straightened in her seat. "After going over the numbers and the supporting document, there is no logical explanation I can come up with. You need to question Mrs. Archer's accountant about the discrepancy."

Four hundred thousand dollars not accounted for. Lauren looked down at her writer, to hide the surprise in her eyes.

She stole a quick look at Chief Newell, whose mouth hung open. *It should be an interesting deposition this afternoon.*

After another ten minutes of questioning the accountant, the deposition concluded at eleven-fifty-five.

"We're starting back up with Mr. Bates at one-thirty, right?" asked Mr. Phillips.

"Yes," said Mr. Whitmore.

Instead of getting in her car and driving home for lunch, Lauren decided to take a walk, then grab a quick bite. She strode to the corner, headed south, the wind, a force of its own, pushing at her back, making her pick up her pace. After walking for two blocks, Slice It Up Pizza came into view. She slowed down. Unwanted thoughts of the trial flooded her mind. Photos of the murder scene had been displayed to the jury on a large monitor in the courtroom. Blood on the dining room floor next to Mrs. Archer's crumpled body, blood spattered on the pizza box were conjured up as the aroma from Slice It Up drifted onto the sidewalk. There were multiple photographs of the pizza box, one with a label stating the contents: a supreme, meat lovers with peppers and onions. And one photo of a pizza inside its cardboard box.

Her thoughts went to the autopsy report. Lauren spun on her heel and ran smack into Sam Overstreet. He stopped and raised his hands but not before coffee escaped from his to-go cup, spilling onto the sleeve of his shirt and hand. "Whoa, whoa." He wiped his hand on his jeans.

"I'm so sorry." Lauren patted her pockets for something to wipe the hot liquid with.

"I'm okay. You just took me by surprise. Where are you going in such a rush?"

"Uh, nowhere. I'm on my lunch break."

"The trial is going on a Saturday?"

"Oh, no, no. I'm doing depositions today. We're on a break and I was just getting some fresh air. I'm so sorry about your shirt."

"That's okay. Really."

Lauren went around him, leaving him to wonder what the big hurry was about.

Chapter Seventeen

$\mathcal{U}$sing her temporary badge and security pin number, Lauren let herself into the courthouse, her footfalls echoing in the large empty building. She knew any answers to questions she wasn't even sure about would be here Monday morning, but when something, an idea lodged in her mind, she couldn't let it go. This time she didn't know what the something was. All she knew was she wanted to look at the autopsy report. Look at it now. If anyone had been with her, they would have tried to talk her out of it, accusing her of being *that* dog with a bone and not being able to let go. And they would be right. But being by herself, she had no one to answer to.

Lauren went to Zoe's desk and straight to the folder containing the exhibits admitted into evidence during the trial. She shuffled through them. No autopsy report. She looked around the room, hoping she just forgot to put the exhibits in order. She went through the documents a second time. No report. She pushed back the panic growing in her chest. She reminded herself she had never lost an exhibit before.

Inside the courtroom, she went straight to the court reporter's table. Empty.

She stood on tippy toes and looked on the judge's bench. There were Tony's handwritten notes on a legal pad, but no exhibits.

Back in Zoe's office she went through the pile of exhibits again, inspecting the sheets of paper clipped together, turning all the pages over, as if she might catch them in the act of playing a mean prank on her.

The uneasy feeling spread to her stomach, giving her a sick feeling. She told herself not to panic. On Monday she would ask the attorneys if one of them had taken it and put it in their files by mistake. But she was sure she brought it to Zoe's office. *Where the heck is it?*

Lauren left the building sorry she ever came, knowing the missing report would bother her until she located it.

She left through the rear exit of the courthouse. She no longer had an appetite but knew she should eat something, as the afternoon would be a long one. Her mind still on the missing report, Lauren didn't see the police chief until he stood a few feet from her. His broad frame blocked the walkway, forcing her to stop. Startled, she sucked in a sharp breath.

He smirked. "Ms. Besoner, you're just everywhere today, aren't you?"

And so are you. "I just – I had to get my spare charger for my writer. I left it at the courthouse," she lied. *Why am*

I even explaining anything to him? It's none of his business what I'm doing here.

"Is that so?"

The only things in her hands were her cell phone, badge and car keys. "See you in a little while." She went to step around him. He mirrored her movement, his barrel chest blocking her. He took a step toward her, looked her up and down, his gaze lingering on her breasts.

Lauren took an involuntary step back.

"You know, Ms. Besoner, you look –"

"*Ray!*"

Lauren and the chief turned in unison at the direction of the voice.

"Are you coming?" Trish Holland gestured to her wrist, indicating the time.

"Yes, hon." Ray smiled at his wife, the lecherous expression absent from his face.

Trish shielded her eyes from the noon sun. "Oh hi, Lauren."

Lauren raised her hand in a half wave.

Ray Newell smiled at Lauren and spoke loud enough for his wife to hear. "Nice chatting with you, Ms. Besoner. I'll see you after lunch." The police chief walked toward his wife and Lauren let out her breath, not realizing she had been holding it in.

When Ray reached Trish, he said something that Lauren couldn't hear. His wife laughed as he hooked his arm in hers, and they walked away.

Chapter Eighteen

*L*auren walked the two blocks to John Whitmore's law office. She reached her car and sank into the driver's seat, opened her palm and saw the impression the car keys left. Her hands shook. *Calm down.* She closed her eyes, leaned into the headrest and breathed in several deep breaths. She started her car. No longer having an appetite, she had enough time to drive home, let Maverik out to do his business, and return for the afternoon deposition.

❊   ❊   ❊

Tension filled the air in the conference room. The attorneys and the parties around the conference table attempted polite conversation while waiting for Mr. Bates but the words sounded rote, forced.

The parties sat, the conference table dividing up the sides. Ray, Lawrence and half-sister Vera on one side, Millie Archer, representative of the estate, on the other. Siblings in a lawsuit. It always brought out the worst in everyone.

Lauren's realtime screen was open and ready for the deposition to begin. Instead of joining in the attempt at conversation, she opened Mr. Black's deposition and started to clean up her untranslates. She concentrated on her laptop and did her best to ignore the fact that Ray Newell was in the room.

Mr. Phillips glanced at the clock on the wall. One forty-five. "Do you have a way of contacting Mr. Bates? See what the holdup is?"

"Yes. I'll be right back," said Mr. Whitmore. He left the conference room, cell phone in hand. His muffled voice could be heard from the hall as he spoke. When he returned he said, "He's not answering. I left him a voice mail to contact me right away."

"Let's give it another ten minutes, see if you hear back from him. I'd like to get this done today." Mr. Phillips let out an exasperated breath.

Five minutes later Mr. Whitmore's phone vibrated on the table. He swiped the screen. "A text from the deponent." He read the message. "He says he's not feeling well and won't be able to make it." He looked up at Mr. Phillips. "And when we reschedule, he wants his attorney present."

He wants his lawyer with him? Interesting.

"Well, that's just great," said Mr. Phillips.

Mr. Whitmore shrugged. He looked at Mr. Phillips and Ms. Trujillo. "What would you like to do, Counsel?"

"I'd like to take a deposition but without Mr. Bates that's not going to happen."

"We'll just have to reschedule," said Vera's attorney.

Mr. Phillips shook his head as he closed his laptop. "I'll call you with some new dates."

Lauren was relieved to be done early, but a little disappointed at the same time. She wouldn't get to hear Mr. Bates's explanation of the missing money. Maybe the deposition would be rescheduled after the trial and she would be hired to report it. She thought of an added bonus of quitting earlier than planned: she wouldn't have to feel Chief Newell's stare upon her.

Chapter Nineteen

*A*fter a quick stop at the grocery store to pick up milk, bread and a few other items, Lauren went home. With Maverik out in the backyard, she fixed herself a peanut butter and jelly sandwich and ate it leaning against the kitchen counter. She let her dog back in and shared some of the crust with him, then went upstairs to her office to send off the morning's depos to her scopist. As she did so, she thought of Mr. Black's testimony.

John's questions were focused on the role Dallas played in keeping the ranch running smoothly. Mr. Phillips's questions were directed toward Mr. Black's personal life. Nothing unusual there and hardly pertinent to the case, thought Lauren. He was divorced. Had two grown sons.

Lauren wondered if Dallas Black had been upset, jealous even, of another man coming in and dating Margaret after they broke up? Did he want more? Did he want to marry Margaret? Did he want to be part owner of the ranch and not just her employee? Even if all those were answered yes, it couldn't possibly matter now. He continued to work for her long after they dated. The romantic relationship was decades-old history.

Lauren thought back to what Mrs. Archer said in her deposition four months ago. There was mention of her neighbor, Nicholas Fischer. She couldn't conjure up the details but did remember she was left with the impression that Margaret's neighbor wasn't a nice man.

Lauren stretched in her chair, gazed out the window. Mr. Phillips's final questions stuck in her mind. Or rather, Mr. Black's answer stuck in her mind. When he was asked if Mrs. Archer ever threatened to fire him, his answer had come quick, almost too quick, she thought. And Margaret wasn't here to contradict him.

At the beginning of every deposition Lauren administered an oath to the witness. And every witness either said yes or affirmed they would tell the truth. She knew some of them turned right around and lied. *Was Dallas Black's last answer a lie?*

Chapter Twenty

Susan looked up from her desk as Lauren hurried past the judicial assistant. The woman's age-spotted hand rested on the phone's receiver. "Well, you decided to show up after all. I was just getting ready to call you. I thought maybe you forgot you were covering court for us today. The jurors are all here. It's almost nine o'clock, you know."

No, I don't know. I'm a dumbass and can't tell time. Lauren turned back. "Of course I didn't forget about the trial."

Susan cocked her head. "Are you okay? You look a little … off."

Lauren touched her cheek, remembering she hadn't had time to apply her makeup. "Yes, I'm fine."

"Zoe has never once been late. Very dependable. So professional."

Yeah, yeah, yeah. Whatever. Lauren didn't comment. Didn't have time to comment. And worse, hated to admit Susan was right. She was cutting it too close. Last night she hadn't set her alarm clock because lately she had been getting up before it went off and used the time to take Maverik for a walk. Get her exercise out of the way at the beginning of the day because no matter how many times she told herself she'd work out after work, her well-intended plans dissolved once she set her keys on the kitchen counter. Hungry and not in the mood to cook dinner ended up being a sandwich, or something microwaved and eaten while sitting on the sofa watching TV instead, or worse, scrolling through her phone on some time-sucking social media site.

The recurring nightmare had returned. It took her over an hour to fall back asleep. When she finally woke, it was to the sun streaming through the crack in her curtains. There was no time for a walk, breakfast or even coffee. And now she was paying the ultimate price, having to listen to Susan's remarks.

In the courtroom she woke up her computer, started the realtime feed to Tony's laptop, then went to collect the exhibits. She turned on the light in Zoe's office. She gathered the folder with the exhibits. The autopsy report lay on top. *What the heck? This was not here Saturday.* There was no time to think about that now. She rushed into the courtroom.

She arranged the exhibits facing away from her and toward the attorneys for their use, then checked the witness list for the day's lineup.

"I'll be right back," she told the bailiff. She needed to use the restroom, knowing it would be a couple of hours before the first break.

He winked. "We won't start without you."

On her way back to the courtroom, Tony stopped her. "Are you okay? You don't look so good."

Lauren displayed a pretend smile. "I'm fine." She felt no obligation to tell him about her sleepless night or the headache she felt coming on.

Tony put on his billowy black robe. "Okay then. Let the fun begin."

Tony's good humor eased some of the anxiousness she felt. She inhaled and entered the courtroom.

*   *   *

"The state calls Detective Silver to the stand," said Ms. Martindale.

The detective, who had been sitting next to Robert Jessup since the first day of trial, came around counsel table and stood before the bailiff, looking him straight in the eye while he swore her in.

She strode confident on two-inch black heels to the witness stand. The dark blue suit she wore complemented her deep-set blue eyes. Once seated, she adjusted the microphone, moving it close to her lips. The simple movement told Lauren this detective felt comfortable. She would speak loud and clear, not afraid of her own voice. Lauren didn't know many people who felt that way, including a lot of the lawyers she encountered in the courtroom.

Detective Silver faced the jurors, gave them a curt nod, placed her hands in her lap, then looked at the attorney in anticipation of the first question.

Ms. Martindale went through the preliminary questions,

name, occupation, training and education. Detective Kristine Silver had worked for the Albany County Sheriff's Department for eight years and had been a detective for the past three. Previous to working in Wyoming she was a peace officer in Lakewood, Colorado for five years.

With the usual opening questions out of the way, the special prosecuting attorney asked, "Detective Silver, on the evening of May tenth, were you called out to 17 County Road 320 to investigate a suspicious death?"

"Yes. Deputy Chavez was patrolling that patch of the county on the evening in question, so he was initially dispatched to the scene. Whenever there's a suspicious death the deputy will notify the detective on duty, which in this case was myself."

"Can you tell us what you did upon being notified by Deputy Chavez of a suspicious death?"

"Yes. I had him secure the scene. Deputy Chavez is part of our crime scene unit, so I had him contact the other members of the unit to meet him out there to begin the investigation process."

Detective Silver took a sip of water from a white Styrofoam cup the bailiff had placed in front of her when she took the witness stand. "I then asked dispatch to contact the coroner and have him meet us at the deceased's home. In the meantime I contacted Sheriff Wolfenden to apprise him of the situation."

"What did you do next?"

"I arrived on scene and I –"

"I'm sorry to interrupt, Detective, but tell the jury who else was there when you arrived on scene, aside from law enforcement."

"Yes. Dallas Black, the reporting party. Ray Newell, the victim's son, who is also Crawford's police chief, as I'm sure everyone knows. He was outside the home with his wife Patricia Holland when I arrived. According to Deputy Chavez he had been inside earlier in the evening."

"Chief Newell is in law enforcement himself. Couldn't he have stayed and assisted with the investigation?"

"No."

"Why not?"

"Two reasons. Number one, as Crawford's chief of police, he has no jurisdiction outside the City of Crawford. This crime occurred in the county." The detective spoke clear and unhurried. "Number two, the victim was his own mother. It would not be proper, even if he did have jurisdiction, to investigate the death of a family member. He was understandably upset, but he could not remain inside the home."

"And earlier you said the crime scene unit was called to the home. What does a crime scene unit do exactly?"

"At my direction, or whoever is in charge, they go to the location of a particular incident, where they take photographs, collect and bag anything that could be classified as evidence."

"Are they trained to know what to look for as far as evidence?"

"Yes. Each member of the crime scene unit has extensive training in evidence collection," said Detective Silver.

"So they're trained in what they should do when they arrive on scene, and don't need any direction from you?"

"Correct. If they have any questions, they will come to me."

142

Everyone in the courtroom listened to the details of the initial investigation conducted by the detective and deputies under her control. How Deputy Matthew Hanson took over two-hundred-fifty photographs, beginning with a picture of the front porch with the front door open, and ending with photos of the victim from a multitude of angles. How another deputy went about bagging and tagging any item thought useful in their investigation, which included Mrs. Archer's cell phone, and even the pizza.

One of the first things Detective Silver did was figure out how the pizza came to be at the house, whether it was delivered or if Mrs. Archer picked it up on her way home, or if it got there some other way. Once she confirmed the pizza had been delivered, and delivered by Daniel Throgmorton, the detective focused her attention on him, as he was the last person to see Margaret alive. He went quickly from delivery driver to a person of interest to main suspect.

"What was it about the defendant that made you suspect him of this utterly heinous crime?" asked Ms. Martindale.

Mr. Dresser stood. "Objection, Your Honor. The phrase —"

"Sustained. Ms. Martindale, please refrain from the use of such inflammatory adjectives and just ask your question."

"Yes, Your Honor." The prosecutor approached the witness stand with an eight-by-ten photograph. "Detective, I have handed you exhibit ninety-two. Please tell the jury what that is."

Detective Silver explained it was a photograph taken of the address on the home. The next hour and a half consisted of Ms. Martindale placing a photograph in front of the witness and the detective describing what the photograph showed. Lauren found herself writing the words while gazing outside, gauging how windy it was by how fast a fat white cloud moved in and out of her vision.

"Your Honor," said Ms. Martindale, "may I publish these to the jury?"

The defense attorney was on his feet. "Objection. They have not been admitted."

"I move then for the admission of exhibits ninety-two through three-hundred-two, photographs taken that day depicting the scene."

"Objection, Your Honor." Mr. Dresser once again stood. "Lack of foundation. Detective Silver did not take any of these photographs. She testified it was Deputy Matthew Hanson from the crime scene unit that took these photos."

"Sustained."

"Your Honor," began the prosecutor, "Detective Silver was there. She –"

"Ms. Martindale, I've been listening to the testimony. You'll need to lay the proper foundation before the photographs can be admitted," said Judge Jenkins.

Lauren wanted to bang her head on something right then, frustrated at having sat through an hour-and-a-half of tedium. The prosecutor trying to cut corners failed. Lauren didn't know if this was deliberate on Ms. Martindale's part, attempting to introduce evidence without setting up the proper foundation, or if she truly didn't realize she had to have the person who took the photographs come in and testify. After listening to the prosecutor's questioning style throughout the trial, Lauren suspected the latter.

She thought about the state's witness list. She didn't remember seeing Deputy Hanson's name on it. If that was the case, the prosecutor would have to call him to get the photographs admitted in evidence, giving Mr. Dresser another reason to object. Ms. Martindale didn't list the deputy as a witness and shouldn't be allowed to testify. If his objection was sustained, none of the crime scene photos would get admitted, and it would be one less thing for the jury to have in their hands when they started deliberations.

Ms. Martindale consulted her notes, and Lauren used those few seconds to turn her head all the way to the left and then to the right, stretching the muscles in her neck, all the while thinking that if the attorney kept missing important steps, the jury just might be forced to find Daniel Throgmorton not guilty.

"While you gather your thoughts, Ms. Martindale, I think this is a good time to take our lunch break." Judge Jenkins looked at the jury. "Ladies and gentlemen, as I release you for the noon hour, please remember my words I spoke at the beginning of the trial. Do not discuss the case with anyone, and do not do any research, online or otherwise, regarding the case."

∗　　∗　　∗

Lauren sniffed the remains of the coffee, held it away from her and poured the bitter-smelling sludge down the drain. She prepared a fresh pot knowing she needed caffeine to keep focused and stay awake in the afternoon.

"Do you believe that woman?"

She turned to see Tony in the doorway, a scowl on his face.

"I'm going to have a serious talk with Randall Graham when this is over."

"What are you going to say to him?"

"I'm going to tell him whoever is sent into my courtroom from now on better know what the hell they're doing or they better stay the hell away."

"Can you do that?"

"I don't care if I can or not." Tony went to the window and looked out. "Ms. Martindale is on her way to screwing this case up royally."

Lauren had to agree with her ex-husband. She wasn't a lawyer but even she knew the prosecutor was making rookie mistakes.

"You know she's going to try and call Detective Hanson to get those photos in. Do you know he's not listed as one of the state's witnesses?"

Lauren nodded. "I know."

"And you know Mr. Dresser is going to object, and I'm going to have to rule in his favor. Shit." He shook his head and strode down the hall.

Chapter Twenty-One

The salad Lauren brought for lunch lay in the clear plastic container, half eaten. She knew she should eat somewhere other than in Zoe's office. Have a real lunch break. But today she had munched on chicken thrown on salad greens. Once she'd eaten the chicken, the greens lost their appeal. She'd gone into the courtroom, grabbed the detective's report and the autopsy report off her table, took them back to Zoe's office and began to read them.

The detective's report didn't shed any light on who else might have committed the murder. Lauren began to read the autopsy report. She flipped from page seven to the next page, page nine. She checked to see if maybe the page was double-sided. No page eight. *I stapled them together myself. It has to be here.*

Tony walked past the open office door, then retraced his steps when he saw Lauren. "Back from lunch already?"

She pointed to the leftover salad, then lay the autopsy report down.

"Anything interesting in there?" Tony gestured with his chin to the detective's report.

"No, not that I can tell."

"I grabbed a quick workout at the gym." He patted his stomach. "I didn't realize this job would have me sitting on my ass so much."

Lauren raised an eyebrow. "Really? Sitting on the bench all day long, five days a week, and you didn't think you'd put on any weight?"

"Didn't expect to pack on the pounds so quick." He cleared his throat. "My metabolism must not be what it used to be."

"You're not getting any younger, that's for sure."

"Ouch. What is up with you?"

"Nothing. Just kidding." Lauren liked knowing she could say these things to Tony and be able to get away with it even though he was a judge. She knew it was because they were once married, but all the same it gave her some odd satisfaction.

She pointed to the autopsy report. "I started reading through some of this. Most of it's beyond my comprehension, you know, the technical jargon, toxicology, stuff like that. Maybe there's something in there that might help the defense." Lauren didn't want to tell him she misplaced a page from an exhibit. She'd search through every piece of paper first before admitting such a thing to her ex-husband.

"What, you're part of the defense team now?" He laughed at his own remark.

"No, I was just – I don't know. I'm sure you think it's silly, but I thought maybe I could find something inconsistent in the autopsy report or maybe the detective's report."

"I'm sure the state has gone over all the evidence with a fine-tooth comb. But with Ms. Martindale at the helm, maybe it's not that silly an idea." Tony picked up the document and tapped it on the palm of his hand. "Nothing jumped out at me when I read this."

"When did you look at the autopsy report?"

"Friday night. After you left I came back here to finish ..." He let the words trail off.

Tony had returned to his office after they parted company instead of going home. They were alike. He also had no one to go home to. Lauren revised the thought. She had Maverik waiting for her. Always excited to see her. Tony didn't have a dog or a cat. *Unh-unh. Don't you dare go feeling sorry for him.*

"I went back on the bench to make sure my laptop was turned off. I don't like leaving it on over the weekend. I saw some papers on the floor near your table. Being the nice guy that I am," he wriggled his eyebrows, "I retrieved it and took it back to my office. This morning I put it on the stack of exhibits for you. I know how you can be when something is not in the exact spot it's supposed to be."

She let out a sigh. "That explains it."

"Explains what?"

"I came here Saturday. I wanted to look at the report but I couldn't find it." She took a sip of coffee. "I got a little panicky."

"You panicked for nothing, Lauren." He raised an

eyebrow. "You came here on a Saturday just to look at the report?"

"No. It was during the lunch break. I had some extra time. I thought I'd, you know, look at it."

"Your OCD is kicking in a little, wouldn't you say?" Tony chuckled.

Lauren ignored the remark because on some level she knew it to be true. "Did you take it apart and restaple it?"

"No. Why would I do that?"

"Uh, no reason."

"Is it all there?"

Lauren debated whether to lie to him or not. "No. There's a page missing."

"Are you sure?"

"Yes, I'm sure."

"That shouldn't be a big deal. Get with Martindale and have her print another copy. She probably has them in electronic form."

"I will. but I'm going to look for it one more time before I do."

Tony handed the document back to her.

"Anyway, I must have spent twenty minutes searching for the damn thing. I went through every single piece of paper in that pile ... *twice*."

He held up his hands, palms out. "Sorry. Hope you didn't lose sleep over it. But you know, if you hadn't come in, on a weekend no less, you would have never known it was *missing*. So if you think about it, it's mostly your fault, wouldn't you agree?"

She rolled her eyes in answer.

"I'll take your silence as agreement. And it wasn't like

it was floating around where someone outside of these walls had access to it."

She opened her mouth to tell him that wasn't the point, the point being she lost sleep over it, but that piece of information would only amuse him.

"Speaking of the report, I've been meaning to tell you, I thought you did a decent job of getting down all those technical terms Dr. Grant was rattling off the other day."

Decent? How kind of you. "A lot of them were already in my dictionary, but she rattled off some words I'd never heard of before."

He patted the doorjamb. "I'll leave you to it. And," he dropped his voice to a deep bass, sounding like the late singer Barry White, "I'll see you in court." Tony obviously thought what he said was funny. The sound of his laughter carried all the way to his office.

Lauren took the autopsy report back to the courtroom. The trial would start back up in ten minutes. She picked up the crime scene photos wanting to make sure they were all in order. She hurried through the graphic ones, slowed down when she came to the pizza box. There were several photos of the box. Closed pizza box, bird's-eye view. Closed pizza box, straight on view. She flipped to the next photo. Pizza box open. Supreme meat lovers inside. The last picture was a close-up photograph of blood on the side of the box.

※　※　※

Judge Jenkins entered the courtroom, gave a slight nod at Lauren. She took the cue, stroked the time on her machine, and waited for him to speak.

"The bailiff has informed me you want to put something on the record before the jury returns. Is that right, Counsel?" Judge Jenkins asked.

Ms. Martindale stood. "Yes, Your Honor."

"Go ahead," said the judge.

"I spoke with Mr. Dresser over the lunch hour, and he has agreed to stipulate to the admission of the crime scene photographs."

Judge Jenkins peered at Mr. Dresser. "Is this correct, you no longer object to the photographs coming in?"

"That's partially correct, Your Honor. We've stipulated to all of them except the ones of the deceased. We continue to object to those and do not stipulate to the admission of them. I have discussed this with my client. We believe the rest of the photographs are of little value and therefore we do not object to their admission."

The judge turned to look at Ms. Martindale. "Is that the agreement?"

"Yes, Your Honor. That's what I meant to say. All photos of the victim will be removed from the stack."

"Very well then. When the jury returns, renew your request to admit them on the record, and those stipulated exhibits will be received," said Judge Jenkins. "And one more thing. Our court reporter needs you to provide another copy of the autopsy report. Apparently there is a page missing."

"Your Honor, I'm sure I provided a complete copy to the court," said Ms. Martindale.

"Matters not. There is now a page missing. Provide her with another copy."

"Yes, Your Honor. I'll provide that at our next break."

"Mr. Johnson, please return the jury," said Judge Jenkins.

*   *   *

After the photos were admitted on the record in front of the jury, the prosecutor turned to a new line of inquiry. "Detective Silver, did you search the defendant's home?"

"Yes, we did."

"And did you find any prescription medication at his residence?"

"Yes. We found Oxycontin and fentanyl."

"What day did you search the defendant's residence?"

"May eleventh. The day after Mrs. Archer was killed."

"Was there anything else that you found during your search of his home?"

"Not at his residence."

Where are the pills? The fentanyl patches? Why isn't she putting that in evidence? Lauren glanced at the jurors, noting confusion on several of their faces. They too were expecting to see the drugs.

"Detective Silver. I'm handing you state's exhibit three-hundred-three," said the prosecutor. She placed a brown bag on the witness stand. "Before you open the bag, please explain the writing and all the markings."

Mr. Dresser stood. "Your Honor, may we approach?

"You may."

Ms. Martindale and Mr. Dresser approached the bench, and the three huddled around a small microphone set on top of the judge's bench. Judge Jenkins pressed a button next to him and white noise filled the room. For a split-second Lauren was in the back seat of her dad's old Ford pickup on a summer vacation. As they made their way out of town, the song on the radio would slowly fade out, replaced with static, and then he would pop in a cassette tape.

Lauren donned a headset and nodded at Tony that she was ready for the sidebar conversation. With the white noise on, the jury would not be able to hear the attorneys or the judge speaking, but Lauren would be able to hear their argument through her headphones.

"Your Honor, I object. Yesterday was the first time I knew anything about a ring. The state failed to disclose this evidence in their pretrial memorandum. I am caught totally by surprise. I must object to it even being talked about."

"Your Honor," said Ms. Martindale, "this ring has only come to our attention the day before yesterday. I let Mr. Dresser know as soon as I found out. My detective has been searching, without any luck, for this ring. We believe it ties into motive and the jury has a right to hear about it."

"If the state only found out about the existence of this ring two days ago, the objection is overruled. You may continue questioning the detective, Ms. Martindale." The judge shut off the white noise.

Eli returned to his seat, his face a mask, his emotions hidden, all except the twitch of his jaw.

Lauren pulled off her headphones, a strand of her hair catching on them as she did so.

*　*　*

The prosecutor returned to the podium, head held high from the victory at the bench. "Please continue with your explanation, Detective."

"This is an evidence bag with evidence that I collected. It has the date the item was collected. I've written my initials and the case number on the tag. If anyone breaks the seal, it will tear where my initials were placed."

The silence in the courtroom was broken by the sound of a pocketknife slicing open the brown sack.

Detective Silver extracted a clear plastic bag. She reached inside the bag and pulled out a ring, holding it for the jury to see, then looked at the prosecutor, waiting for the next question.

"Detective Silver, tell the ladies and gentlemen of the jury whose ring this is."

"Margaret Archer's."

"And how do you know that?"

"Speaking with Mrs. Archer's daughter, Mildred Archer, she advised a ring was missing. A ring the victim often wore. She provided us with a photograph of the ring."

"What did you do once you learned of this information?"

"Myself, along with Deputy Chavez, canvassed the pawn shops here in town, without any luck. We recently widened our search to Cheyenne. We contacted several of the pawn shops there, showed them a photograph of the ring. We eventually got a hit a couple of days ago."

"And what is the name of the pawn shop where you found the ring?"

"Harley's Pawn Shop."

"Judge, I offer the ring into evidence," said the prosecutor.

"Objections, Mr. Dresser?" asked the judge.

"None other than the objection I made at the bench, Your Honor."

"The ring is admitted," said Judge Jenkins.

"May I pass it to the jury?" asked Ms. Martindale.

"Why don't you hold off. The jury can take it back with them during their deliberations," replied Judge Jenkins.

"Yes, Your Honor."

She hasn't tied the ring to Daniel, thought Lauren.

"So, you recovered the ring. Can you tell us about who pawned the ring?" asked the prosecutor.

"The owner of the pawn shop showed us his surveillance video for the time in question. We were able to make a positive ID of the individual."

Ms. Martindale appeared to be looking over her notes, letting this fact sink in with the jurors. A deliberate tactic of building suspense, as if this were some thriller novel and she wanted the jury's full attention.

Ms. Martindale handed Detective Silver a black thumb drive. "Can you please identify what is on this?"

"This is a copy of the surveillance footage from Harley's Pawn Shop."

"Your Honor, may we approach again?" asked Mr. Dresser.

"Yes."

The white noise came on again. Lauren barely had time to place the headset on her ears before Mr. Dresser spoke. "Again, I object. We knew *nothing* about any surveillance until last night. I was able to view it but I've not had any time to go over this piece of evidence with my client. I certainly haven't had time to question the pawn shop owner. And frankly, Your Honor, I think the state has been holding back –"

Ms. Martindale interrupted. "The state has done no such thing."

"– evidence it could have easily given –"

"That is way out of line for Mr. Dresser to –"

"Ms. Martindale, let Mr. Dresser finish. You'll be given an opportunity to answer once he's done."

Lauren heard the prosecutor's heavy sigh through the headphones.

"This should certainly have been disclosed long ago, Your Honor. We vehemently object to this surveillance video being admitted into evidence."

"Response?" asked Judge Jenkins.

"Your Honor, as I previously said, we only discovered this two days ago. As soon as we learned of the surveillance video we secured it, made a copy of it and delivered it to Mr. Dresser last evening."

"Again, I have no reason to disbelieve the state, so at this time Ms. Martindale may continue laying the foundation for the video."

The prosecutor went through the steps of identifying how the video was obtained, and after establishing chain of custody, the thumb drive containing the video was admitted into evidence.

Mr. Jessup placed the thumb drive into his laptop, opened the video file, and projected it on a large monitor. Every juror's attention focused on the screen as they watched a man enter the pawn shop. The individual in the grainy video had stringy dark hair down to their shoulders and wore a red T-shirt over loose-fitting jeans.

The footage continued to play, and everyone watched the person approach the store clerk, reach in the front pocket of their jeans and produce a ring, laying it on the counter. After several minutes, the clerk could be seen counting out an indeterminate amount of cash and handing it to the person.

The figure turned to leave, their face now in full view of the camera. Ms. Martindale paused the video, letting the jury take a good look at the thin yet very recognizable face of Daniel Throgmorton.

"Your Honor, at this time the state has no further questions of –"

A loud thud sounded in the courtroom. Several jurors gasped, and the elderly juror sitting closest to the prosecutor's table put a hand to his chest.

"I'm so sorry, Your Honor. Slipped out of my hand," said Mr. Jessup. He pushed his thick-framed glasses up on his nose.

Ms. Martindale swung around to look at her co-counsel who was bending over in his chair, picking up a large book. Its spine read *Wyoming Rules of Criminal Procedure*. When he straightened up, book in hand, he angled his head, making *come here* movements with his eyes.

"One moment please, Your Honor." At counsel table, Ms. Martindale bent to confer with her second chair. She straightened, turned and cleared her throat. "Your Honor, one more question. Detective Silver, the man whom you investigated, the man you brought in for questioning, the man who is in the surveillance footage, who had possession of Mrs. Archer's ring, is that man in the courtroom today?"

"Yes, he is."

"Would you point him out for the jury and describe what he's wearing."

"Yes." Detective Silver pointed in the direction of Daniel. "He's the man sitting next to Mr. Dresser. He has brown hair. Wearing a blue button-down shirt, a black-and-white striped tie, and gray slacks."

"Your Honor," said the prosecutor, "I ask the record to reflect that the witness has identified the defendant, Mr. Throgmorton."

"The record will so reflect," said the judge.

"No further questions of this witness." Ms. Martindale took her seat next to co-counsel.

"I assume you'll have a fairly lengthy cross-examination of this witness, Mr. Dresser?" said the judge.

"Yes," replied Mr. Dresser.

"Well, it's close enough to five o'clock, I think we'll adjourn for the day and let you start fresh in the morning."

*　　*　　*

Tony stood by Susan's desk when Lauren came out of the courtroom. "Did you see what almost happened in there?" Her ex-husband spoke so loud she thought the bailiff would walk in any moment to tell him there were still jurors in the jury room, and to lower his voice.

"What did I miss?" asked Susan.

Lauren laughed. "Martindale almost sat down without identifying Mr. Throgmorton as the person involved in all this."

"*Yes*. She was that close," Tony gestured with his thumb

and index finger, "to blowing their case. Martindale, she's
… she's unbelievable."

"Quick thinking on Jessup's part, dropping that book,"
added Lauren.

"I'm going to have a word with Mr. Jessup before we
get on the record tomorrow morning. He better not pull
any more stunts like that or I'll hold him in contempt."

"I wish I could be sitting in there. I miss all the good
stuff," said Susan. She threw out her lower lip and pouted.

Tony didn't notice.

"State ended on a strong note. That ring was a surprise
to Mr. Dresser," said Tony.

Lauren nodded. She was thinking the exact same thing.
Eli had not known about a ring. He was taken by surprise.
Is there anything else Daniel was keeping from his attorney?

160

Chapter Twenty-Two

The stack of exhibits was growing. Lauren had to press them against her chest to keep them from toppling and spilling to the floor as she walked to Zoe's office. She deposited them on the desk, then returned to the courtroom, closed out her file and backed it up to the cloud. She took the list used to keep track of the exhibits, went back to the office, sat in Zoe's chair, and cross-referenced each one on the list confirming they were all accounted for.

She kept a tight watch over every exhibit admitted into evidence, double-checking and often triple-checking them to make sure none were missing. She couldn't stop herself from being overcautious.

Tony rapped on the doorjamb. "Hey. Mind if I come in?"

She looked up. "Of course not." *It's not like I can stop you. This is no longer my office.*

He sank into the chair opposite her, his robe thrown over his shoulder. "I think the state is closing in on this case. What do you think?"

"I'm thinking the same thing. I don't know if Eli is going to put his client on, but if he does then he'll have to admit to stealing the ring. Unless he says a friend gave it to him and he didn't know it was stolen."

Tony nodded his agreement.

"Lauren paperclipped some of the loose exhibits as she talked. "Do you think he'll take the stand?"

"Don't know. But if he does he opens himself up to his criminal history, if he has one. Once he starts testifying, he has to continue. He can't all of a sudden plead the Fifth when the state starts asking about his prior run-ins with the law. Eli will do his best to keep his client off the stand if he's got priors, I'm sure."

"It doesn't look good that he stole the ring, does it?" Lauren had been surprised to see Daniel on the video footage. All this time she believed he was innocent. How did he get her ring? Maybe she was wrong. Maybe he was capable of murder. No, she thought, it's just more circumstantial evidence. Stealing doesn't mean he did it. Unless she caught him and he panicked. Lauren didn't want to think about that.

Tony rubbed the back of his neck. "Eli's got his work cut out for him."

"If he doesn't testify the jury is going to be left wondering about it."

Her ex nodded. "And he could get on the stand and lie about how he came into possession of the ring. Or maybe he has a plausible explanation." Tony leaned forward in the chair, elbows on his thighs. "Either way, it's not looking good for Mr. Throgmorton."

"You sound like your old prosecuting self, you know that?"

"I was good, wasn't I?" His mouth twitched with a slight grin, his mischievous blue eyes giving his words double meaning.

Lauren raised an eyebrow in answer.

"Oh, come on. You know I was a good prosecutor. I won over ninety-five percent of all my cases."

"You're right," Lauren mumbled. "Can't argue with the facts."

He sat up straight in the chair with an *I-told-you-so* look on his face.

Lauren pulled her messenger bag out of the drawer. "How much longer do you think the trial is going to last?"

Her ex-husband shrugged. "There's a few more things Ms. Martindale needs to get in evidence but she must be close to being done."

"I wonder if Eli is going to call any witnesses. I didn't see a defense witness list. I assumed that's because he has none. But maybe he's holding back and he'll have someone come in to testify that Daniel didn't even deliver a pizza to Mrs. Archer that night. Maybe his car broke down and someone else had to take over his route."

"And Eli would keep that piece of evidence to himself all this time *why?*"

She could think of no good explanation. She gave him an impish shrug. "For dramatic effect?"

"More like wishful thinking on your part. Why do you want this guy to be innocent? I don't get it."

"Up until today I was sure he was. But him having Margaret's ring … maybe he is guilty. If he is it certainly isn't first degree murder. It certainly doesn't look like it was premeditated, because if it was he botched that up pretty good."

"Lauren, he could have been high at the time. We don't know."

"But I really like Dominick, and he feels bad for having fired his nephew. If Daniel ends up in prison Dominick's going to blame himself for the rest of his life. I tried telling him it's not his fault, but he won't listen to me."

"There's no reason the guy should blame himself." Tony slouched in the chair, stretching his legs, crossing them at the ankles and looking at the ceiling.

"I told him that exact same thing. More than once."

The two were quiet for a moment.

"And I think that whole Newell-Archer family are … odd."

"What do you mean?"

"I told you I took Mrs. Archer's deposition last spring."

Tony nodded.

"Her kids were trying to get her declared incompetent, but she died so the conservatorship no longer mattered. At least I thought it wouldn't matter but that's what this new lawsuit is about. Sort of. I think. All of her children, except the youngest one, are challenging the will and her estate based on her being incompetent at the time it was drawn up."

"I knew her will – it's actually a trust – was being contested. I haven't read the pleadings in the case yet but it's on my docket for some preliminary motions next month."

"The depositions I took Saturday, one was of the ranch manager, Dallas Black."

"He testified in our case. He was the one who called nine-one-one, right?"

"Yes."

"Was he in her will?"

"He is."

Tony did a slow nod of his head. "Sounds more and more interesting. And it'll be my first contested trust case."

"I don't know if this will come up in the case but Mr. Black, who now works for her neighbor, a guy named Nicholas Fisher, he said he threatened to sue Mrs. Archer. And after she died, he told him he was thinking of suing the estate."

"Why?"

"Fisher said Margaret had agreed to sell him the ranch and then backed out at the last minute."

Tony stroked his chin. "This Fisher guy having a separate lawsuit against the estate could complicate things. Could even have an impact on the assets inside the estate. Was a contract produced during the depositions? Anything to prove what Fisher is claiming?"

Lauren shook her head. "Just a verbal commitment."

"If nothing was ever put in writing, doesn't sound like he would have a leg to stand on."

"The Newells, Ray and his brother, hired an accountant to do an audit of the ranch assets and what should have been in the estate. I took her depo too on Saturday."

"What did she have to say?"

"She said that the Newell Ranch profit and loss statements didn't add up." Lauren tried to remember the exact

165

words. "She said no decent accountant would have made the mistakes that she saw. She implied that Margaret's accountant, who also kept her books, had left things out on purpose. Over the last five years it came to three or four-hundred-thousand dollars."

Tony nodded and whistled. "Who was her accountant?"

"Alden Bates."

Her ex shook his head. "Don't know him."

"We were supposed to take his depo too but he was a no show. Said he was sick. And," Lauren paused for dramatic effect, "he wants his lawyer to be there when they reschedule. Anyway, whatever was going on, Mrs. Archer – and even Mr. Black – made it sound like she had a bunch of greedy kids who couldn't wait for her to die."

"Her ranch manager said that?"

"Well, no. But he wouldn't have, not with them present for his deposition. He did hint at it though."

Tony nodded his understanding.

"Mr. Black also talked about a company that wanted to start a wind farm on her property, but she wouldn't have anything to do with it. He testified he heard Mrs. Archer and Ray arguing about it. Ray thought she should sell the land, that she was getting too old to run it, even with the ranch manager's help."

"What are you suggesting? That Ray, Crawford's chief of police, killed his own mother so they could move forward with developing the land?"

She had given it some thought, that maybe one of her children might have had something to do with her death, but Tony saying the words out loud made it seem farfetched. "No. Maybe."

"Sounds like you're fishing, Lauren. And I don't think you're going to get any bites with that theory. I think –"

Susan appeared in the doorway, gave Lauren a disapproving look and said, "Oh, here you are, Your Honor."

"Are you leaving, Susan?" Judge Jenkins asked over his shoulder.

"Unless there's something else you need me to do, Judge." Susan sighed, letting out a deep breath. "It's been a long day."

He raised his hand in a backward wave. "No, I'm good. See you in the morning."

"Have a good night," added Lauren.

Susan looked at Lauren, her lips pressed tight. She turned and teetered down the hallway in her two-inch high-heeled shoes.

"Sounds like a long, drawn-out battle over the Archer estate is brewing." Tony grinned. "I'm sure the attorneys involved are going to love that."

"I'm sure they will." Lauren dropped her cell phone into her messenger bag.

Tony stood. "I didn't mean to keep you. Maybe I can interest you in a drink? A drink just between friends?"

"Thanks, but I'm really tired."

"Of course. Go home. Rest your fingers."

Rest my fingers? She did a mental head shake. *My fingers could go forever. It's my back, my neck, my shoulders and my brain that need the rest.*

Chapter Twenty-Three

$\mathcal{L}$auren pulled out a bag of salad greens from the refrigerator, tossed it in a bowl and added carrots, tomatoes and cucumbers. Even with the large puddle of ranch dressing she doused it with, couldn't disguise the fact she was eating a salad. Out of necessity.

Maverik sat patiently at her feet. She tossed him a carrot, which he caught midair. "You're the only one I know who gets excited for a carrot." She laughed as he crunched the crisp veggie.

The waistbands of all her skirts left their marks around her stomach and she couldn't wait to get home and slip on a pair of sweats or yoga pants. But the marks were a reminder she had to make healthier choices at mealtime. She thought this extremely unfair because when she arrived home after working hard all day, she deserved to eat a satisfying meal, which translated into carb heavy. Salad rarely lived up to her expectation of satisfying.

She put her dish in the dishwasher and went upstairs to her office. She cracked open the window several inches to hear Maverik out in the backyard. When he tired of sniffing all the dirt, grass and bushes he sniffed earlier, he'd nudge the doorknob with his paw. If that didn't catch her attention quick enough, he would proceed to scratch at the back door. She painted the door in May and it was already in need of a new coat of paint.

End-of-summer scents piggybacked on the warm twilight air, tempting her to go outside and forget about doing a little research. She turned away from the window and fired up the laptop.

When she left the courthouse at the end of the day, she had run into Dominick. He had been on his way to see Daniel. They exchanged quick pleasantries as the baker wanted to visit his nephew before the jail staff shuffled the housed inmates to the small dining hall for dinner. The sight of her friend's face saddened her. He seemed to have aged since the start of the trial. His salt and pepper hair had more salt coursing through it. It may have just been her imagination, or it may have been the angle of the sun and the time of day making the gray more noticeable.

When Lauren had been at the bakery a few days earlier, there hadn't been anything new to share with him. He had looked disappointed. The prosecuting attorney continued to present her case. Until this afternoon, Lauren didn't think the state's case was all that solid. Seeing Daniel on that video left her with mixed feelings.

She opened her court reporting software and clicked on the file containing the deposition transcript of Mrs.

Archer, the one taken mere hours before her death. Not sure if she would discover anything useful, she took her time scrolling through the document, hoping there would be some words on the screen that would point to another possible suspect. Someone she could tell Eli to look into.

On the first run-through she pulled a notebook out of the side drawer to jot down anything which caught her attention.

Scratching sounds came from below. Lauren went downstairs and let Maverik in. She dug into an open bag of peanut butter cookies, took two and started up the stairs. Maverik raced ahead of her, trotted into the office and lay under the desk panting.

She closed the window and sat down. On the second, more thorough reading, she stopped on page thirty-two and re-read the testimony.

"Dallas had been a good hand." Further down, *"He had run the ranch well."* Lauren found herself reading through several more pages. She stopped to give her eyes a rest and thought about what she had been reading. A pattern emerged in the words Mrs. Archer used. She spoke in the past tense.

She looked out her window for a few seconds, then scrolled through the next few pages, stopping randomly.

Page thirty-seven. *"He used to be at the ranch by seven in the morning to begin work."*

Page forty-five. *"We rarely share a meal anymore."* Had there been a reason for Margaret to have phrased it that way? Lauren jotted down the words *had* and *used to* and put Dallas's name next to them.

Mr. Phillips had not picked up on Margaret's choice of words. After further study of the deposition, Lauren realized Mr. Phillips never asked Mrs. Archer if the two were still on good terms.

Lauren remembered there was testimony of a new neighbor. She used the search function in her court reporting software and went to that section. Reading a few pages refreshed her memory. The man wasn't actually a new neighbor. Malcolm Fisher had owned the property to the south of Mrs. Archer. He passed away two years prior and left everything to his only child, Nicholas. Malcolm's estate included two thousand five hundred acres of land.

After his father's death Nicholas Fisher returned to the home he grew up in and took over his father's ranch. He approached Margaret and offered to buy her property. All of it. Though she thought the offers were generous, she told Mr. Fisher no, she wasn't interested in selling. Nicholas approached her two more times, asking if she had reconsidered his offer to sell him the land.

Page fifty-nine of the transcript. *"The last time Nicholas Fisher came to my home he said if I was smart I'd sell. 'People your age have accidents all the time. What if you were outside all by yourself and fell? There would be no one here to help you. Think about it.'"*

Lauren thought back to Mrs. Archer's reaction when she spoke those words. Yes, the elderly woman held her head high, indignant that Mr. Fisher would say such a thing to her. But there had been something else lurking in her sharp blue eyes. Fear.

Chapter Twenty-Four

*O*n the piece of paper with Dallas Black's name Lauren added the name Nicholas Fisher followed by a question mark.

She wrote down a few basic facts she learned from Mrs. Archer's testimony.

Margaret Archer. Longtime homesteader/ranch owner. Married three times. Widowed twice, divorced once.

Husband number one, Lawrence Newell, died when sons were adolescents. Two children, Lawrence Jr., and Raymond.

Husband two, Charles Babcock. Divorced after three years of marriage. One child, Vera Mann.

Husband three, Harold Archer. Married to Margaret ten years before passing. One child, Mildred ... Millie Archer.

Newell Ranch. Twenty thousand acres. Formed by Margaret and Lawrence Newell, Sr. Fifty-one percent owned by

Margaret. The forty-nine percent left divided equally amongst all children.

Lauren sat up straight in the chair, did a few stretches while thinking what else to add to her list.

Flipping to a new sheet of paper Lauren listed Margaret's children, with a mini bio beside each of them.

Mildred Archer. Dental assistant. Never married. Goes by Millie. Close relationship with her mother. Lives in Crawford. Not part of the involuntary guardianship attempt.

Lawrence Newell. Eldest of Margaret's children. Junior high math teacher. Married. Two kids. Lives in Colorado. Not involved in ranch. Rarely visited.

Raymond Newell. Married. Not involved in ranch. Visited occasionally.

Vera Mann. Married. Cashier at grocery store. Lives in Cheyenne. Not involved in ranch. Rarely visited. Recent empty nester.

Lauren went back to the keyword index, scanned the list for the name Alden Bates. She went to each page and line where the accountant's name appeared. She wrote the accountant's name down on a fresh piece of paper, underlining it twice. She added, *"Mr. Bates is no longer my accountant."*

In response to Mr. Phillips's questioning, Mrs. Archer testified that she hired another accounting firm. *"I told Alden I no longer wished to engage his services. He wasn't happy when I told him, but that was my decision."*

Lauren jotted down that Mr. Bates had gotten his marching orders less than a week before her death. After reading a few more pages on the topic of the accountant, Margaret kept the reason for letting Mr. Bates go vague, saying that *it was necessary*. After thinking about the accountant, Ms. Carlson's, testimony, Lauren jotted down the word *embezzlement* and underlined it.

She leaned back in the chair. Did Mrs. Archer discover what Alden was doing? It wasn't proven but it appeared the accountant was stealing from her. Could Mr. Bates have killed Mrs. Archer to keep her from exposing what he was doing?

Lauren massaged the sides of her face and around her eyes. As she powered down her computer, she thought about what she should do, if anything, with what she'd learned from the recent depositions. Even if it has meaning she couldn't give the information to Eli. It wasn't hers to give. She could, however, suggest he contact John Whitmore and ask the attorney if he would share the contents of his client's testimony and the testimony of Carissa Carlson. She had no idea if Mr. Whitmore would divulge attorney-client matters but it wouldn't hurt for him to ask. And she would also remind him that Nicholas Fisher was a client of Sean's, who he shared office space. Eli could talk to him and perhaps learn something useful.

Lauren was about to text Eli and offer her suggestions, but Maverik's sudden bark startled her. He rushed out from under the desk, swiveling her chair as he ran to the window, front paws on the sill. He whined, raced out of the room and down the stairs. Lauren peered out the window. Night had fallen and the only thing she could see was her own reflection in the glass.

The sound of a car engine coming to life made her rush down the stairs. In the kitchen Maverik alternated between jumping and barking at the kitchen door. Lauren turned on the outside light and let him out. He charged toward the back fence in pursuit of a set of vanishing taillights.

Lauren joined Maverik and peered out over the fence down the alleyway. The vehicle turned left at the corner and disappeared.

She walked as fast as she dared in the dark toward the safety of her house, Maverik close by her side. Once in the kitchen she secured the lock and deadbolt. Then she did something she hadn't done in a long time: she checked every window to make sure it was locked, ending in the basement, Maverik hugging her thigh as she went. Taking in the stark, bare area where there had once been cardboard boxes filled with yet-to-be unpacked items, that autumn evening rushed into her thoughts. She could still feel the cold of the cement floor, the searing pain in her ankle and shoulder, lying helpless, unable to do anything but watch Judge Murphy's killer nonchalantly set fire to her basement. That feeling of helplessness and terror haunted her subconscious.

As she made her way up the basement stairs she wondered, was it just a coincidence someone had been outside her yard? The city greenway lay beyond the alley that ran behind her home. There were several access points to reach the greenway on this side of town. A few houses down at the end of the block, there was a paved path that ran between two homes. People used it to reach the city-owned walking area. Someone probably parked behind the house for convenience, someone out for a late evening stroll.

Lauren tried to convince herself that's all there was to the incident. In fact, it couldn't even be called an incident.

Don't go getting yourself all worked up for no reason. Especially right before bed.

Chapter Twenty-Five

*L*auren approached Ms. Martindale. "Did you print off another copy of the autopsy report?"

The prosecutor looked up from her laptop at counsel table. "No, not yet. Don't worry, I'll make sure you get it."

How hard is it to print off another copy? "Okay." Lauren returned to her chair, wrote the date and time on her writer and waited for Tony to take the bench.

"Detective Silver, you may retake the witness stand. You remain under oath from yesterday," said Judge Jenkins. "You may cross-examine the witness, Mr. Dresser."

The detective, dressed in a charcoal gray suit, strode to the witness stand. Her blonde hair, worn loose, trailed down her back.

Lauren stole a sideways glance at her ex-husband, who was doing his best not to out-and-out stare at the detective.

She did a mental head shake. *You always did have a thing for blondes.*

* * *

Everyone who was in attendance yesterday heard pretty much a replay of the testimony as Mr. Dresser rehashed what the detective had already testified to.

When it sounded like he reached the end of his cross-examination he asked, "Detective, were there any fingerprints of my client found in the home of Mrs. Archer?"

"Yes, there were."

"Where were they located, Detective?"

"On the doorknob of the front door, both inside and outside."

"Anywhere else?"

"On a dining room table."

Mr. Dresser scribbled a note on his yellow legal pad. Lauren could tell he was using the tactic to cover his surprise by the answer. Since the state did not bring up the fact his client's prints were anywhere other than the doorknob, he was expecting to hear a "no" from the detective.

He looked up from his pad. "So his fingerprints weren't found in Mrs. Archer's bathroom?"

"No."

"And his fingerprints weren't found on the medicine cabinet?"

"No."

"And you didn't find his DNA on Mrs. Archer, did you?"

"No."

"And you didn't find his DNA on any items in her home, did you?"

"No, I take that back. His prints were found on the dining room table."

"But he admitted to being there that night? He didn't deny it, did he?"

"Since we identified them there would be no reason to deny it –"

"Yes or no, Detective? He didn't deny being there that night?"

"No."

"And during your investigation you searched Mr. Throgmorton's residence?"

"Yes."

"Did Mr. Throgmorton give you permission or did you have to obtain a search warrant?"

"He gave us permission."

"Would you take that as a sign that my client had nothing to hide?"

Detective Silver thought about the question. "Not necessarily, no."

"And what did your search of his home reveal?"

"We collected his clothes, his work uniform that he was wearing the night in question, and the shoes he was wearing."

"And can I assume those items were sent off to the crime lab for testing?"

"Yes, they were."

"I don't see them here." Mr. Dresser made an exaggerated sweep of his arm around the courtroom, then looked at the detective. "Is there a reason they're not here in evidence?"

"The defendant's clothing didn't reveal anything negative or positive."

"Negative or positive. Interesting choice of words. When you say there was nothing positive, is that another way of saying there was not one shred of evidence on my client's clothing connecting him to the death of Mrs. Archer?"

The detective tugged at the sleeve of her suit. "You could say that."

"I did say that. Would you agree?"

Detective Silver tilted her head from shoulder to shoulder as she thought about the question. "Yes."

"So the crime lab found no traces of the victim's blood on Mr. Throgmorton's pants, shirt, shoes or socks, correct?"

"Correct."

"If my client had killed Mrs. Archer, surely there would be some trace amounts of her blood on something he wore, wouldn't you agree?"

"Possibly."

Mr. Dresser appeared to be studying the legal pad in front of him. "Did you find anything in his home that you determined was the weapon used to kill Mrs. Archer?"

"We found no weapon." She went on to clarify her answer. "We did not find a weapon that matched the injuries Mrs. Archer sustained."

"You testified on direct that you found Oxycontin and fentanyl in my client's home."

"Yes, we did."

"Did they belong to the victim?"

"Possibly. I don't know."

"*Possibly*. What did the name on the label of the prescription bottle or packet that contained the fentanyl patches say?"

"There was no pill bottle, no prescription label."

"Where did you find these medications?"

"On his kitchen counter. The fentanyl patches were loose, not packaged, as were the Oxycontin pills."

"Did you ask my client about them?"

"Yes. He said they were left over from an old injury he sustained." The detective looked at Mr. Throgmorton, then back at the jury. "I couldn't verify his statement because he didn't remember where he got the prescriptions filled nor could he remember what doctor prescribed them."

"So you also can't testify they were Mrs. Archer's prescription medications, can you?"

"No, I can't."

"Detective, Mr. Black is the one that discovered the body and called nine-one-one, is that right?"

"Yes."

"Did you ever consider him a suspect?"

"Not a suspect as such. Mr. Black had a solid alibi for the time of Mrs. Archer's death. He'd gone to a movie. He provided us with the ticket stub. And we checked the surveillance cameras they have at the movie theater. He was there."

After a handful more questions Mr. Dresser said, "No further questions." He grabbed his legal pad and went and joined his client.

Ms. Martindale returned to the podium and spent a half an hour on redirect examination of the detective before returning to her seat at counsel table.

Lauren wanted to turn and give a thumbs up to Eli. Even with the prosecutor asking follow-up questions of the detective, a chance to strengthen her case, the defense exposed several holes in the state's case, filling the space with doubt about his client's guilt.

She thought of testimony like a debate. One side gets up and argues and their words sound so convincing that you find yourself nodding your head as they speak. But then their opponent begins to talk and you find yourself agreeing with them, saying to yourself, I never thought of it that way.

Today Eli tipped the scales of justice more in his client's favor, thought Lauren. But would twelve strangers agree with her?

Chapter Twenty-Six

The crunch of gravel under the Volvo's tires announced to Lauren they had reached their destination. After sitting in court all week, she took advantage of the weather forecast for Saturday and invited her aunt to go on a hike with her. Horseshoe Lake was a twenty-minute drive from her home.

The gravel parking lot was deserted except for an older blue Chevy Suburban and a white two-door Honda Civic.

Lauren opened her car door and Maverik climbed on her lap, squeezed between her and the steering wheel trying to get out first. She grabbed him by his collar before he had the chance to leap out. "Not so fast." Lauren nodded to the passenger floorboard. "Can you hand me that leash please?"

Aunt Kate handed the lead to her, exited out the passenger side, pulled the sunglasses down from the top of her head and waited for her niece to secure Maverik. She looked up at the sky. "Looks like a perfect day for a walk."

Lauren turned her face to the blue sky and warm sun. "It does." She went to the passenger side, took out the sandwiches her aunt brought and placed them in her pack alongside the trail mix she brought. "I thought we could hike to the lake. According to the app it's a mile and a half, and it says the trail is easy." She looked at her aunt. "What do you think?"

Kate adjusted her sunglasses. "Three miles round trip. I think I can handle that."

"Good. And we'll take a break and eat once we get to the lake. And we can always turn around sooner and eat here if it's too much for you." She pointed to a metal picnic table sitting under the canopy of a mature pine a few yards away.

"Good idea," said Kate.

Before they started up the trail, Lauren pulled out a package of trail mix and offered some to her aunt.

"No thanks. I'm still full from breakfast."

A loud pop breached the air around them. Kate turned to Lauren. "Was that a gunshot?"

"I don't know. Kind of sounded like a car backfiring to me." Lauren waited and listened, but the sound wasn't repeated. They looked at one another and shrugged.

They reached the trailhead after walking a short distance. A tall wooden sign standing off to the right read, *Horseshoe Lake – two point five miles.* Lauren kicked at the dirt. "Two and a half miles?" Lauren pulled her cell phone out of the backpack and tapped on the screen. She backed up several feet hoping to get better reception. "It says one and a half." She showed her aunt the phone.

Kate nodded. "But like you said, we don't have to go the whole way."

Lauren pocketed the phone. "If you're sure."

"My doctor says I need to exercise more. Let's not waste time standing here talking about it. Let's go." Kate nodded at her niece's wrist. "Your Big Brother watch will tell you."

"You mean my fitness watch?"

"Yes. That thing does more than just tell you how many steps you take. I read on the internet where it collects all kinds of data. It can even tell if you quit sleeping with your husband." Aunt Kate gave her a knowing nod of her head.

Lauren snorted. "What?"

"Don't laugh. And then pretty soon you'll see ads on your Facebook page for divorce lawyers in your area."

Lauren laughed harder. "I'll try and remember that if I ever get married. Married again, I mean."

As the two women walked the path, Maverik stayed by Lauren's side, the leash slack between them. She looked down at him. "Good boy. When we get a little further up, I'll let you explore." She gave him a stern expression and pointed her finger at him "But you have to stay close."

The trail, which started out wide and flat, narrowed and steepened as the women walked further into the Medicine Bow-Routt National Forest, stands of aspen trees lining the path. Lauren unhooked Maverik's leash after they had went a quarter mile. He bounded off into the dense foliage. When she could no longer see him, she called out his name. He reappeared, his body quivering with excitement. "Good listen." She pulled out a dog treat, offered it to him. It was gone in one bite. Maverik thrust himself once again into the shrubs.

185

They fell into an easy cadence. "So how was your trip? Is Glacier National Park as beautiful as everyone says it is?" asked Lauren.

"Gorgeous. Amazing. There's not enough words to describe it." Aunt Kate shared her RV travel adventures with her niece via text message. "We had a wonderful time, but …"

"But?"

"Jack and I have decided that while we like traveling in the motorhome, we could use a small break from all the togetherness. And as long as we still have the alpacas, we shouldn't be gone so much. It's not fair to keep asking you or Sam to watch over them."

"Are you starting to get on each other's nerves? Is that what you're saying?"

Aunt Kate put her thumb and index fingers together. "Just a little. So we're going to park the motorhome for a while."

Lauren nodded, wondering if any of it had to do with Aunt Kate's backseat driving, which she witnessed firsthand as she drove them up the twisty highway.

*   *   *

"I didn't realize how out of shape I am." Kate stopped. "I don't know how …" She bent over, hands on her thighs. "… I let you talk me into doing this." Her chest heaved as she tried to catch her breath.

"You were the one who said you needed to get back in shape."

Kate shook her head. A bead of sweat dripped off her nose.

"I'm sorry. I thought you'd be able to handle this trail. The app has it marked as easy."

"Does it now? I suppose … it's all relative. It's easy for you … I can see that."

"Let's sit for a minute and then head back, okay?"

"No, no. I'm fine. Just need … to catch … my breath."

Lauren bounced on toes tucked into a pair of neon orange cross-trainers. When she looked at her aunt, she stopped. "I think we should go back. You don't look so good."

"I'll be fine. But how much further do we have?"

"We've gone a mile, so a half mile more."

Aunt Kate straightened, dabbed her face with the sleeve of her shirt and reached for her water bottle.

Lauren had made her way over to a gray flat boulder ten yards off the dirt-packed trail. Kate joined her on the rock. The air was thick with the scent of sagebrush. A family of quaking aspens provided shade from the midday sun. Kate unscrewed her water bottle and took a long drink.

"Do you hear that?" Lauren tapped her aunt's arm.

Aunt Kate held the bottle midway to her lips and listened.

The noise came from further up the trail. The whine of an animal.

"Maverik," Lauren called out.

The intensity of Maverik's whine increased until it turned into high-pitched barking, breaking into the quiet.

She looked at her aunt. "I wonder what he's gotten into."

The two women made their way onto the path, Lauren half running. She followed the sounds of Maverik's barking. When she reached a fork in the trail several yards further up, the barking stopped, the air around them once again silent.

"Maverik, come."

She waited for her aunt to catch up. They turned off the trail and onto freshly matted grass that meandered to the right. They wound their way past granite outcroppings and over toward clumps of sagebrush, some with broken branches.

Maverick's black-and-brown bushy tail stuck up from the low-growing twisted branches, whipping back and forth with a frenzy.

"Maverik, come."

He ignored the command. She reached down, hooked the lead to his blue collar and gave it a tug. "So much for letting you go off leash, mister. What was I thinking?"

Kate came up and stood next to her. She let out a sound, somewhere between a croak and a yelp. She held out a shaky arm and pointed.

Lauren looked in the direction her aunt was pointing. A man lay face up on the ground, arms outstretched. Blood pooled around his head like a devil's halo.

Kate spun around, retreated several steps, bent over and vomited.

Lauren squeezed her eyes shut, hoping the image of the man wouldn't find a place to nest in her mind and return as a recurring nightmare, but she knew she hadn't looked away soon enough.

Maverik strained against his collar while whimpering.

"Oh, my goodness. Oh, my goodness. Oh, my goodness." Aunt Kate spoke the words like a mantra.

The ground beneath Lauren's feet was like a magnet holding her hostage. She blinked hard and looked around. The earlier welcome breeze disappeared. Nothing moved. Not a lone aspen leaf, not a chipmunk foraging on the ground. Nothing.

She fumbled in her backpack until she found her cell phone, then dialed nine-one-one. The call failed. "I don't have any reception. Try yours." Lauren looked at her aunt. She stood unmoving, repeating her mantra. "Aunt Kate."

Her aunt blinked.

"See if you have cell service."

Kate dug inside her black fanny pack and extracted her cell phone.

While she waited for her aunt to confirm if she had service, a magpie, its outer black feathers shiny as wet paint, landed on the man's chest. The bird strutted across him as if he were packed earth, a grassy area or an outcropping. Just another surface to walk on.

Her aunt turned away to block the glare of the sun. "I don't have any bars."

"Maybe a text will go through. Try texting Jack."

"He's in Cheyenne." Kate tapped on her phone, then moved away from Lauren, trying to see if the phone would catch a few bars. A moment later she returned. "I texted Sam."

"Good thinking."

Seconds later Kate's phone vibrated. She read the screen. "Sam wants to know where we are."

Where the hell are we exactly? Think, Lauren. She inhaled, trying to slow her breathing and calm her mind so she could focus on their exact location and describe precisely where they were.

"Lauren, how far did you say we were from Horseshoe Lake?"

"About a half mile away. We parked on the east side of the lake at Beaver Trailhead. We're about a mile from there."

Kate texted the information to Sam. "He's notifying dispatch. And he's on his way."

Lauren relaxed a little knowing Sam would be here soon. It made it easier to keep down the handful of trail mix she ate earlier. She gripped Maverik's leash tight so he wouldn't destroy the ... was this a crime scene? Whatever it was, she couldn't let her dog do more damage than he already had before they found the poor soul who lay there. "I'm going to go back down the trail and wait for a sheriff or Sam. I can show them where ... where we are. You stay here."

Aunt Kate shook her head. "No. We ... we should stay ... stay together. Let's both get out of here." Lauren looked once more at the man. The magpie pecked at the shirt, then spread its wings and took flight, carrying a shiny object in its beak.

Lauren averted her gaze from the man's head and the blood-stained grass around it and concentrated on the rest of him. Just beyond the fingertips of his right hand lay a nine-millimeter gun glinting in the sun.

"Come on." Aunt Kate grabbed her arm and uprooted her from the spot on which she stood.

She looked over her shoulder as her aunt tugged her away. He wore a button-down shirt with the sleeves rolled up and black slacks. And then there were his shoes. Black tips with a herringbone pattern in the center.

190

Chapter Twenty-Seven

Kate and Lauren retreated a few yards from the body. Kate abruptly sat on one of many granite outcroppings dotting the landscape. They still were within sight of the body. Beads of perspiration appeared on Kate's forehead and upper lip.

"Are you okay? You look awful."

Her aunt covered her mouth, then ran behind the boulder, twigs snapping underfoot, and threw up again.

The sound made Lauren's stomach lurch. She sat on the trunk of a fallen pine, put her head between her knees and took several deep breaths.

Aunt Kate walked toward Lauren, her face drained of its normal healthy glow.

Lauren stood, fumbled in her pack for her water bottle and put it in her aunt's hand. "Here."

Her aunt took the bottle and Lauren turned her attention

to Maverik, who had turned to face the trail. He pulled at the lead and let out a loud bark.

"Maverik, ssh."

He barked louder and then did something Lauren had never seen him do before: curled his upper lip, exposing his large canines.

From the direction of the lake came a man. Beads of sweat shone on his forehead. He held a gun in his hand, pointed at Kate and Lauren.

Maverik stretched the limits of his lead. Lauren gripped it tighter not wanting Maverik to get in front of the gun. The killer must have returned. The man stepped closer.

Chief Newell? What the hell? Lauren knew they were in the county and it should have been Sheriff Wolfenden or one of his deputies responding to their call, not Crawford's police chief.

Ray Newell scowled at the two women. "You're the ones that called this in?"

Aunt Kate answered, her voice shaky. "Yes."

"We were up there." Lauren pointed behind her. "And we came across ..." she didn't know how to finish the sentence. Came across a horrible sight? Came across a dead man? Came across a body? They all seemed so inadequate to describe what happened.

"What are you two even doing here?"

"We were out hiking," answered Kate.

"The body's off the trail. Over there." Lauren gestured with her head to where the man lay.

Chief Newell stomped through the brush making his way over to the body. Kate and Lauren trailed behind.

Lauren started to speak. "We were just –"

"Quiet." Chief Newell bent over the body, then glanced at Lauren over his shoulder. "And I see your dog has already fucked up the scene."

There could be no arguing his statement. Large paw prints were pressed in the damp grass and dirt all around the body. What else had Maverik disturbed as the man lay there, oblivious to the flies that landed on him?

Kate put a hand to her throat. "We … we just stumbled upon him while we were walking."

"We didn't touch anything." Lauren's voice sounded unnaturally high in her ears. "Like my aunt said, we were hiking toward Horseshoe Lake."

The chief snorted at her explanation.

"How did you get here so fast?" asked Lauren.

Chief Newell didn't respond. He remained crouched in front of the man, making it easier for her to see large patches of scalp between the steel-gray buzz cut.

Lauren strained to see beyond the chief. She watched as he reached his hand out toward the barrel of the gun. She whispered to her aunt, "What's he doing?"

He straightened, shoved his hand in his pocket, then moved close to Lauren. He hissed in her ear. "What did you say?"

"I just … nothing. I didn't say anything. I just thought …" The words vanished off her tongue.

He holstered his firearm and waved his arms at the women, shooing them away like a swarm of gnats. "Step back. Both of you. But don't leave."

Really? Don't leave? Lauren took a step back.

The distant sound of sirens split the quiet air, their

sound a prequel to the barrage of activity soon to descend upon the trail.

"We're just going to start walking back. I think the sheriff's deputies will have a better time of finding us," said Aunt Kate.

Lauren followed her. They walked about a hundred feet. Kate swayed, bumping into Lauren's shoulder.

"Aunt Kate, are you all right?"

"Yes. I just need to sit down." She took a step, leaned into her niece and slumped to the ground.

Lauren grabbed her aunt's arm in time to prevent a complete face-plant into the dirt path.

"Aunt Kate! Aunt Kate!" Kneeling next to her, Lauren patted her aunt's cheek. No response.

Maverik nosed in and licked Kate's face.

"No, Maverik." Lauren positioned herself between her aunt and the dog, then rolled Aunt Kate on to her back. *Now what do I do?* Lauren tried to remember what she'd learned from a CPR class she took, but her mind drew a blank.

Lauren gripped her aunt's limp hand. "You're going to be okay." She spoke the reassuring words trying to convince herself they were true.

"Lauren," came a deep voice from behind her.

She looked over her shoulder.

Sam knelt on one knee beside Lauren. He pressed two fingers to Kate's neck, then stood. "The paramedics are on their way. I'll notify dispatch to send another ambulance for whoever you found. I'm sure your aunt will be fine. It's probably the heat and what you two discovered."

His reassuring words should have been a comfort but

they weren't. She felt she were to blame for her aunt lying here; either from having pushed her too hard on this hike or for suggesting the hike in the first place. If they had stayed home, her aunt would never have been subjected to such a horrific sight.

"I don't know. Maybe she's having a heart attack. She told me the hike was too much for her. And she was sweating. And then we came across …" Lauren nodded in the general direction of the body.

"The EMTs will check her out. Sit tight." He squeezed her shoulder, then stood and looked around, catching sight of his boss coming down the path. His brow furrowed.

"Maybe he can explain how he got here so quick." Lauren gestured at the chief.

Sam shot her a look that said, *not now*, then walked toward his boss.

"And tell him not to touch anything. This is out of his jurisdiction." She muttered those words under her breath. The Albany County Sheriff's Department will tell Chief Newell the same thing he said to her moments ago about disturbing the scene. With all that was happening, it gave her little satisfaction.

He had done his own tromping around the body, and more than likely destroyed footprints left by the killer. It seemed rather careless on his part. And maybe he would explain to Sam what he was doing in the area, how he happened upon the scene so quick. Would the chief of police tell Sam he touched the gun?

Chapter Twenty-Eight

The squeaking of metal made Lauren stop her pacing in front of her aunt. Lauren looked to see two EMTs maneuvering a portable gurney up the rutted path. They made quick work of strapping Kate to it and rolling her down to the trailhead and the awaiting ambulance. Lauren and Maverik walked alongside, Lauren telling her aunt everything would be fine. Kate remained unresponsive.

When they reached the ambulance, the petite female EMT asked, "Do you want to ride along with your aunt?"

"Yes. Wait, no, I can't. I'm sure you don't allow dogs." She pointed at Maverik.

The EMT shook her head.

"Are you taking her to Crawford Memorial?"

The female paramedic nodded. "Yep."

Before loading Kate into the ambulance, Lauren reached out and touched her aunt's cheek. "I'll be there soon."

The ambulance turned out of the parking area at the same time two deputy sheriff cruisers pulled in, one behind the other. They exited their cars and approached Lauren.

"The man ... the body is up that way." Lauren pointed in the direction of the trail. "It's a little ways in."

"Why don't you show us," said the older deputy.

She guided them to the area. Chief Newell and Sam Overstreet stood side by side a few feet from the body.

"We'll just stay here." The younger deputy motioned for Lauren to remain. "I need to get your statement, Ms.?"

"Besoner. Lauren Besoner."

The older deputy continued up the trail to the body.

Lauren squinted at the younger deputy's name tag – Rodriguez – as he flipped open his notebook.

"Can you tell me what happened?" he inquired.

Lauren explained to him how her and her aunt had come to find the man, and Maverik's role in possibly disturbing the scene. She wanted to share that information with him before Ray Newell did. She added the police chief tromped around the scene as well. No reason her dog should take all the blame.

Five minutes into her narrative, Sam approached them. "Do you need any more information from Ms. Besoner?"

Deputy Rodriquez flipped the notebook closed. "I have what I need for now, but you'll need to come by the station and give a more detailed written statement." He pulled out a business card and handed it to her. "Please come by as soon as possible. The sooner the better."

Lauren pocketed the card. "I'm going to go to the hospital and check on my aunt. I'll stop by after that, if it's not too late."

"We're open twenty-four seven. But thank you, Ms. Besoner." The deputy made his way up the path toward his partner.

"Let's go. I'll walk you to your car." Sam touched her on the shoulder.

"Thanks. But if you need to stay I can walk back to my car by myself."

"No, I'm done here. Besides ..." Sam gestured toward the trees with his arm "... we don't know if whoever is responsible for this is still out here." He took the leash out of her hand and draped his free arm around her, pulling her in to him as they walked.

Adrenaline still flowed, but Lauren let herself be guided down the trail. For the first time since discovering the man, she felt her body relax, glad Sam was here walking her to her car, safe in his embrace.

They walked in silence, their footsteps falling softly on the hardpacked earth. The parking area where their vehicles sat came into view. When they reached the driver's side of her car, he faced her and pulled her in for a hug. He spoke, his breath warm on the top of her head. "I'm sorry you had to come across that."

"Me too." Her words were muffled against his chest.

"Are you sure you're okay to drive? I can take you home."

She looked into his eyes and without answering, leaned in and kissed him. For a fraction of a second Sam's full lips pressed into hers, but then he turned his head away as if she had slapped him across the face.

Lauren stepped back and bumped into the Volvo. She grabbed the door handle, opening the driver's side. She yanked the lead out of Sam's hand. "Maverik, inside." He scrambled in and she followed, almost catching her foot in the door as she closed it.

"Lauren, wait."

Those were the last words she heard before starting the engine and slamming the car in reverse and turning it around. She sped out of the parking lot, the tires spewing gravel in their wake.

The more distance she put between herself and Sam, the more her heart rate slowed. "Why did I do that? Why Maverik? Tell me." Keeping her eyes on the road, she kept talking. "I am such a loser. That's why."

Maverik, who had recovered from being jostled as they sped away, started to climb on her lap.

"No, no. It's okay." She rubbed the side of his face. "I'm okay. You just lay down."

He sat in the passenger seat, eyeing her.

She swiped at her wet cheeks. *Breathe. Just breathe.*

She checked her speedometer. Sixty-five miles per hour, well over the speed limit. With the ambulance already on its way to the emergency room, Lauren didn't let up on the gas pedal.

Chapter Twenty-Nine

On the drive to the hospital Lauren couldn't help but wonder why Crawford's police chief had arrived so soon on scene. Did he just happen to be in the area hiking? Lauren thought about the things that were absent. He hadn't been carrying a backpack, a water bottle, anything suggesting he had been hiking. And if he was just out for a casual walk, how did he know to respond to the call? Cell reception had been spotty when she and her aunt were trying to reach nine-one-one.

The fact he was carrying a firearm was no surprise. Lauren assumed most law enforcement did even when they were off duty. Had he been in the area all along? He hadn't even tried to hide his hostility when he saw her and her aunt.

As Lauren followed the curves in the road, the image of the dead man's shoes resurfaced. She'd seen those shoes before. But where? The man's eyeglasses lay next to his side, black frames, one lens cracked. She started to do a mental checklist of the man, but it made her stomach heave. She stopped herself from conjuring up any more images.

Fifteen minutes later she pulled into the hospital parking lot, parked the Volvo in the shade of a row of Chinese elms and lowered the windows, enough to let fresh air in and not let Maverik out. She looked at him. "Be a good boy."

She checked her phone before getting out of the car. There were several texts from her uncle asking what was going on, asking why Kate wasn't answering her phone. She texted Uncle Jack and let him know his wife was at Crawford Memorial Hospital, to meet her there and she would explain everything.

She reached the entrance to the emergency room. As the doors swished open it came to her where she had seen those shoes before.

Chapter Thirty

The sight of a salt-and-pepper braid hanging off the end of a gurney caught Lauren's attention. Aunt Kate. An orderly and a nurse were wheeling her down a corridor. They turned right, and Lauren went after them. She was about to make the same turn when a voice called out.

"Miss. Miss. Come back. You can't go down there."

She stopped and looked over her shoulder to see a nurse standing under an admissions sign. "You can't go back there."

Lauren walked over to the tired-looking older woman perched on a stool behind a tall counter.

"Can I help you?"

"That's my aunt." She pointed toward the hallway. "I just want to see if she's all right."

"You have to wait here, but while you wait you can fill in some of your aunt's information." With efficiency she grabbed a pen from a gray mesh pen holder, tucked it under the clipboard's top with a form already placed in it, and handed it to Lauren. The woman returned her attention to the computer monitor in front of her.

Lauren sat in one of the molded plastic seats in the waiting area. The invisible odor of disinfectant filled her nostrils. She wrinkled her nose and began to fill out as much of the paperwork as she could. Just as she handed the clipboard to the woman, her phone pinged. A text from Sam wanting an update on Kate's condition. And a reminder not to forget to go to the sheriff's office and write out a statement. She deleted the message and went to stand by a bank of windows.

The blue sky had turned gunmetal gray, perhaps paying homage to a man recently deceased. Rain would not be far behind. Wind whipped fallen leaves and dried bits of grass into little eddies in the parking lot. From where she stood she could see her car and Maverik in the driver's seat, nose out the partially open window. At least he won't be hot while he waits for me, she thought.

Unable to relax she paced the small antiseptic waiting area. She was making another lap around the room when she heard a *swoosh* and turned to see the emergency room doors open.

"Uncle Jack."

He spotted Lauren and rushed to her. "What's happened to Kate?" Jack asked.

Lauren was explaining the events that led to Aunt Kate's trip to the hospital when a tall slim woman approached, stethoscope draped around her neck, its end tucked in the breast pocket of the white lab coat she wore. "Are you Mr. Alexander?"

"Yes," said Jack.

"I'm Dr. Wakefield." She extended her hand to Jack. "Your wife is resting comfortably. All the preliminary tests run so far have come back negative. There is little need to be concerned."

Jack looked at the ceiling. "Thank the Lord."

"It was most likely a fainting episode from the excitement, coupled with hiking at that altitude. I understand she was at Horseshoe Lake?"

Lauren nodded.

"At your wife's age that's akin to the making of a perfect storm."

Jack looked at Lauren. "We better not mention the age thing to her."

Knowing her aunt would be all right, Lauren allowed herself to smile at her uncle's attempt at humor.

"We want to keep her overnight for observation."

Jack nodded his agreement with the plan.

The physician glanced at her clipboard, then gave them Kate's room number. She wished them a good evening, then disappeared down the hall to handle her next emergency.

As they rode the elevator to the third floor, Lauren finished her account of what transpired at Horseshoe Lake.

Lauren read off the numbers at each door until they reached 326. Jack opened the door to a room pretending to be something it was not. A place someone would voluntarily spend time in. The flat-screen TV on a pastel-colored wall and a vase containing faux flowers on a corner table did nothing to disguise the faint hum of the vital signs monitoring equipment at Kate's bedside.

Aunt Kate, propped up in the bed, opened her eyes and attempted to smile. Jack hurried to her bedside.

Lauren held back. All the events that happened that day hadn't been her fault, but she felt guilty all the same. If they hadn't gone on a hike, if they stopped and turned around sooner, Aunt Kate wouldn't be lying in a hospital bed right now. Her face still looked ashen. Lauren wanted to leave, but she would stay long enough to assure herself the doctor was right, that her aunt was okay.

After several minutes of listening to Aunt Kate talk, along with Jack's hovering over her bedside, Lauren knew he would be there until hospital personnel told him visiting hours were over.

Lauren tapped her uncle on the shoulder. "I'm going to leave. I need to go to the sheriff's department and write out a statement. And Maverik is in the car waiting for me."

He nodded.

"Jack, if you two need anything, anything at all, text me." She leaned over, hugged her aunt, then her uncle.

"Sure thing. You go on. I'm going to stay here a while longer," said Jack.

Chapter Thirty-One

*M*averik ran around the backyard while Lauren filled his bowl with kibble. After calling him in she downed two ibuprofen with a glass of water, then locked up and drove downtown to the Albany County Sheriff's Department.

She entered the small ante room, more like a large cubicle, a light in the ceiling needing replacement, and approached a thick glass partition meant to keep the occupants on the other side safe. Lauren went to the intercom and was about to speak into it when a woman of about thirty, close to her own age, came up to the counter. "Can I help you?"

"Yes. My name is Lauren Besoner. Is Deputy Rodriguez here? He wanted me to come in and make a statement."

The woman turned her head and looked around the room. The tops of one or two heads were visible behind computer monitors. She yelled, "Hey Joey, there's some-one here to see you."

Nice system they have for announcing visitors.

Deputy Rodriquez raised his head over the monitor on his desk. "Uh, thank you, Nichole." He came over and stood next to the woman. He lowered his voice and spoke to her. "Just come and get me next time. This isn't an all-night diner. You don't need to shout."

Nichole shrugged. "Sorry."

Somewhere a button was pressed, unlocking a door next to the glass window.

Deputy Rodriguez held the door open. "Thank you for coming down, Ms. Besoner. How is – it's your aunt, right?"

"Yes."

"How is she doing?"

"She's doing okay. They're keeping her overnight for observation."

"Probably just a precaution."

"That's what the doctor said."

"She can give me her statement once she's out of the hospital. If you'll come right over here." He led her to the desk opposite from where he had been sitting and mo-tioned for her to take a seat. He reached into his desk drawer and pulled out sheets of lined paper, handed them to her, along with a pen. "I just need you to write down the events leading up to the discovery of the body."

"I know who he is. At least I'm pretty sure I know who it is."

Deputy Rodriquez cocked his head. "You do? Why didn't you say so earlier?"

"Because I just remembered where I saw his shoes from. You saw them, right?"

"I did. Definitely not hiking boots. What about them?"

"They're unusual. I'd bet nobody else in Crawford has a pair like them. It didn't come to me until I was leaving the hospital that I remembered where I'd seen them before."

The deputy grabbed a sticky notepad off his desk along with a pen. "So, who is this guy? Or who do you think he is?"

"His name is Alden Bates."

"And you know him how?"

"He shares office space with my – he has an office at Gentle Breeze Counseling, but he's a CPA."

He jotted down the information.

"Does that mean you hadn't identified him yet?" Lauren asked. "Didn't he have a wallet on him, a driver's license?"

"I can't share any details, but I can say we ran a couple of vehicle plates that were parked by the lake." He slapped the notepad against the palm of his hand. "I'll give my detective this information."

He nodded at the sheets of paper in front of her. "Take your time. I'd like it to be as complete and accurate as possible. Any little detail you remember, write it down."

"Okay."

"Can I get you some coffee?"

She shook her head.

"Smart answer. The coffee around here tastes like crap. Would you like some water?"

"Yes, thank you."

He left her with the blank sheets of paper.

Lauren picked up the pen and wrote. She started from the time she parked her car, and she and Aunt Kate began their hike at Beaver Trailhead. She made sure she included Chief Newell showing up but hesitated about adding what he had done. What exactly had he done? It looked like he touched the barrel of the gun. But had he? She hadn't had a clear view and couldn't be a hundred percent sure. *He can explain what the heck he did. He would be giving a statement ... if he hadn't already.*

The deputy returned with a cup of water and placed it next to her.

"Thank you."

"I'll leave you to it." Deputy Rodriguez turned his attention to the computer monitor on his desk.

When Lauren could think of nothing else to put in her statement, she brought it over to the deputy. It felt like she was turning in a test paper, hoping she passed.

"If you'll just sign and date it, you'll be done here."

She scribbled her name, along with the date, and handed it to him.

"I gave you my business card, right?"

"Yes."

"If you think of anything else, don't hesitate to call. Day or night. But try not to call at three in the morning." He smiled at her.

"I won't bother you –"

"That was just a joke."

"If I think of something else, I'll call you."

"And if I don't answer, leave me a message and I'll get back to you as soon as I can."

Lauren nodded.

"Have a good evening."

She wanted to ask him how such a thing was possible now, but knew his comment to be nothing more than automatic politeness.

The thunderstorm which threatened the skies earlier had come and gone while she wrote out her statement, leaving the potholes in the roads filled with water. As she drove home, thoughts of the day's events were already replaying in her mind. It left her with an uneasy feeling that settled in the pit of her stomach.

Chapter Thirty-Two

$\mathcal{S}$unday morning Lauren busied herself with sanding down rough boards for her next pine beetle kill project. At noon she texted Jack. *Did Aunt Kate get to come home? I want to come by and see her.*

Her uncle's reply was immediate. *Yes. Discharged this morning. Feels fine. We'll be here.*

Lauren slid into the warm interior of the Volvo, reached over to the passenger seat, grabbed her sunglasses, and drove out to see her aunt.

An Albany County sheriff's vehicle sat in her aunt and uncle's driveway. Jack hadn't mentioned anyone being there with them. Maybe the deputy just arrived.

She recognized Sam's pickup parked next to the sheriff's vehicle.

Damn. Lauren let the Volvo idle, considering whether to turn around and leave. She could stop by later.

She smacked the steering wheel. "Don't be stupid. I can't leave without seeing Aunt Kate. Sam can just leave." After her mini pep talk, she rummaged in her messenger bag for nothing in particular, glancing out the windshield every few seconds. Finally, she turned off the engine.

Lauren rapped on the storm door, then opened it. "Hello?"

"Come on in," called her uncle.

Inside, voices floated from the kitchen, and she made her way to them.

Uncle Jack stood as she entered the room. "Lauren, have a seat." He grabbed a coffee cup out of the dish drainer and poured coffee into it. "Here." He placed it on the kitchen table in front of an empty chair. He took the milk out of the refrigerator, placed it by the mug, along with a sugar bowl.

Lauren was about to protest but said instead, "Thanks, Uncle Jack." She bent over, giving her aunt an awkward hug, then maneuvered herself so her back was to Sam, and sat down. She nodded hello to the deputy, who smiled in return. "I hope this isn't a bad time, but I had to see how you were doing."

"Of course it's not a bad time. And I'm doing fine. Just fine. Glad to be out of the hospital. I *hate* hospitals." Kate gave a little shudder. "So many sick people."

Lauren sighed with relief. Aunt Kate making a joke meant she must be feeling better.

Deputy Rodriguez flipped his notebook shut and rose. "I'm finished here. Thank you again for answering my questions, Ms. Alexander."

"Of course," said Kate.

"If I can get you to just sign and date your statement, I'll be on my way."

Kate signed her name on the page in front of her. As she wrote the date she said, "I can't believe summer is already gone." She handed her statement to Deputy Rodriguez. "And thank you for coming here and not making me come down to the station. I appreciate that, Deputy."

He took the statement. "I thought you might still be recovering from everything that happened yesterday. But all the information we can gather, as quickly as we can, does help in our investigation, so I was happy to come out here." He turned to leave.

"Deputy Rodriguez, was the man Alden Bates?" asked Lauren.

"Yes. We confirmed his identity."

Sam, who had been leaning against the kitchen counter, straightened, "You knew the guy?"

Lauren directed her answer to her aunt and uncle. "He shares – shared office space with my therapist."

Kate's eyebrows arched. "Therapist? You're seeing a therapist? You never told me anything about seeing a therapist."

"I've been meaning to, but with you and Jack being gone so much lately, off seeing the country, I never found the right time." She shrugged. "I decided to take your advice and talk to someone about..." Her voice trailed off. She didn't want to go into details with the deputy present, and especially with Sam being there. He already knew the general reason for her going but the details were certainly none of his business.

"Folks, thanks again for your cooperation." Deputy Rodriguez smiled at Lauren. "Ms. Besoner, nice to see you again."

Lauren returned the smile.

"I'll walk you out, Deputy," said Jack.

"I should go too," said Lauren.

"Nonsense," said Kate. "You just got here. And I want to hear about this therapist. Who is it?"

"Her name's Patricia Holland." Lauren watched as her aunt's face went through several emotions, landing on surprise, close to shock. "What? You have been bugging me since last fall to talk to someone."

"It's not that, Lauren. I'm just surprised who you picked to go see. That's the chief's wife?"

"Yes." Lauren nodded in Sam's direction. "It was his idea."

"It was," Sam agreed.

"She's been very helpful, Aunt Kate. She really has."

"I'm glad to hear you decided to seek some counseling." said Kate. "Is she helping you with some of your issues … I mean with your mother?"

Lauren looked at her aunt's mug. "Let me pour you another cup." Before Kate could object, Lauren stood, reached for the coffeepot and refilled her aunt's cup. As she placed the mug in front of her aunt, Lauren shook her head and motioned with her eyes, as if to say, *Not in front of Sam.*

"So, you're feeling better?" asked Lauren.

"Yes, much," said Kate.

"I'm so relieved to hear that," said Lauren. "You scared the heck out of me yesterday."

"That certainly wasn't my plan," said Kate.

Sam moved around the kitchen table, tapping Kate's shoulder as he passed by on his way toward the living room. "It's good to see you're feeling better and out of the hospital. I have to go to the station but if you need anything, call or text me, okay?"

"I'm sure I'll be fine. Jack's here if I need anything." Kate began to stand.

"No, don't get up," Sam said.

Over her shoulder Kate said, "Thanks for stopping by, Sam."

Lauren pretended to be absorbed by something happening outside the kitchen window.

When they heard the front door open and close, her aunt said, "You weren't very friendly to Sam."

"I wasn't? I guess I'm still not myself after what happened yesterday." Lauren made small talk with her aunt until Jack entered the kitchen. "I'm going to get going. You should rest."

"Thank you for stopping by," said Jack and Kate in unison.

"Of course. I wanted to see how you were doing."

Lauren sat in the driver's seat and blew out a long breath. *Seeing Sam wasn't awkward at all.*

Chapter Thirty-Three

*M*iguel's parking lot only had three cars parked in it. Lauren's stomach grumbled as she pulled into the parking lot and went inside. After placing her order, she stood off to the side, palming the plastic square card with the number ninety-four on it, thinking about Sam. Would it always be like this? Running into him, feeling embarrassed, awkward?

Lauren chided herself for dwelling on that moment, but she excelled at replaying an event over and over in her mind, asking herself, *Why did I do that?* Or, *Why didn't I do that?* "Stupid," she mumbled.

"Come here often?" a husky voice spoke from behind.

The voice startled her. She turned to see Eli, head cocked, thick eyebrows raised.

"Hi. I didn't see you come in." She nodded. "And, yes, I come here often." Then added, "More often than I should I'm afraid."

"I could see you were off somewhere in your own little world." He went to the counter, placed his order and returned to stand next to her.

"Ready for your trial to be over?" Lauren asked.

"I have to say yes, I'll be relieved when it's done." He shook his head. "This is my first murder trial. The pressure is immense."

"I can't imagine how that feels. Such a tremendous responsibility."

"Very, very stressful. My client is depending on me to keep him from spending the rest of his life in prison." He rubbed the back of his neck. "I'd be happy with a good ol' divorce right about now."

"I don't envy you."

"Tell me, what's your sense of the case? Have you gotten a feel for the jury?"

"You don't want to ask me. I'm wrong more often than I'm right on figuring out which way a jury is leaning."

"Okay. Let's not talk about work. Let's talk about something normal."

"Normal?"

"Yes. How's your weekend been?"

Lauren let out a snort of laughter. "So far it's been freakin' insane."

"I take it not in a good way?"

"No, in a bad way. I'm laughing at the word 'normal' but it's not funny. Do you know an accountant in town named Alden Bates?"

"Yes. He did my taxes when he was at Lerner and Associates."

"Were you two close?"

217

He thought a moment. "No, I wouldn't say close. We were on a pool league together a few years ago. When we won we'd all stick around and have a beer or two, but we didn't win often so I didn't do much socializing with him." He gave a little laugh. "Why do you ask?"

"He's dead. My aunt and I found him –"

"Number ninety-four," called out a thin teenage girl behind the counter. She handed Lauren a brown paper sack. "Thank you for coming in."

Eli looked at the to-go bag. "You going to eat that here?"

Lauren shrugged. "I can. Sure."

"Good. Then you can tell me what happened."

She grabbed several napkins from the dispenser, filled a tiny plastic cup with salsa and weaved in and around the tables until she found one without any prying ears close by.

A minute later Eli slid his lanky frame into the chair across from Lauren, his long legs bumping into her short ones. "Sorry."

"I imagine that happens a lot."

"As a matter of fact, yes, it does." He pulled his legs away and banged his knees against the underside of the table, making his tray jump a little.

She suppressed a laugh.

"Tell me about finding Alden." He unwrapped one of three beef and bean burritos, took a bite and reached for a napkin from his stockpile to stop the hot sauce dripping down his hand.

Lauren looked at the food on his tray. *How can he get away with eating all that and still be so skinny? It is so not fair.*

This would be the fourth time relaying the events that transpired on the hike she and her aunt were never able to finish. First to the deputies on scene, then to her Uncle Jack, and then finally writing out a statement.

"It's pretty upsetting finding a body." She unwrapped the hard-shell taco and doused it with the tiny cup of salsa. Telling of the events before had felt surreal. Even now she had a hard time believing what happened. Lauren retold the story, of what started out to be an enjoyable afternoon, hiking with her aunt, plans for enjoying a picnic lunch, but ended abruptly with the discovery of a dead man.

Eli, burrito in hand, stared at her. He placed his free hand on hers. "Are you sure you're okay?"

Lauren smiled inside, touched by the concern in Eli's coal-black eyes. "I'm okay. And I'm so thankful my aunt's okay too. She's home resting. I was just at her house checking on her. I was *so* scared when she passed out."

"I'm sure you were." He crumpled the wax paper from his first burrito, unwrapped the second one, dipping it in a side of nacho cheese sauce.

"Eli, do you know Trish, the police chief's wife?"

He shook his head, then swallowed. "What about her?"

"She's a therapist here in town, goes by Patricia Holland."

"Patricia Holland is the chief's wife?"

"Yes. So you do know her?"

"Yes – no. I don't know her know her. She has offices a couple of doors down from me. And I've seen the campaign signs around town. What about her?"

"She shares office space with Mr. Bates."

"Oh. I hadn't been over to his new place since he moved."

"Don't you think it's strange, Crawford's police chief being first on the scene?"

"Technically you were first on the scene."

"If you're going to make remarks like that, technically Maverik, my dog, was first on the scene."

"You were the first person on scene."

"You're in the right profession," Lauren smiled, "always arguing. Yes, I was the first person, but you know what I mean."

"I'm not a fan of the chief, but why do you think that's so strange?"

"He just happened to be there? In the middle of the woods? Walking by himself?"

"Could happen." Eli took a long swallow of his soda. "You were there."

"And he showed up so quick. We didn't have good cell reception right there. My aunt had to go search for a signal."

Two young children, a boy and a girl, approached the table next to Lauren and Eli's, arguing over who would sit next to their dad. He followed them with a tray loaded with food and beverages.

Lauren leaned across the table and lowered her voice. "He was pretty angry when he saw us."

"Try showing up at the police station sometime looking for information about a case." Eli's head did a knowing nod. "The man is a real asshole."

"Makes me feel a little better. I thought he just didn't like me."

"And now that I'm representing the guy who he thinks killed his mother, I try my best to stay out of his way." He took another swallow of soda. "But what are you suggesting? That he had something to do with Alden's death?"

There was more she wanted to say but not here where she'd have to raise her voice to be heard over the boisterous family sitting next to them. She gave a sideways glance at the table.

Eli nodded his understanding. They made small talk as they ate, then put their food wrappers in the trash. Eli carried his drink with him as they went outside.

Lauren stood by her car, keys in hand, Eli facing her, leaning against a faded gray minivan. "Is that yours?" She nodded at the vehicle.

He raised his shoulders, a look of embarrassment on his face. "Temporarily. I borrowed it from a friend of mine."

"Yours in the shop?"

"No. I've been pulled over twice by the police chief since I took on Danny's case. He gave me a speeding ticket both times."

"Ow. That sucks. Were you speeding?"

"No. Not the second time, anyway. And I was only going two miles an hour over the speed limit the first time. He wasn't even on duty the second time. It was around ten o'clock in the morning. Comes up to my window in some ugly-ass Hawaiian-print shirt and asks me if I'd been drinking." Eli continued, his voice charged with anger, "Tells me to breathe on him." The anger reached his eyes. "That is so effed up. But hey, I'm Northern Arapaho. The white man knows we all drink a six-pack of Budweiser for breakfast, right?"

Lauren's eyes widened at his tone. An awkward silence fell until she moved so she was standing next to him and nudged him with an elbow. "We don't *all* think that."

He let out a slow breath. "I know. Anyway, the speeding tickets were getting expensive. I don't need anyone's help putting points on my driving record."

Lauren tried to lighten the mood. "And think of all the perks to driving around in a minivan."

"Such as?"

"Fighting off all those single women. I'm sure you're irresistible when they see you pulling up in such a sensible vehicle."

Eli tugged on an imaginary shirt collar with both hands. "Yep. I've been fighting them off ever since I got behind the wheel."

"What's your friend driving? Not your car, are they?"

"Hell no. I wouldn't do that to her. She has another vehicle she can use." He shoved his hands in his pockets. "So, what were you saying inside about Crawford's asshole police chief?"

Lauren picked up the conversation she had let go of inside. "I'm not exactly sure what I'm saying about the chief, but I think it's strange he was there in the middle … not in the middle of nowhere but we were off the trail and so was he. I keep asking myself what he was even doing there."

"Did you ask him?"

"*No way.* He was yelling at me about how my dog had destroyed evidence at the crime scene. I didn't think it was a good idea to challenge him about why he was there." Lauren looked at the pavement, then into Eli's eyes. "I don't know if I should tell you this – nah, I shouldn't. Never mind."

"Hey, you can't say something like that and then not tell me."

She stayed silent for a moment, then blurted out, "When the chief was squatting by the body, he touched the barrel of the gun."

Eli tilted his head toward Lauren, and he lowered his voice. "You saw him do that?"

"Yes. Sort of. I think I'm pretty sure that's what he did."

"Did you just hear yourself? 'Sort of,' 'I think.' So you're not positive?"

"He was squatting in front of the body, but that's what it looked like to me. I was going to ask him what the heck he was doing, but I lost my nerve."

"Smart of you not to piss him off."

"I was going to tell Sam, but I didn't think he would believe me."

"Sam Overstreet was there too?"

"He arrived later. He's my aunt's neighbor. She texted him when we came across the body."

"Why wouldn't he believe you about something like that?"

"He knows I don't like the chief." She looked at him. "You're right though. I can't swear that he moved the gun. But maybe he did. Maybe he moved it closer to Mr. Bates's hand."

"Why would he do that?"

She leaned against the minivan, her back warming to its touch. "Maybe he wanted it to look like a suicide. Maybe the police chief had something to do with his death."

"Whoa, whoa, whoa. A lot of maybes going on here. You don't really believe that, do you? Why would he want to kill the guy?"

"Because ..." *That was the question. Why would he?*

"Bates shares office space with the chief's wife. Maybe there's a connection there somehow."

"Like what?"

The wind which had been absent, now picked up. Lauren hugged herself. "Like the chief just found out Trish and Alden Bates were having an affair. We both agree the chief isn't a very nice guy. He could have killed Mr. Bates out of jealousy. Or …"

"Or?"

"I can't give you any details. All I can say is Mr. Bates was also Mrs. Archer's accountant up until a week or so before her death."

"So you think the chief lured him there and killed him?"

Lauren shrugged. "Maybe."

"How did he do that? Suggest they go for a friendly hike to have a quiet talk about him screwing his wife?"

Lauren shifted to keep the sun out of her eyes. "No. Mr. Bates certainly wasn't dressed for a walk around the park. And neither was Ray Newell. I know you can reach Horseshoe Lake a different way than my aunt and I went. If you approach it from the south, there are several pull-out spaces where you can park right at the edge of the lake."

"I know where you're talking about. A few of them have picnic tables and built-in fire pits. That's where I usually park when I go there. It's a great place to snowshoe in the winter." Eli tipped his cup and took the last swallow.

"Then I suppose a person could meet somebody out there and not be all decked out in hiking gear."

Eli nodded in agreement. "So you think he lured Bates there, confronted him about the affair and shot him. And he brought two guns with him because?"

Lauren thought about the question. "Because he planned to make his death look like a suicide. It could have been Alden's gun, and they were arguing."

"Did you hear any gunshots when you were there?"

"No. Wait, wait. Come to think of it, when we first arrived, we did hear something that sounded like a gunshot but at the time I thought it was a car backfiring. Aunt Kate thought it might be a hunter. Though now that I say that, it's too early for hunting season." Lauren turned and looked up at Eli. "Isn't it? Doesn't it start the first of October?"

"Don't know. I don't hunt here. I hunt on the rez."

"Maybe this whole thing somehow ties into who killed Mrs. Archer."

"How?"

"I don't know. I said maybe. But couldn't you use this information to throw suspicion on someone else?"

"It's not that easy, Lauren. I have to have a good faith belief someone else was responsible before I can offer up an alternate killer theory. Otherwise when someone is accused of murder you could throw anyone's name out there and say, 'Mr. Smith did it.' I could even throw out your name."

Lauren narrowed her eyes at him in mock anger.

Eli held up his hands in surrender. "Bad example. But you get my point. You can't just say Mr. Smith did it, not without some piece of evidence that points to Mr. Smith."

"I learned a lot – more like heard a lot – about Margaret Archer during her deposition. I can't give you details but maybe you could talk to her attorney. I'm sure you know John Whitmore."

"I do. I worked in his office one summer as an intern in my third year of law school. Very smart man."

"Maybe you can ask him some questions, not so much about the specifics of the lawsuit but about the dynamics of the family relationship." Lauren didn't think it would be unprofessional of her to bring up Mrs. Archer's neighbor. "When you talk to him ask him about Nicholas Fisher."

"Nicholas Fisher?"

"Yes. He's Sean's client. And –"

"Right, right."

"His property is right next to Mrs. Archer's. When I was reviewing her deposition the other night I came across –"

"Is that how you spend your evenings?"

Lauren looked at the asphalt before her eyes met Eli's. "Sometimes."

He gave a small laugh. "You're as bad as me."

"Anyway, Mr. Fisher's name came up. Margaret testified he wanted to buy her land, but she didn't want to sell. He said some threatening things to her."

"Like what?"

"I don't remember the exact words but along the lines of 'a woman your age could fall and get hurt.' Mrs. Archer tried to make it sound like it wasn't a big deal but I think it scared her."

"I'll contact John, see if he can shed some light on what was going on between them."

"Do you know anyone at the sheriff's department that you can ask about how the investigation is going? If they have any leads about who might have killed Mr. Bates?"

"I have a friend on the force … I suppose we're still friends, but ever since I got heavy into defense work, we don't have the same interaction like we used to."

"That's too bad. Because I was thinking if Mr. Bates's murder is tied in with Mrs. Archer somehow, then maybe the same person killed them both. And if that's the case, it can't be Daniel since he's sitting in jail."

Eli nodded. "Makes sense."

The two were silent in their own thoughts as an older Honda Civic with teenage hormones behind the wheel sped into the lot, jerking to a stop in the parking space across from where Eli and Lauren stood. Two boys and two girls spilled out of the car, talking and laughing as they bumped into one another.

"I wouldn't be badmouthing the chief but since he doesn't seem to like you either, I thought it would be okay to share what I know," said Lauren.

"And why are you on his shit list?"

"He and my dad had some issues in the past. Years ago my dad was on the Casper City Council."

"Oh. Is that where you grew up, Casper?"

"Yes. Did you know Ray was also Casper's chief of police years ago?"

"No."

"I don't know any details of what happened, all I know is he stepped down or was asked to step down. According to my aunt my dad was somehow involved."

"How long ago was that?"

Lauren thought for a moment. "I'm not sure exactly. Had to be over twenty years ago, maybe more. I didn't know anything about it until last year."

"You would have just been a kid back then. Besides, twenty years is a long time to hold a grudge."

"It is a long time, and why hold it against me? All I

know is he dislikes me. He had been pressuring Sam to charge me with Judge Murphy's murder."

"Really?"

"Sam Overstreet didn't come right out and say it, but the chief was his boss and must have had some say in the direction of the case, but it was Sam's investigation, not his."

"I've had a few dealings with Overstreet. Rumor back then was you were being investigated for Judge Murphy's death. I assumed it was routine because you discovered her body." Eli looked down at Lauren. "If that man can hold a grudge for over twenty years, and you think he's behind this murder, that's some pretty serious shit. And if he is, Lauren, you better be damned careful."

Lauren hugged herself tighter. "You think he'd do something to me too?"

"Well, you were there, you found the body. Maybe he thinks you saw something." Eli patted her on the shoulder. "But it's more likely the chief had nothing to do with Mr. Bates's death and the only thing he's guilty of is being an asshole."

"Whatever he is, I don't trust him. And I'm going to stay away from him." Lauren moved to unlock her car.

"Listen, I appreciate everything you've told me. I've got some digging to do."

"Happy to help."

"Maybe I can make something of it. Figure out an angle that will help Daniel."

She opened the car door. "How is he doing?"

Eli hung his head and spoke. "Not great. He knows it's not looking good for him, especially after they introduced

Margaret's ring into evidence. I'm doing my best but there's just so much circumstantial evidence against him."

"That's just it. It's circumstantial. Nobody saw him do it."

"Lauren, you've been listening to the same testimony I have, so don't go sugarcoating it. You know people get convicted on circumstantial evidence all the time."

"True."

"That damn surveillance video of him at the pawn shop didn't help either."

She nodded. "It's Dominick I feel bad for. He's been pretty hard on himself, thinking none of this would be happening if he had just given his nephew another chance." Lauren hurried to explain. "Not that he thinks his nephew did it. Just that he wouldn't have been there that night if he hadn't fired him."

"Dominick's not the only one who feels bad." Eli looked out across the parking lot, his gaze unfocused. "I don't usually talk about my clients and whether I believe them or not, Lauren, but Danny is different. I believe this kid when he tells me he's innocent." Eli slid his hand down his face and his next words came out a hoarse whisper. "But I don't know if I can pull off a not guilty verdict for him."

✳   ✳   ✳

On the drive home Lauren thought about Eli, and the sadness his voice carried when he spoke about the possibility of letting down his client. He called him Danny, not Daniel, not Mr. Throgmorton. They had become close.

And then she thought of Ray Newell. She didn't want to think someone appointed to uphold the law could be a cold-blooded killer. She shivered, gripping the steering wheel tight. A cold-blooded killer who might want to do her harm.

Chapter Thirty-Four

S moke filled Lauren's nostrils and stung her eyes. She breathed in, began to cough uncontrollably, then bolted upright. Her chest heaved as she looked around trying to orient herself. She listened for any sounds, sniffed the air for any unusual smells. When her breathing returned to near normal, she patted her nightstand until she found her phone and looked at the time. One-fifteen. The familiar nightmare receded in her mind.

Now wide awake, she pushed the fluffy comforter away, reached for her robe and went into her home office. She fired up the laptop. Time to do something until mental exhaustion set in. Perhaps a little research of her own would shed some light into who would want to kill Mr. Bates.

Lauren rubbed her eyes, opened the internet browser and typed in "Alden Bates in Wyoming." One hit. After

half an hour and visiting numerous websites, a more complete picture of Mr. Bates formed in her mind. His life
began on a ranch outside of Rock Springs, Wyoming and
ended, literally, outside of Crawford.

He'd attended the University of Wyoming and obtained a bachelor's degree in accounting. After college he
returned to Rock Springs and worked for a small accounting firm until he relocated to Casper and continued
working as an accountant.

The State of Wyoming's website for professional accountants showed his CPA license to be in good standing.
When Lauren clicked on the local obituary page, it showed
he was survived by three children, two grandchildren, his
mother and a brother.

Further typing had brought her to the Casper Chamber
of Commerce website, where the name Alden Bates
showed up as a past board member. It didn't give the dates
he was a member. Could he have been on the board during
the same time Ray Newell was on Casper's police force?
Casper was a big enough city that their paths might never
have crossed. But maybe they had known each other. And
if they did, did it mean anything?

The final search brought Mr. Bates to Crawford, where
he'd lived for the past ten years, opening his own solo accounting firm not long ago. Before opening his own business, he
had been with a large accounting firm. Large being a relative
term for the size of Crawford. Lauren remembered Mr. Bates's
disciplinary hearing, the events surrounding the matter
prompting him to strike out on his own.

Lauren moved her bare foot and felt the softness of
Maverik's stomach. Somewhere during the online search

he must have come in and settled himself under the desk. She massaged his belly with her toes while thinking. Born in Rock Springs. Moved to Casper. Moved to Crawford. Funeral arrangements were taking place in Rock Springs. He was to be buried in his hometown. In her mind Lauren drew a line from town to town to town. "Mystery solved. I created a triangle. Yay for me." Maverik lifted his head, looked at her, blinked, then lay his head back down.

"Okay. It means nothing. It means even though I can't sleep I'm obviously too tired to think straight."

The next search Lauren chose was of Raymond Newell. She didn't expect to find anything new or surprising. Having taken the deposition of his mother, she knew where he was born, where he grew up, how many siblings he had. She already knew he was married to Trish who went by Patricia Holland, her maiden name, Lauren assumed. What she didn't know was if he had been married before, and if any of those types of details were important.

With her elbows on the desk, she cupped her face in her hands and stared at the screen and the letters which spelled Google in their primary colors.

After thinking about who or what to search next, she had another thought. *Why am I wasting my time? Is any of this going to matter?*

Her thoughts turned to Dominick, which led her to think about Daniel. He had grown thinner since she first met him at the bakery, his complexion dull with an almost gray tinge. Incarceration in the county detention center would do that to a person. It wasn't like the jail had an outdoor patio with deck chairs and inmates could lounge in the fresh air.

She looked at the time on the monitor. Two-forty-five. Lauren leaned back in her chair, yawned and blinked several times. "I better get some sleep. A couple of hours is better than none, right?"

Maverik lumbered out from under the desk and followed her to the bedroom.

She pulled off her pink robe, laid it on the foot of the bed and slid into the soft folds of the flannel sheets.

Chapter Thirty-Five

"Good morning." Lauren powered on her laptop. After two nights in a row of nightmares and little sleep, that was all she could muster to say to Tony. Her eyes felt heavy, her mind in a fog.

He was on the bench looking at his computer screen. "Morning." He tapped on his laptop keys, then looked over the bench at her. "We were so busy yesterday I didn't get to ask you about your weekend. You worked Saturday, right?"

"No, that was last weekend."

"Oh, right, right. I remember now."

"Saturday turned out to be a horrible day."

"What do you mean?"

Lauren started the realtime feed as she spoke. "You probably heard about someone being found dead over by Horseshoe Lake?"

"Yes. It was on the news Sunday night. Said the death was suspicious. Is it someone you know?"

"No – yes. Aunt Kate and I were the ones who found him."

"You're kidding?"

"Wish I was, but sadly it's true." Lauren tried to make light of it. "Sort of put a damper on the rest of the week-end." She explained in detail what happened Saturday, including the fact the chief of police showed up.

"Chief Newell was there? Strange."

"Yes, I thought so too."

"Did he say what he was doing there?"

"No, he didn't share anything with me. And I didn't ask. For some reason he doesn't like me."

"It's interesting you say that. I noticed him giving you a few odd looks when he was on the stand. Do you know him? I mean personally."

"No. But it's nice to know it's not my imagination."

He turned his attention to something on the monitor, then looked over the bench at Lauren. "That also explains all those untranslates I saw on my screen when he was on the stand. His behavior must have rattled you."

"Maybe a little." *So he did notice my crappy writing. Dang.*

"I think I'll keep my distance from you. Death seems to have a way of following you around." He smiled letting her know he was joking.

He didn't see her roll her eyes. *You just do that.* She looked at the clock on the wall. Plenty of time for some coffee. She would need the extra caffeine. She went into the break room and poured herself a cup of coffee.

Tony came up behind her. "Don't mind if I do," he said.

She shrugged, handed him the mug in her hand and reached for another. She concentrated on adding milk and sugar to the coffee.

Tony examined Lauren's face after she handed him the coffee. "You look like you've been up all night. Are you okay?"

"I'm fine. Just tired. Had a hard time falling asleep last night."

A skeptical look crossed his face, but he said, "Perfectly understandable after what's happened."

Understandable, yes, she thought, but it wasn't the reason for her looking so haggard. Last night she'd had a new nightmare. The details escaped her other than she once again sat up straight in bed, disoriented and scared. It was the second night in a row sleep had been elusive. She wondered if nightmares would be a new normal. She pushed the thought aside, not wanting something else to worry about.

❄   ❄   ❄

The testimony of the first witness, an evidence custodian at the sheriff's department who spoke loud and distinct should have been easy to take down on her writer, but Lauren couldn't seem to find her rhythm, her groove, where normally pressing all the right keys on her machine came without a second thought. The mistakes were there on her screen and Tony's as well.

At the lunch recess Lauren took her sandwich outside and sat at the lone metal bench. As she unwrapped the chicken salad sandwich – last night's grilled chicken breast – her cell phone pinged. She pulled the phone out.

Patricia had sent a text. *Heard you found Mr. Bates. I have opening this evening if you need to process what happened.*

Lauren tapped out a response. *Yes thank you.*

As she chewed the first bite her phone pinged again.

See you at five thirty. If that works.

Lauren replied with a thumbs-up emoji, and felt her shoulders relax now that she had a plan of action. She wanted someone to talk to. She wanted to find out if Patricia thought the new nightmare was tied to finding Mr. Bates. She didn't need a professional to tell her as much but what she wanted was reassurance. Reassurance that when something bad happened it wouldn't mean she was destined to sleepless nights brought on by nightmares.

As she slid her phone back into her pocket, she wondered if maybe seeing Patricia tonight was thoughtless. After all, she and Alden shared an office. They seemed on friendly terms with each other. She might be mourning his loss.

She touched the phone in her pocket, weighing whether to cancel the appointment. *Quit overthinking it. She's the one who reached out.* She remembered her conversation with Eli at Miguel's on Sunday afternoon. Was it possible Patricia and Alden were sharing more than office space? She gave that some thought as she chewed the last bite of the sandwich.

She shoved the plastic wrap in her coat pocket, closed her eyes and tilted her head toward the sky.

* * *

At the three o'clock break Lauren went to Zoe's office to grab a snack out of her bag, grateful not to run into Tony and have him ask her again if she were okay. It seemed to be his code for saying, *Why are you writing like shit and making me guess at what those letters on my screen mean?* It would be yet another remark on her ability to take down the proceedings accurately. Or more pointedly, her lack of ability.

She walked past Susan's desk. The secretary's computer screen was dark and her light jacket missing from the coat rack. Gone for the day. Some things never change, thought Lauren.

In the courtroom, the defense attorney stood up to cross-examine another employee of the sheriff's department in charge of evidence. The deputy answered Mr. Dresser's questions at warp speed. When he stepped down from the stand, Lauren relaxed her jaw which unbeknownst to her had tightened on its own during the witness's testimony. She stole a glance at the clock on the wall. An hour and a half left before quitting time. She could only hope the next witness would be someone who spoke slow. Very. Slow.

Chapter Thirty-Six

$\mathcal{P}$atricia texted Lauren advising her the lock on the office door was broke, but she could park her car in the rear of the building and enter through the back door near the kitchen area. At five twenty-five Lauren pulled alongside a late model gray Ford F250. A new Escalade sat parked next to the truck. Lauren walked around the truck, admiring it. The tinted windows prevented her from seeing inside.

She went up a small set of steps to a landing, turned the knob of the back door, entering a small kitchen that doubled as office space. An overhead light lit up the small area. A copier sat on a stand near the doorway that led into the hall. Against the copier, arms folded across his chest, stood Ray Newell.

Lauren stopped at the sight of him. "I have an appointment with your wife. That's why I came in." *Why am I explaining this to him?*

"Yeah, my wife said she had one more appointment." He gestured with his arm for her to pass.

She walked past him, keeping her eye on the prize, the office at the other end of the hallway. She was almost out of the kitchen when the chief spoke, his voice husky. "You look just like your mother, you know that?"

Lauren stopped but didn't turn around.

He moved in close to her and whispered, "Right down to those pretty hazel eyes."

The desire to run down the hall was strong, but she made herself walk at a normal pace, like he hadn't even been there, like he wasn't even watching her now.

Ms. Holland came out of her office. "Lauren, come in. Can I get you something to drink? Coffee, water?"

"No. I'm fine. Thanks."

"Have a seat. I need some caffeine. I'll be right back."

She took a seat in the designated client chair and used the time Patricia was gone to take a deep breath. She had to calm down. *Breathe. What the hell is wrong with him? Breathe. Breathe.*

From where she sat she could see into Mr. Bates's office. The door was open and there were two strips of crime scene tape stretched across the opening, creating a big X.

When her therapist returned, Lauren asked, "What happened?" gesturing to the tape.

"Someone broke in. Must have been around the time Alden was killed. That's why I had you come in through the kitchen. Whoever broke in damaged the lock on the front door. And they ransacked Alden's office. Nothing of mine was touched, thankfully."

"That's scary. Do the police have any idea who did it?

241

Is that why your husband's here?"

"No, not yet. And no, Ray just stopped in to check up on me. He's been worried ever since it happened. Detective Overstreet is investigating it. He said it was more than likely Alden's killer came looking for something. I have no idea what that would be. I do know Mr. Bates's computer is gone."

"Sam's investigating it then?"

"He's the one who responded, so I assume so."

"Do you have an alarm system? Or one of those surveillance things set up?"

"No. But I'll definitely put something in soon. It's very unsettling to find," Ms. Holland gestured with her hand toward the crime scene tape, "that."

"I can only imagine."

Patricia grabbed a notebook off her desk.

"Thanks for seeing me on such short notice. I appreciate it."

"I try to be available when my clients need me." Patricia set her coffee cup on the low table and sat down. "After Ray told me what happened with you finding Alden, I wanted to reach out in case you needed to talk to someone. I thought your nightmares might have returned. Have they?"

"Yes. I was going to call you so I appreciate you reaching out to me." Lauren explained how she had been coping before the discovery of the body, and how the event triggered a new nightmare.

"I know it's unpleasant, but I'd like you to tell me what happened. Please don't leave anything out. Any detail might help."

Forcing herself to concentrate on why she was there, Lauren described everything that happened in as much detail as she could, but omitted the interaction with Chief Newell, his reaction at seeing her there, and him possibly touching the gun. "Am I going to have nightmares every time something bad happens? I thought I was tougher than that."

"I don't believe it's a matter of how tough you are."

"The one good thing about the nightmare – if there is such a thing – it wasn't my usual one."

"What was this one about?"

"I can't remember any details. I just recall I was in the woods searching for something, but someone started chasing me. I remember the feeling of panic when I woke up. I felt like I was still in the dream." Lauren, her palms up, shrugged. "It's hard to explain."

Patricia nodded. "Well first I would say coming across a body partially hidden in the bushes is certainly a rare thing for anyone to experience. And you've come across a violent crime twice now. This last event, seeing the body, and perhaps seeing – seeing something that your mind is trying to tell you through your dreams or nightmares, something out of the ordinary."

Something out of the ordinary? Lauren didn't follow the therapist's train of thought.

"Judge Murphy's death was less than a year ago, right?"

"Yes, last October."

"And now this event happening, relatively soon I would say, it might explain why the nightmares have returned." Ms. Holland wrote a note on her pad. "We could try something that might help but you have to be open to it."

243

Lauren's thoughts returned to the comments the chief made as she passed him in the kitchen. *Why did he say that to me?*

"Lauren?"

"Sorry. What did you say?"

"We could try hypnosis."

Lauren's eyes widened at the suggestion. Before deciding on a therapist she had checked out Gentle Breeze's website and knew hypnosis was offered, but in her mind being hypnotized came close to the outer fringes of legitimate therapy.

"It is a recognized treatment. And I'm trained in it."

"I don't know –"

"Oh, no, we wouldn't do it today. But it is something to think about. In the meantime, I think it would be helpful to do some free association about the event."

"Free association?"

"Yes."

"I didn't know that was an actual thing that therapists did."

"It can be effective. I'll throw out some words and you say whatever comes to mind. There might be something you saw and for some reason you're blocking it out and your subconscious is bringing it back through the nightmare."

"Okay." The frown lines between Lauren's brows deepened.

"You say okay, but I see skepticism on your face."

"It's … it's just I've gone over what happened several times. Not only writing a statement out to the police but going over in my own mind *every* detail. The whole afternoon feels like it's on a continuous loop in my head, playing over and over."

"I understand. But it's different from a therapeutic point of view. Plus if you're able to remember something else, some small detail might be important to the murder investigation."

"I'm pretty detail oriented. I don't think I left anything out." Lauren glanced at the doorway, wondering if the chief had slunk down the hallway and was just outside the door listening.

"From your body language I get the sense you're holding something back. Is there something in particular bothering you tonight?"

Uh, yeah. Your husband. Lauren twisted her hands in her lap. "No. There's nothing … It's just … It's been a very long day, and I have a headache and …" Her voice trailed off.

"I see."

"I should have rescheduled this. I'm so sorry. I feel like I'm wasting your time."

"No, no. I understand." Patricia set her notepad down.

Lauren rose from the chair and started to leave. "I did want to say I'm sorry for your loss."

Patricia cocked her head. "*My* loss?"

"Alden. Mr. Bates." Lauren nodded in the direction of his office.

"Thank you. It was terrible what happened to Alden. I just couldn't believe it when Ray told me."

"I was surprised to see your husband there. I mean he seemed to come out of nowhere." Lauren hoped her voice sounded conversational, void of any accusatory notes.

Patricia shook her head. "That's Ray. Can't keep track of where he's at sometimes. Turns out it was a good thing he was there. The killer might still have been in the area. You and your aunt could have been in danger."

"Yes. We were lucky. Had you known Mr. Bates a long time?"

"Yes, a few years now. We shared this office space, but I wouldn't say we were close. Still, it's upsetting when I think about what happened to him."

Lauren nodded.

"He was my late mother-in-law's accountant, but you knew that already. Ray mentioned you were the court reporter at the depositions in the estate matter. You must know a lot of things, listening in on other people's lives all day."

Listening in? "I don't think of it like that. Your profession is more listening in, I would say."

"Except people make a conscious decision to seek out my services whereas in your profession you just..."

Whereas I just what? Eavesdrop? Lauren didn't like the tone in Patricia's voice. She was probably reading more into the therapist's words than were there. Drained from the day's work, uneasy about what the chief said in the kitchen, Lauren needed to leave. She pulled her car keys from her purse.

As if reading Lauren's thoughts, Patricia said, "I didn't mean to make it sound like you enjoyed knowing other people's business."

Lauren put on her professional courtroom expression of disinterest. "It doesn't matter to me what I hear. What's important is to get down every word that people say. Ninety percent of the time, once a job is done, I forget about it because it's not worth remembering. Most litigation is pretty uninteresting."

"Think about the hypnosis, Lauren. And restart your biofeedback if you haven't already."

"I have been doing that."

"Good." Patricia scrolled through her online calendar. "Let me see what I have available for next week."

"When are you closing your business?"

"I haven't made up my mind on when exactly."

"How about if I call you when I know what my schedule is like?"

"Sure. But you shouldn't wait too long. I can tell you're not yourself tonight, but I know I can help you if you talk about it rather than keep it bottled up."

"I'll call you."

"Have a good evening, Lauren." Patricia turned her attention to her computer screen.

Chapter Thirty-Seven

*L*auren patted her face dry with a towel. She looked at her reflection in the mirror as she replayed what Ray Newell said to her the other evening. She'd been obsessing over his words, unable to concentrate at work and losing several more night's sleep.

Their paths had never crossed until the death of Judge Murphy. During the investigation Aunt Kate's explanation of the history between the chief and her father made sense but that's what it was. History. The deliberate remark he made about her looks left her with questions.

Lauren padded into the kitchen, picked up her phone and called the one person who would have answers. After the third ring she heard the familiar upbeat voice say, "Hello."

"Hi, Dad."

"Lauren, hi."

"I'm not interrupting anything, am I?"

"No, no. I'm just sitting here watching TV."

"I just called to see how you're doing," said Lauren.

"I'm doing fine, Sweetie. Is everything all right with you?"

"Yes, yes. Everything's great."

"Good. You just caught me off guard. I thought something might have happened. Unusual for you to be calling me, especially on a Friday night."

"I know I don't usually call but it's been a while since we actually talked."

"It has. Texts are nice, but it's good to hear your voice."

The two of them talked a few minutes before Lauren asked, "I know it's last minute but are you working tomorrow?"

"No, I'm off this weekend."

"Do you have plans?"

"No, not really. What did you have in mind?"

"I thought I'd come see you. Maybe we could have lunch or something?"

"I'd love to see my little girl."

Lauren pictured him winking, something he always did when he called her his "little girl."

"What time can I expect you?"

"Around ten-thirty, eleven."

"I should be out of bed by then." Her father laughed.

"Right. You probably haven't changed a bit. Still up before the sun rises."

"Well, sweetie, old habits are hard to break. Especially when you get to be my age."

"Yeah, yeah, old man, whatever you say," Lauren teased. "I'm looking forward to seeing you."

"Same here. You drive safe."

"I will. Love you, Dad."

"Love you too."

When they disconnected, Lauren wondered if she should have explained the real purpose for her visit, but she didn't want him suddenly coming up with an excuse for her not to come. Or telling her outright he refused to talk about the subject. It was time, she told herself, that he open up and tell her about Melissa. Tell her about her mother.

She looked at her phone. Should she text her next-door neighbor Jeff and see if his daughter Tess could watch Maverik? Or should she take him with her? The half Border Collie, half your-guess-is-good-as-mine dog went for plenty of rides with her, but they were all around town. All short trips. This one, he would be spending two-and-a-half hours in the car on the way up. Same time for the drive home.

Tess said she loved to watch him and Lauren felt comfortable leaving him, knowing she would do a good job. She punched in the number for her neighbor and tapped out a text. Five minutes later the phone pinged. Lauren had her answer.

With arrangements made for Maverik, she spent the remainder of the evening thinking about how she would bring up the subject of her absentee mother without her father becoming too upset.

Chapter Thirty-Eight

The front door to her childhood home had a new coat of paint. At least it was new to Lauren.

When was the last time I came home? Now was not the time to feel guilty for not visiting often enough. Several reasons ... excuses ... popped into her head for not making the drive. *Quit it. I'm here now.*

She raised her hand about to wrap on the teal-colored door when it swung open. A small fawn-colored dog dashed out, then ran inside, then back out again. Lauren stepped into the foyer and into her father's bear-like embrace. When he released her she looked around the room, taking in its familiarity, even its smell. The smell of home.

Her father shouted over her head. "Trouble, inside. Now."

"Trouble?"

"Yes, Trouble. He came with the name."

The dog obeyed. He circled Lauren, sniffing her pants feverishly.

"Come on in the kitchen." Her father continued talking as they made their way through the living room. "Did you bring Maverik with you?"

"No. My neighbor's daughter is watching him."

"I had forgotten how nice it is to have a dog."

"Isn't Stacy still allergic?"

"Yes, but she doesn't live here anymore. She can handle being around him for a couple of hours."

Lauren reached into a cupboard and took a glass out and held it up at her father.

He nodded.

Lauren grabbed a second glass, popped ice cubes into them, opened the refrigerator door and smiled to herself. A large pitcher of iced tea sat on the top shelf. A staple at the Besoner household. A plate with hamburger patties sat on the shelf below alongside a package of unopened hot dogs.

She took the jug out and filled their glasses. "Are we having lunch here? I wanted to take you out, my treat. I didn't want you to have to cook."

"After we hung up I called Stacy. She wants to see you too. She'll be here a little later with the kids. I thought it would be more convenient just to stay here. It's been such a long time since I fired up the grill. You don't mind, do you?"

"Of course not. A burger sounds great." Lauren pulled out a stool and sat at the granite-top island. "When did you get Trouble?"

Gregory Besoner rubbed his clean-shaven chin and thought. "It's been five months now."

So it's been at least five months since I visited. Not going to win any daughter-of-the year awards. "He's so cute. What is he?"

"He's a long-haired Dachshund mix. He's five years old."

"What made you decide to get a dog?"

"I didn't. My friend Rocky – you remember him, don't you?"

Lauren nodded. "Yeah, I remember him. Hunting buddy. Poker buddy. You two are good friends."

"We were. Anyway, he was diagnosed with cancer last year. When his condition deteriorated to the point of him going into hospice care, he asked me if I'd take his dog."

"Oh."

"He didn't have any family that could take him. How could I say no?" Gregory looked at Trouble. "You're a fun little guy to have around. Once we got a few ground rules established, that is."

"Such as?"

"No sleeping in the bed with me. No peeing in the house." He raised a bushy eyebrow at the dog. "Now we're good."

"That's great. I mean, you taking him in. Not, you know, that your friend …"

"I know what you meant." He looked into the glass he held. "Rocky passed away … it's been four months now. He sure was a good friend."

"Why didn't you tell me?"

"What's to tell? It's not like you could have done anything being so far away. Besides, your sister fussed over me enough for the two of you."

Even though Stacy had been there for him, Lauren felt guilty. Not only had she not kept in contact with her dad, she also hadn't been there for him when he was grieving the loss of a good friend. She told herself it was easy for her sister. Stacy lived right here in Casper. Just a few miles away. A spark of anger flickered inside her. Stacy never said anything to her about Dad's friend passing. The spark extinguished itself just as quickly when she tried to remember the last time she called to talk to her sister and couldn't.

"Tell me, how are things in Crawford? How's work? And how is that sister of mine doing with all those alpacas?" He laughed.

"Aunt Kate and Uncle Jack are fine. And their pack seems to be growing little by little."

"Good to hear. I've been thinking of driving down and visiting them one of these weekends."

"You should."

"And of course I'd stop in to see my favorite daughter." He winked.

Lauren laughed. "Right. Favorite daughter." She sipped on her tea. "I have an extra room. You should stay with me."

"I might just do that."

"I'll plan on it then. As far as work, freelancing is always up and down, not steady like the official job I was used to, and lately it's been down. But right now I'm subbing in court," she nodded, "So it's all good."

Gregory raised an eyebrow. "You're working for your ex-husband?"

"Yes. But just temporarily. I'm covering a murder trial right now while his court reporter is on maternity leave.

It's an interesting case. Has it been in the newspaper here?"

"I remember reading about it in the *Casper Star*. It was a murder of an elderly woman?" Gregory pulled out a stool and joined Lauren at the island.

"Yes."

"That's what you're covering?"

"Um-hum. I know the defendant's uncle, Dominick DiMartino. He owns Dominick's Bakery."

"Oh. And do you think this guy did it?"

"Before the case started I was sure he was innocent. But now ... even though the state's attorney hasn't been doing the greatest job of presenting her case, I'm beginning to wonder." Lauren shrugged.

"Anything else exciting happening in Crawford?" her father asked.

"Did Aunt Kate tell you what happened?"

"I haven't spoken to my sister in a couple of weeks. Why? What's happened?"

"I can't believe she didn't call you and tell you as soon as she felt better."

"Felt better? Is Kate okay?"

"She's fine." Lauren described finding Mr. Bates and watched her father's face go from worried to shocked. She ended by saying, "It's still upsetting to think about."

"I'm sure it is. You're okay though? And Kate?"

"Yes."

"Then let's talk about something else."

"When is Stacy coming over?"

"Around eleven-thirty."

Lauren looked at the clock on the stove. Her sister

255

would arrive in an hour. She cleared her throat. "The trial I'm covering … the woman who was killed was someone named Margaret Archer." She waited a beat to see if the name meant anything to her father. "Do you know her?"

"I only know three people in Crawford." He chuckled.

"The woman was Ray Newell's mother."

"Ray Newell. Is that so?"

"Yes."

"I haven't heard his name in years." Gregory was quiet for a moment. "That must be where he's originally from. Crawford. Hmm."

"Yes." Lauren placed a hand on her father's forearm as he went to get up. "I have to ask you something."

He sat back on the stool. "Shoot."

"It's about my mother."

Chapter Thirty-Nine

*H*e looked at her for a long moment. "Why? Why after all this time would you ask about her?"

"Because she was my mother. I want to know more about her. I … I need to know."

He drained the last of his drink. "I don't understand. What do you want to know? If she was a good mother? We both know the answer to that question. Honestly, there's nothing to tell."

"Yes, there is." Lauren sounded, even to herself, like a sullen teenager minus a foot stomp. "You've never talked about her. Never. You never let me or Stacy talk about her or ask questions about her."

"You don't need to go getting upset." He put his glass in the sink and said over his shoulder, "She walked out on me when you girls were little. End of story."

The sound of the refrigerator hummed in the suddenly

quiet kitchen. Lauren went to the sink and stood by her father. "Will you at least answer one question?"

He shook his head, as if to say, *You don't give up, do you?*

"Do I look like her?" It was a question she needed an answer to, a question she drove one-hundred-seventy miles to get an answer to.

Stacy looked like their dad. They both shared the same ginger wavy locks and ocean-blue eyes. Lauren stood apart from them with her hazel eyes and straight, chestnut-leaning-toward-mousy-brown hair. Her sister even took after their dad in height, standing five foot eight in her stocking feet, five inches taller than Lauren.

"I need to know, Dad."

He turned around, his back against the sink, and ran a weathered hand down his face. "Why? Does this have something to do with Ray Newell?"

"Sort of."

Her father's voice rose. "Has he said something to you?"

"No. Not exactly."

"What do you mean, 'not exactly'? Has he been bothering you?"

Lauren heard the protectiveness in his question. No way would she tell him how Ray had been making her feel. If her dad knew, he would jump in the car, drive to Crawford and do ... do what? Whatever he did might get him arrested. Crawford's police chief would love for that to happen.

"Is that the real reason you're here?"

Guilty as charged. "No, no. It's just I've run into him a few times. When the police were investigating Judge

Murphy's death, he thought I was … involved. I think he pressed for the detective on the case to arrest me."

"Lauren, you never told me this. Why didn't you ever say anything to me?"

"Because … it was natural for the police to consider me a suspect. But Newell seemed to take it personally. Aunt Kate told me you were partly responsible for him losing his job as Casper's chief of police. Or at least involved. I assumed that was why he disliked me."

"I was on the city council when he was Casper's police chief. I was involved in discussions regarding his conduct. The matter was brought before the whole city council, but the mayor had the final say. And he asked Ray to step down as police chief. But my goodness, that was over twenty years ago. And it has *absolutely* nothing to do with you. What's going on? What's he said to you?"

She hesitated, not wanting to upset him.

"Tell me what said."

"That I look just like my mother." Lauren watched her father's ruddy cheeks drain of color, afraid he might pass out. She was silent a moment, then continued. "And since the whole time growing up the subject was taboo around here, I had no response. I mean, none. I just walked away so he wouldn't see me with a deer-in-the-headlight dumbass look on my face."

Her father walked to the kitchen island, gripped the edge so hard his knuckles turned white. "What else did he say?"

"That was it." She wouldn't mention the smirk on the chief's face. Or how it made her feel. Lauren drew in a breath, exhaled and spoke, doing her best to keep her voice even and calm. "So I want to know. I have to know, Dad. I don't want to be blindsided like that ever again."

He let out a resigned breath. "When your mother left for the last time, it was hard on everyone. You and your sister were both too young to understand what happened. And then as time went by, you girls adjusted so well to her not being around, I thought not bringing her up, not talking about her was the best thing for all of us. I just wanted to protect you."

He shook his head. "Her leaving had *absolutely nothing* to do with you. Nothing at all. It's not something children need to think about."

"That's just it. Whenever I brought it up and you refused to talk about it, I thought it was because of something I said. Or did."

He looked at her. "Sweetie, no. It had nothing at all to do with you."

"But I was just a kid, so of course I thought it was somehow my fault. What was I supposed to think?"

"Why would you –"

"Of course I know now I had nothing to do with her leaving. But for years I was convinced I was the reason she left. That I must have done something to make her stop loving us."

Her father gathered Lauren in a tight hug. He spoke into her hair. "Nothing could be further from the truth."

She folded into his embrace, inhaling his familiar scent.

He released her and busied himself by pulling the hamburger patties and hot dogs out of the refrigerator and setting them on the counter. He opened the sliding glass door.

Trouble raced into the kitchen at the sound, nails dancing on the tiled floor. He raced past Gregory onto the patio. Lauren and her father followed.

Gregory opened the lid of the grill as if he were opening up the hood of a car to check its oil levels. He took a wire brush and scraped its already clean surface.

With the brush in hand he pointed to a clump of aspen in the far corner of the yard. "Do you remember when we planted those?"

Lauren smiled. "I do. Stacy and I said we'd dig the hole for them but gave up after a few minutes because the ground was so hard."

"Yes. It was three months after Melissa ... after your mother left."

The pained expression on his face almost made Lauren say, *No, you don't have to do this.*

"They were a couple of feet taller than you when we planted them. Look at them now."

Lauren smiled at the memory, then turned her attention back to her mother. "Earlier you said, 'the last time she left.' So she'd done that before?"

He nodded. "Your mother and I always had a rocky relationship. The first time she left I was working in Gillette, in the oil fields. I got a call from your Aunt Kate – thank goodness she was still living here in Casper – when I returned to the motel. Melissa just dropped you girls off at my sister's. Said she needed her space. She didn't think she was cut out to be a mother."

"Wow. How long was she gone?"

"A month or so. Of course, I came home right away. Ended up quitting oil field work. No way I could work on a rig and raise you two at the same time. I found work here." He looked down at his hands. "When I worked as a roughneck I was gone anywhere from seven to ten days at a stretch. It was hard on your mother, being home alone with two little ones."

He must have loved her mother a lot, for even now it sounded like he was defending her.

"I didn't know you worked in the oil fields."

"Yes. It was hard work. Didn't miss it after I gave it up. Anyway, when she finally came home we agreed we'd try to work on the marriage. I tried, I really did, but for some reason I just couldn't make her happy. Even though I didn't work out of town any longer we still fought a lot."

"I don't remember you fighting."

"No, you wouldn't have known." He scrubbed the grate with fast and hard strokes. "You were too little to know what was going on. We tried to keep it from you." He set the bristle brush on the table.

Lauren waited for him to say more. There had to be more. "So, what? Did she tell you she was leaving for good the last time?"

He shook his head. "No, I didn't know. We'd had another argument the night before, but I never thought... never thought she'd leave like that, without any explanation, not even a goodbye."

The wind picked up, the leaves on the quaking aspens speaking a language all their own.

Lauren's mind went back to that afternoon in March, the last time she saw her mother. "I vaguely remember her taking us to Aunt Kate's house, telling us to be good, to mind Kate, and she'd be right back."

She gazed out into the backyard, then turned to her father. "So that's it, Dad?"

"That's it. Not much else to say." He shrugged.

"What does her leaving have to do with Ray Newell? I don't understand."

Her father slumped into one of the deck chairs. Trouble jumped on his lap, trying to lick his face. "No. Stop." The dog stopped and Gregory scratched under the dog's chin.

"A few months before she disappeared for good, I'd found out your mother and Ray Newell had been having an affair."

Chapter Forty

*O*f all the things her father might have told her, might have said, those words never crossed her mind. "She had an affair? With *him*?"

He nodded. "Yes."

Lauren had asked for the truth. And her father gave it to her. And now? Now she was sorry she ever brought the subject up.

"She worked part-time for the police department then. As a receptionist."

"Was he the police chief by then?"

"Yes."

Lauren had heard enough but her father continued.

"She lost her job because they caught her syphoning drugs, cocaine to be exact, stored in the department's evidence locker. Melissa admitted it."

Lauren's eyes widened.

"She was a different person by then. I think Ray might have been into drugs too, but it could never be proved."

"How was she able to do that?"

Gregory rubbed his chin. "Easy enough for her to get her hands on drugs in those days. They didn't have the safeguards like they do now. Anyway, after they fired her, she broke down and told me about the affair with Ray. And I blew up. We had one hell of a fight."

Lauren watched sadness creep into his blue eyes, making him look older and suddenly vulnerable.

"I stayed with Kate for a few days. Melissa got in contact with me. Said she'd be willing to get help for her drug problem. Wanted to get back together. Try and make the marriage work. I agreed." He shook his head with resignation. "I tried to make it work, but it's hard when something like that happens. It's hard to ever have that trust back."

"I know what you mean."

Gregory looked at his daughter. "I guess you do. I never trusted her after that. And she could tell I didn't." He looked out over the backyard and then at Lauren. "Before she left she'd gone back to using."

He set Trouble on the ground and stood. "It wasn't long after your mother walked out on us for good that Ray was asked to step down. And even though I had absolutely nothing to do with the original complaint being brought against him, he accused me of being behind it. Said it was my way of getting even with him for him having an affair with Melissa."

"Just because you were on the city council at the time?"

"Yes. But it was his own doing. The mayor had complaints from the public and from his own officers about the way he treated ... or mistreated them. It wasn't one single incident. It had nothing to do with your mother. But he never owned up to any of it."

"From what little I know of him that's not surprising."

"He blamed your mother for the breakup of his marriage." He shook his head. "Like it was all Melissa's doing. He was as much to blame, if not more. But he didn't see it that way. His wife found out, divorced him, and left town with their two kids. Went back to ... not exactly sure where she was from, but that was another thing he blamed Melissa for. Him never seeing his kids again."

I'm a painful reminder of all the things Ray Newell lost, thought Lauren.

Her dad went inside and returned with the plate of hamburgers and hot dogs and began placing them on the clean grill. "I saw him the day after he handed in his resignation to the mayor. He accused me of 'masterminding' his demise, as he put it. Said I went behind his back and talked the officers into lying." He closed the barbecue lid.

"He's such an ass."

Her dad arched an eyebrow.

"Well, he is," said Lauren.

"By then there was also a question about missing evidence. Drugs, to be exact. It was never proven he was involved. But I often wondered if he was capable of something like that." He took in a deep breath and exhaled loudly. "'And that,' as Paul Harvey would say, 'is the rest of the story.'"

"Paul Harvey? Who's he?"

Greg laughed. "A radio commentator. Before your time."

He went inside with Lauren and began gathering plates from the cupboard. Lauren pulled open the utensil drawer, and they went about setting the table, each lost in their own thoughts.

The information, the history her father divulged, was a lot to take in. It explained the chief's behavior toward her. Didn't make it right but at least she understood his twisted reasoning for disliking her. Maybe even hating her.

As for learning about her mother, it left her with mixed emotions. Relief to finally know what happened all those years ago. And hurt and anger that a mother, her mother, could walk out and leave her children behind.

After Gregory placed the last plate on the table he said, "We can talk about this more later if you feel the need, but let's not do it while your sister is here, okay?"

Lauren shrugged. "Okay. But one more question. Not really a question. You know the person that Aunt Kate and I found? Ray Newell was there too. Afterwards I mean. He showed up before any other law enforcement. I don't even know why he was there."

"What are you saying?"

"He was angry that we were there. Do you think it's possible – Never mind. I don't even know why I'm asking."

"He was at the crime scene and you're wondering if he could be the killer?"

Could that possibly be? "I suppose so."

"I haven't seen that man in over two decades. I didn't know him well even back then. I have no idea what he's capable of."

"But he's in law enforcement."

"You work in the court system. You know all kinds of people commit all kinds of crimes."

Lauren nodded in agreement.

"You need to be extra careful, Lauren. I don't like this one bit. Maybe you should come stay with me for a while."

"I'm in the middle of a job. I can't do that."

"What about that friend of yours, the one Kate's told me about, Sam? He's a police officer, right?"

"He is but Ray is his boss."

"Doesn't matter. Talk to him. See what he has to say."

That's not going to happen any time soon. "Maybe I will. Thanks, Dad."

They were quiet for a long moment, her dad studying her face, concern evident in his eyes. Then he said, "Let's just have a nice, enjoyable meal together. It's been too long since I've had both my girls home at the same time. I just want to enjoy the day without … without those memories. Do it for your old man."

"Okay. But just one more question."

He blew out an exaggerated puff of air. "What?"

"Do I? Do I look like her?"

Gregory tilted his head toward the ceiling and closed his eyes.

"I mean I have a few memories of her, but I can't picture her face anymore."

After a moment he looked at her, sadness in his smile. "You're the spitting image of your mother."

*   *   *

Lauren pulled the plastic Ziploc bag containing a dozen

snickerdoodles Stacy had baked onto her lap. Concentrating on the road, she felt for the tab, opened the bag, grabbed one of the cookies and bit into it. The sugar-cinnamon combo danced on her taste buds. "Mmm-mmm-mmm." She closed the bag and tossed it onto the back seat, keeping them out of reach so she wouldn't eat them all before arriving home.

The afternoon with her father and Stacy went by fast. Lauren thought she would find it hard not to say anything to her sister about what she'd learned about their mother, but with her niece and nephew monopolizing all her time, it turned out not to be a problem. The afternoon turned out to be fun despite what she learned from her dad.

When she'd hugged her nephew and niece goodbye, it was with a promise to come watch one of Cole's soccer games soon and attend Ally's next piano recital.

She had stood in the doorway, hugged her father tight and whispered in his ear. "Thanks, Dad. I know that was hard. Love you."

He kissed the top of her head. "Love you more. Drive safe." He thrust a manila envelope into her open messenger bag.

Chapter Forty-One

$\mathcal{L}$auren pulled into her garage, gathered the bag of cookies from the back seat along with the envelope that her father had given her. When she stopped at the convenience store to gas up for the drive home, she almost opened it but managed to resist the urge. Now she couldn't wait to get in the house.

Maverik had his own agenda, which included being let out. Lauren put on her UW hoodie, turned on the outside light, stepped out and watched her dog run amongst the caragana bushes that ran the length of their backyard, between her and her neighbor.

Twila Nash's porch light came on, and a moment later, Percy, her Papillon, could be heard making his way through the low shrubs to the fence which separated their property. One yip from Percy, a short bark from Maverik, and the game was on. The dogs raced up and down the fence line, the bushes rustling as they ran.

The old woman stepped onto her porch, her dyed red curls lit up like an old Ronald McDonald head underneath the porch light. The threadbare robe she wore didn't look like it would keep the cool night air out.

"Percy," Lauren called. He ran to her. She reached over the fence, scooped him up and hugged him. "How are you doing?" He answered with licking her face and squirming in her arms. "I need some hugs from you. Then I'll let you go." She squeezed him, ruffled his large ears, then set him down.

The squeaky wheels of her neighbor's oxygen tank signaled her making her way to the fence. Enough light shone from Lauren's deck she could see her approach. "How are you, Twila?"

Her neighbor coughed a phlegmy cough, then answered. "I'm upright so I must be okay."

"How's Percy been?"

"He's fine. Keeps me on my toes."

"He feels like he's put on a little weight."

"Yeah, he don't go hungry. Always begging for table scraps. He was on the thin side when you had him."

Lauren couldn't argue. After the death of Judge Murphy, somehow Lauren ended up caring for her boss's Papillon. He spent the first week with Lauren trembling and having such an upset stomach he lost two pounds. Being a tiny breed to begin with, two pounds was weight he couldn't afford to lose.

"What's going on at your place?"

"Nothing. What do you mean? I just got back from Casper."

"I saw a car just sitting outside your house earlier, for a really long time. And I knew you weren't home."

Of course you did. You somehow know whatever is going on over here.

"I couldn't see inside the vehicle, my eyes not being as good as they used to be. Plus it had those tinted windows everybody seems to have nowadays. Just sat parked there for a good half hour. Even though your dog was inside, I heard him barking. The *whole* time. Would not shut up. That's what made me look out my window in the first place." Twila harrumphed. "Got Percy all wound up too."

"What kind of vehicle was it?"

"I don't know. It was big like one of them SUVs everybody around here drives nowadays. Come to think of it, it looked like the kind of newer vehicles the police department spent my tax dollars on. Maybe it was your fella. That's probably who it was."

Puzzled, Lauren asked, "My fella?"

"You know who I mean, your detective." After seeing the questioning look on Lauren's face, Twila added, "I think it was that detective, the one who was here when your house almost burned down."

"Oh, him." *Why would Sam just be sitting outside my house?* Mrs. Nash had to be mistaken. Recently the Crawford Police Department had purchased a fleet of three SUVs ... if three qualified as a fleet. Sam drove one, but SUVs were almost as popular as pickups in Crawford. It didn't narrow down who could have been parked outside.

"Anyway, I thought you'd want to know. In case you want to call him and tell him you're home now."

"Thanks."

Mrs. Nash cocked her head. "Come to think of it I saw that same car parked behind your fence in the alleyway a couple weeks ago. And you *were* home that night. Your lights were on. I thought it was strange, him parking back there all secret-like."

Twila leaned closer to the fence and peered at Lauren from thick-lensed glasses. "Is your fella a married man? Is that what's going on here?"

"There's no –"

"That's why he parked out back, isn't it?"

"No. And Sam is not married. And he's not my boyfriend. We're just friends." *Not even that at the moment.*

"Whatever you say."

"What night was that, do you remember?"

"No, I don't. Do you think I write these things down? Who do you think I am, some kind of personal assistant of yours or something?"

"No. It's just –"

"I wouldn't have noticed except I had just let Percy out. I turned the porch light on and waited for him to do his business. He took longer than usual. Must have spied a rabbit or something. Trying to get his little self in trouble. The rabbits around here are bigger than he is. Anyway, that's when I seen the vehicle. When Percy came inside I turned off the outside light and I thought I could make out an outline of a person behind the wheel."

Lauren couldn't think of any reason why Sam would park and sit outside her backyard. What Twila said made no sense. But Lauren remembered the night that she herself saw a vehicle parked out there.

"When I was upstairs in my bedroom, I happened to look out my window and he was driving away. No headlights on." Twila pointed a finger at Lauren. "You need to tell your fella he should pay more attention when he's driving at night like that. That's just plain dangerous."

Sam hadn't been in her home after dark. Was it Sam that Twila was talking about? If so, why would he just sit there in the dark? And if it wasn't Sam, who was it? Lauren hugged herself.

"Come on, Percy. That's enough running around out here in the dark." Without so much as a good night, Twila turned and shuffled to her house.

* * *

After calling Maverik inside, Lauren started to text Sam, *Were you at my house*, then deleted the message, not wanting him thinking this was an excuse to have contact with him. She put her phone down, picked up the manilla envelope and undid the metal clasp on the back. She reached inside and pulled out three photographs. Lauren leaned against the sink and studied each one. The first showed a woman in her late teens with a Mona Lisa smile for the camera. Glossy brown bangs fell into gold-flecked hazel eyes. The next photo showed the same woman but heavier with a bored expression on her face. She held a baby wrapped in a pink blanket, and a red-haired toddler hugged her knee. Lauren turned the photo over. The block lettering – her father's – looked crisp, recent. It read, *Lauren, three months old. Stacy, three years old.*

The last picture showed the woman with dyed blonde hair and a deep artificial tan sitting in a recliner smoking a cigarette. Two little girls, she and her sister, sat on the living room floor playing with dolls.

She fished inside the envelope to make sure she had taken them all out and pulled out a sheet of paper folded in half.

Lauren, sorry it took so long to give you the answers you needed. As you can tell you do resemble your mother. But only on the outside. You've become an awesome young lady. I'm very proud of you. Love Dad.

Lauren looked at the first photograph once more. She stared at the stranger. At her mother. At herself.

Chapter Forty-Two

"You may call your next witness," said Judge Jenkins. Ms. Martindale stood. "The state rests, Your Honor."

It was Friday afternoon. Lauren thought the case would have gone to the jury by now but every time Tony said, "You may call your next witness," the state did.

Lauren looked at the jury. Relief or something similar looked back at her. She presumed all the jurors were eager to end their civic duty and return to their daily routines. And like her, they probably had the same question on their minds: whether the defendant would testify. If he didn't take the stand, they might start deliberations this afternoon. And if he did decide to testify, they would return Monday to finish the trial. Unless her ex did something her other judges never did, let the jury deliberate over the weekend.

"Ladies and gentlemen, this is a good time to take our afternoon break. Bailiff, please escort the jury out."

Everyone in the courtroom rose collectively. The jurors scooted out of the jury box and single-filed out of the courtroom, the bailiff closing the door behind them.

"Before we recess, Mr. Dresser, do you have something to put on the record?" asked Judge Jenkins.

The defense attorney approached the podium. "Yes, Your Honor."

"Go ahead then," said the judge.

Mr. Dresser pulled the microphone toward him and proceeded to give his reasons why the judge should acquit Daniel Throgmorton of murder.

Lauren had never reported a case where an acquittal had been granted. There was always a first time, but this case was not destined to be it.

After the judge ruled against the defense, he said, "We'll take our recess now. When we return, Mr. Dresser, I'll hear from you about whether your client intends to take the stand and testify. We have ten minutes before the jury returns. Court is in recess."

"All rise." The bailiff's loud voice filled the air.

Tony held a diet soda in his hand. He stood near Susan's desk. "Well, we're in the final stretch. The jury is going to get this case either late this afternoon or first thing Monday morning, depending on if Mr. Throgmorton takes the stand. It would be nice if it were wrapped up today." He turned to Lauren. "Is that your take on it also?"

Lauren nodded. "Yes."

"Is the defendant going to testify?" Susan put down her

cell phone and looked to the judge for an answer.

"We'll know after the break. Even if he does, he won't be on the stand very long." He turned to Lauren. "Do you think he's going to testify?" He held his arms out, like the scales of justice, weighing the odds. "Or no?"

"I think he'll testify." Lauren took a drink of her bottled water. "He shouldn't but I think he will. He's going to want to tell his side of the story, tell the jury he didn't do it even though he doesn't have to."

"I know. Even though I admonish the jury that a defendant has the right to remain silent... still. Eli let that one potential juror go, the one who kept insisting they needed to hear both sides before they could decide." Tony shook his head. "If it were only that simple. Everyone just gets up and tells the truth. But I don't think he will testify. Eli will talk him out of it. Shall we wager a little bet?" Tony raised an eyebrow.

"A bet?" Lauren asked.

"Yes. If I'm right, you have dinner with me."

"I –"

"Wait. Hear me out. Just a dinner between friends. Your choice of restaurant, of course."

"No thanks. I don't want to bet." Lauren didn't feel right making light of the whole situation. *And I'm not ready to be friends with you. I may never be.*

"Okay. All bets are off." Tony shrugged. "But if the jury gets the case late this afternoon, I'm going to let them decide if they want to stay into the evening and deliberate. Are you okay with that? Even if they come back, say, ten, eleven o'clock tonight?"

"I can come back. But you do know anything after six

o'clock I charge triple my normal per diem rate, don't you?"

"That seems a little extreme, don't you think?" Susan sounded indignant, as if she was being asked to pay the money out of her own pocket.

Lauren suppressed a giggle. "I was kidding, Susan."

"Hmmph." Susan rolled her eyes.

❋ ❋ ❋

"Let the record reflect we're in session but without the jury." Judge Jenkins looked at the defense attorney. "Have you discussed with your client whether he intends to take the stand and testify, Mr. Dresser?"

Mr. Dresser walked over to the podium. "Yes, Judge. I have discussed it, and Mr. Throgmorton wants to testify. Your Honor, since I have advised my client not to take the stand, I would ask you advise him on the record of his right to remain silent."

"Of course. Mr. Throgmorton, please join your counsel at the podium."

Daniel walked over to Mr. Dresser, who stood a good ten inches taller than his client.

"Mr. Throgmorton, I understand you wish to testify on your own behalf," said the judge.

"Yeah, I do, Your Honor."

"Your counsel has informed me he has spoken to you and his recommendation is to not testify. After discussing it with Mr. Dresser, do you still wish to testify on your own behalf?"

Mr. Throgmorton nodded. "Yes."

"If that is the case I must advise you once you start testifying your Fifth Amendment right is no longer available to you. In other words, if state's counsel questions you about your criminal background, or any other relevant question, you will have to answer. You will not be able to refuse to answer based on the fact it may incriminate you in another matter."

Judge Jenkins pointed his gavel at the defendant. "Do you understand once you start testifying, you will have given up your right to remain silent?"

The defendant glanced at Mr. Dresser, who shrugged, his way of saying, *It's your call.*

"Yes, I understand. I still want to testify. I think if I just explain my side of the story –"

"Let me stop you there," said Judge Jenkins. "I don't need to know the details of why you decided, just that you understand the implications of testifying."

Mr. Throgmorton furrowed his brow.

"Can I have a moment with my client, Your Honor?" asked Mr. Dresser.

"Certainly. You may step away from the podium and speak with your client."

Lauren glanced around at the participants in the courtroom. Ms. Martindale and Mr. Jessup were looking at the defendant and Mr. Dresser. The bailiff stood by the closed door of the jury room, inspecting his fingernails. Lauren could hear Tony tapping away on the keys of his laptop.

The air in the courtroom was a cocktail of all the perfumes, colognes and aftershaves intermingled over the course of the trial.

Lauren looked at the clock on the wall, knowing it

would be at least another hour and a half before she could breathe in fresh air. Or longer.

"Your Honor, we're ready to proceed," said Mr. Dresser. "My client just needed some terminology explained to him. Thank you."

"Having again discussed the matter with your lawyer, do you wish to testify?"

"Yes, sir," replied Mr. Throgmorton.

"Very well then. Bailiff, return the jury, please."

The jurors walked in single file clutching their water bottles and notebooks.

When the jury panel was seated Judge Jenkins spoke. "We are again present in the matter of the State of Wyoming versus Daniel T. Throgmorton. Let the record reflect counsel for the state and the defense are present, as well as the defendant, as is the jury panel.

"The state having rested, does the defense wish to call any witnesses at this time?" asked Judge Jenkins.

Mr. Dresser stood. "Yes, Your Honor. The defense calls Daniel Throgmorton to the stand."

The room grew quiet as the defendant stood and walked toward the bailiff.

He wore a white button-down shirt underneath a black suit which swallowed his gaunt frame. The clothes were loaners, perhaps from his uncle Dominick. Either way, Daniel did his best to swagger to the witness stand, but the brown oxford shoes, two sizes too big, made it impossible.

While the bailiff administered the oath to Mr. Throgmorton, Lauren jotted down his name on the witness list she kept beside her laptop, then swiveled her chair to face the young man whose fate would soon be determined by twelve people he didn't know.

She stole a quick glance at the spectators who came to watch the trial. Dominick sat in the long bench closest to the door. Their eyes met. He acknowledged her with a sad smile.

Mr. Dresser approached the podium. "Mr. Throgmorton, tell the ladies and gentlemen your name and where you live, please."

Daniel lifted his chin and looked at his attorney. "My name is Daniel Throgmorton. I live at –"

"You can just state the town you live in." Mr. Dresser cut him off before he answered where he presently resided, at the detention center. Living in a jail cell sent the jury a preconceived message. Guilty.

"I live here in town, in Crawford."

"And where did you grow up?"

"I was born in Brooklyn, New York. But we moved around a lot. Like to different parts of the city." He nodded, as if satisfied with his answer.

"When did you move to Crawford?"

"Uh, I ain't too sure when I moved here. A year and a half ago, maybe two." Again, he nodded.

After asking a few more general questions, Mr. Dresser said, "Daniel, you know why you're here, so I'll get right to it. Did you kill Margaret Archer?"

The defendant shook his head. "No."

"Did you deliver a pizza to her house on May tenth of this year, the night she was killed?"

"Yes. I delivered her usual."

"And what was her usual?"

"A medium supreme meat lovers. No, wait. That night it was a large."

"Was it usually a medium?"

"Yeah, most of the time."

"Do you know why it was a large that night?"

The defendant shrugged. "No. Maybe she was real hungry. Or expecting company."

"And she was alive when you arrived?"

Mr. Throgmorton looked at his attorney as if to say, *What a stupid question. Of course she was.* "Yeah, she was alive when I got there."

"And she was alive when you left her residence?"

"Yeah."

"Had you had any dealings with Mrs. Archer aside from delivering food to her?"

"She was a regular at my uncle's bakery. I waited on her a couple times, I think."

"Does anything stand out about that? Did you two ever exchange words or have an argument?"

"No. Didn't really pay much attention to her. She was just another customa."

Mr. Dresser nodded. "I know it's going to come up so I want to ask you, have you been in trouble with the law before?"

"Yeah."

"When and what kind of trouble were you in?"

"When I was younger. You know, like smoking pot, doing a little … doing drugs."

"Now, we might as well address the elephant in the room."

Mr. Throgmorton's forehead creased.

"The male in the surveillance video from the pawn shop, was that you?"

The defendant lowered his gaze. "Yes."

"And did you steal Mrs. Archer's ring?"

The answer came out in a whisper. "Yes, I stole the ring."

Judge Jenkins spoke up. "I'm sorry, I didn't hear your answer."

The defendant leaned into the microphone "I said yes, I stole the ring." Before Mr. Dresser asked another question he added, "But I didn't kill Mrs. Archer."

"Why did you steal the ring, Daniel?" asked Mr. Dresser.

"So I … I needed … I had a drug problem back then. I pawned it and used the money to buy meth."

Mr. Dresser did a slow, understanding head nod. "Did you steal it the evening of her death?"

"No. It was a different night. A couple of weeks before maybe. I … I don't remember when. I wasn't planning on stealing from her, but when she went to get her purse to pay me I saw it just laying on a table next to her couch." He shrugged. "So I took it."

Eli looked at his legal pad which sat on the edge of the podium. "Let's go back to the night in question. You said you were working delivering pizza."

"Yes."

"Where did you work?"

"Sol's Pizza."

"How long had you held that job, delivering pizza?"

Daniel scratched his chin. "I don't remember exactly. Maybe like six months, seven months. Coulda been longer."

"Did you enjoy your job?"

"It was okay. Just a job. Tips were decent."

"What time did you go to work on the day in question?"

"Four o'clock."

"What time did your shift usually end?"

"Midnight."

"So that night did you deliver pizza to anyone other than Mrs. Archer?"

"Uh-huh."

"For the record you need to say yes or no."

"Oh, yeah, I delivered pizza to other people."

"Did you have a conversation with Mrs. Archer that evening when you delivered the pizza?"

"Yeah, a little. She had me step inside like usual –"

"So you were in her home?"

"Yes. She would always tell me to come in while she went and got her bag. She always tipped me in cash." He nodded, remembering. "She thanked me for the pizza. Asked me how I was doing. Told me, have a good evening like she always did. Handed me a tip. Yeah, that was about it."

"And you said you'd been to this address before? Delivered to this address before?"

"Uh-huh – I mean, yes."

"This night, was there anyone else there besides Mrs. Archer?"

"No. Just her."

"Was she usually alone when you made your delivery?"

"Most of the time. Once in a while there would be some dude there."

"This 'dude,' can you describe him?"

The defendant took a moment before he answered. "No. He was just some old guy."

"Can you say how many times you saw him there?"

Mr. Throgmorton shrugged. "No. Maybe once or twice a month. I really don't know."

"And other than being, as you say, an old guy, can you give any more of a description?"

"Had gray hair. Tall-ish. Thin."

"Did you ever have an argument with Mrs. Archer? Did you and she ever exchange words?"

"No."

"Did you like Mrs. Archer?"

Daniel's eyes widened slightly, like he had never thought about that before. "Uh, I guess so – I mean yes. She always gave me a good tip. Not like some of my other customers. They think since they already paid a delivery fee they didn't have to tip." Daniel shook his head. "Cheap bastards – oh, I'm sorry." The defendant's eyes darted to the jury and back to Mr. Dresser. "Hard to make a living that way. I think Mrs. Archer kinda knew that." He smiled at some memory, then added, "She was nice that way."

Mr. Dresser flipped through the pages of the legal pad. "No further questions, Your Honor."

Chapter Forty-Three

"Questions for the witness, Ms. Martindale?" asked Judge Jenkins.

"Yes, Your Honor." The prosecutor approached the lectern, head high. "Do you often steal from people you like, Mr. Throgmorton?"

The defendant's pale face turned bright red. "Uh, no. It's just –"

"You answered my question. Thank you." She removed one of many pink sticky notes off the legal pad in front of her. "Mr. Throgmorton, what did you do for employment before working for Sol's Pizza?"

"Worked at my uncle's bakery."

"Is that Dominick's Bakery here in town?"

"Yeah."

"Why did you leave that employment?"

"Why did I leave?"

"Yes. Why were you no longer working for your uncle?"

The defendant thought a moment. "Me and my uncle just didn't get along, I guess. And I ... I didn't like getting up so early."

"Did you quit or were you fired?" asked the prosecutor.

"He – we both agreed maybe I wasn't cut out for the job."

"Where did you work before working for your uncle?"

"Uh, I worked odd jobs. Back in New York. Yeah."

"Mr. Throgmorton, how many times did you deliver pizza to Mrs. Archer's residence?"

Mr. Throgmorton looked at the ceiling, then at the prosecutor. "I don't remember exactly. Maybe three times a month, I guess, for six months."

"Did she order pizza the same day every week? Or was it sporadic?"

"Sporadic. What do you mean?"

"Did you always deliver pizza on the same day? Say every Monday? Or did she order randomly?"

"I don't remember."

"Would you consider her a regular customer of Sol's Pizza?"

"Yeah, I suppose so."

"Did you ever go to Mrs. Archer's residence for any other reason?"

"What do you mean?"

"Did you ever go to Mrs. Archer's home and you were not delivering pizza? Did you ever go there when she wasn't home? You told us you knew her from your days working at the bakery. Did she ever ask you to help her? Have you come over, move a piece of furniture? Mow her lawn? Did you have any reason to be at her home when you weren't working for the pizza place?"

Mr. Dresser stood. "Objection, Your Honor. Compound question."

Before the judge ruled, Ms. Martindale spoke. "I'll break the question down, Your Honor."

"Please do," said the judge.

"Mr. Throgmorton, did you ever, even once, for any reason, go to Mrs. Archer's home other than to deliver a pizza?"

"No."

"Can you tell the jury why your fingerprints were found on Mrs. Archer's dining room table?"

"I must have touched it when I put the pizza down."

Several questions were asked and answered.

The prosecutor pulled a sticky note off her notepad, then looked at the defendant. "I'd like to ask you some questions about the ring. You admit you stole Mrs. Archer's ring?"

"Yeah."

"And you said you stole it with the intent to sell it for drugs, is that correct?"

"I already said that before. Yeah."

"And where did you say the ring was when you stole it?"

"On a table next to the couch."

"I see. And it was just lying there and so you just took it?"

Mr. Throgmorton shrugged. "Yes."

"And you want this jury to believe the victim never confronted you about stealing the ring?"

"Yeah, because she didn't."

"And you maintain you didn't steal it the night she was killed?"

"I didn't take it that night."

"Are you sure about that? It sounds like you spent a lot of time high on drugs. Could you be mistaken?"

Mr. Dresser stood. "Your Honor, I object –"

"I'll withdraw the question, Your Honor." The prosecutor took a sip of water from a cup on the podium. "Who was your employer when you lived in New York?"

""I wasn't working. That's why I came out here. My uncle offered me a job in his bakery. Thought I'd see what Crawford was like."

"And your uncle is Dominick DiMartino?"

"Yeah. He's my mom's brother."

"Mr. Throgmorton, isn't it true you had just been released from the Vernon C. Bain Correctional Facility in New York City before moving to Crawford?"

"Yeah, I was in prison."

"What were you in prison for?"

"What was I in prison for?"

Lauren knew from past witnesses, repeating a question was a person's way of stalling, a mental flipping of a coin. Heads, they would tell the truth. Tails, they would lie.

"Yes. What *illegal* thing did you do that caused you to wind up in prison?"

Burglary. And possession with intent."

"Burglary. I see. And possession of what?"

"Heroin."

"Did you say 'with intent'?"

"Yeah."

"What does 'with intent' mean?"

"It means to sell it."

"So you're a drug dealer. I see. Now –"

Mr. Dresser stood. "Objection, Your Honor. There's no evidence my client was a drug dealer."

"Sustained. Questions please, Ms. Martindale, not commentary," Judge Jenkins said.

"Yes, Your Honor." The prosecutor looked down at her notes as she asked her next question. "What did you steal that you ended up serving time for?"

The defendant scratched his head. "Uh, I don't remember."

"You don't remember. I see. But whatever it was, you spent time in prison for it?"

"Yes."

Ms. Martindale flipped a page in her legal pad. "Let me see if I can refresh your memory. Isn't it true you were serving time, not for burglary, but for robbery?

"Well, the lady came home while I was, you know, in the house, so they got me for robbery. She wasn't supposed to be home."

"So it was a planned burglary that went wrong?"

Mr. Throgmorton waited a beat before answering. "I guess you could say that."

"And you stole jewelry from that elderly woman also?"

"Yeah, I guess."

"You guess. Did you steal jewelry or not?"

"Yeah, I did."

"Not just any jewelry but you stole two very expensive rings and a necklace?"

"I don't remember exactly, but I'm sure you know what I stole."

"How long ago did this happen?" asked Ms. Martin-dale.

"Maybe four years ago. I'm not for certain."

"Is there some medical condition you have which causes you to have trouble remembering things from four years ago?"

The defendant's dark eyebrows creased together. "No. I'm just not good with dates is all."

"And you also stole a gun during that robbery, didn't you?"

The defendant nodded.

"Is that a yes, Mr. Throgmorton?"

"Yes, I took it. I didn't mean to steal it. It was just there so ..."

"I see."

Lauren stole a glance at Eli. He sat at counsel table, jotting something in his legal pad.

Ms. Martindale held the sides of the podium and leaned in, her blonde hair falling forward. "What happened that night is you delivered a pizza, you saw the ring lying around and decided to steal it, isn't that true?"

"No. I –"

"Did Margaret Archer see you steal the ring? Is that what happened?"

"No."

"She caught you putting her ring in your pocket, didn't she?"

"No. I didn't –"

"She confronted you with trying to steal it, didn't she?"

"No."

The prosecutor's questions piggybacked the defendant's answers. Lauren's fingers moved over the keys of her writer matching the speed of the words being volleyed back and forth.

"And when she turned around to call the police, you panicked and grabbed whatever was handy, didn't you?"

"No."

"What was it, an iron skillet? Whatever it was, you struck her in the back of the head, didn't you?"

Mr. Throgmorton's voice rose. "No."

An iron skillet, a possible weapon. That sounded plausible to Lauren. Mrs. Archer was found near the kitchen. Did that mean it wasn't premeditated? That someone had an argument with her and it got out of hand?

"And while she lay there on the floor dying you decided to go to her medicine cabinet where you knew her pain-killers were kept and steal them, didn't you?"

"No, I never –"

Mr. Dresser stood, cutting off his client's answer. "Your Honor, I object. There is absolutely no evidence any prescription drugs were removed from the victim's home. Much less by my client."

Lauren captured Eli's words and they displayed on her monitor, but they did not do them justice. They could not show the anger in his voice.

"Objection sustained," said the judge. "The jury will disregard Ms. Martindale's question." He returned his attention to the realtime feed on his laptop but not before eyeing the prosecutor and giving an imperceptible head shake.

"In that case, Your Honor, I'm done with this witness," Ms. Martindale turned on her high heels, hair bouncing back over her shoulders. She stopped and swung around. "I'm sorry, Your Honor. One more line of questions, if I might."

"Of course."

She returned to the podium. "You said you delivered pizza that night to other customers, is that right?"

"Yes," said the defendant.

"Did you make any deliveries after the delivery to Mrs. Archer?"

The defendant looked at the ceiling while contemplating his answer. "No. She was my last customer."

"Why was she your last customer? Was it close to the end of your shift?"

"No."

Ms. Martindale approached the witness box, holding a piece of paper. "I'd like you to take a look at that document. Have you seen it before?"

Daniel shook his head.

"Is that a no?"

"Yes. I mean no. I mean yes, it's a no."

"This came from Sol's Pizza on the night in question. It shows the time Mrs. Archer called in her order. What time is on that document?"

The defendant studied the piece of paper before answering. "Six o'clock."

"Yet she was your last delivery. Why is that?"

The defendant looked down at his hands, then spoke into the microphone. "Because I didn't feel good. I texted my boss and let him know I was going home."

"No further questions," said the prosecutor.

"Redirect, Mr. Dresser?" Judge Jenkins asked.

"Just briefly, Your Honor." Mr. Dresser stood at the podium. "Just to reiterate, Mrs. Archer was alive when you left her residence?"

"Yes, she was." Mr. Throgmorton nodded at the memory. "And she must have been real hungry that night. She was pulling out a slice before I was out the door." He looked at Mr. Dresser and continued. "She reminded me of my grandma that way. My mom always brought home a pizza for us on payday." Mr. Throgmorton spoke to his attorney as if they were the only two people in the room, and he was sharing an anecdote with a buddy. "And my grandma always had the first slice. Always. She would say, 'I have to test it. Make sure it's good enough for you kids to eat.' Then she'd laugh."

"Thank you, Mr. Throgmorton. I have no further questions."

"Very well. You may step down, Mr. Throgmorton."

"No further witnesses, Your Honor. The defense rests." Mr. Dresser joined his client at counsel table and sat.

"Ms. Martindale, does the state have any rebuttal evidence it wishes to present?"

"No, Your Honor," Ms. Martindale replied.

"Very well then." The judge looked down at his notes, then turned his attention to the jury. "Ladies and gentlemen, this case is almost yours, but there is still some work that needs to be done outside your presence, so at this late hour I will excuse you and have you report back Monday morning at nine o'clock when you will hear final arguments from both sides."

Judge Jenkins's remarks elicited various facial expressions from members of the jury: relief, surprise and annoyance. Lauren knew some jurors were just happy to go home while others, knowing there was no more evidence, were eager to stay and begin deciding Mr. Throgmorton's fate.

The judge added, "Again, I remind you, do not read any newspaper accounts of the trial, do any online research, or discuss the case with anyone."

As the jurors filed out of the courtroom, the judge said, "Counsel, we'll take a brief recess, then start on the jury instructions you've each submitted."

❋   ❋   ❋

Lauren went to the witness stand and checked to make sure no exhibits had made their way there and not been returned to her. Then she walked over to the prosecutor's table. "Did you have a chance to print me off another copy of the autopsy report?"

Ms. Martindale turned to Mr. Jessup. "Did you bring it down with you?

He shook his head. "I forgot. I'll run upstairs and get it for you. Sorry."

"Thank you, said Lauren. "I want to have all the exhibits before I leave tonight. I have to give them to the bailiff Monday morning."

"We understand how the process works." Ms. Martindale sighed, then turned her attention to her laptop screen.

You are such an ass. Lauren pressed her lips together, knowing if she didn't say the words in her mind they would be spoken out loud. *You are a professional. You are a professional. You are a professional.* She repeated the mantra in her head as she exited the courtroom to use the restroom.

Lauren gulped down a glass of water. She was still annoyed at the comment Ms. Martindale made. *What was her problem? I politely asked for it. More than once. And she never gave it to me.* She thought, was that just who the woman was naturally? Naturally sarcastic? Condescending? Or did it have something to do with the exhibit itself? Was there something in it she didn't want the jury see? Lauren dismissed the idea as absurd. Eli was entitled to everything the state had.

*   *   *

Lauren returned to her workspace. A sheath of papers stapled together lay face down on her open laptop. She thumbed through the autopsy report. Page eight was there, as were all the rest. Having the exhibit in hand eased the anger that had been building up, but the notion of a page missing on purpose lingered in her thoughts.

Chapter Forty-Four

$\mathcal{L}$ auren looked at the vacuum cleaner cannister filled to capacity with Maverik's hair. It didn't surprise her. She had not thoroughly cleaned her house since the trial started, and so she spent the bulk of Saturday vacuuming, mopping, dusting, and doing laundry.

She foraged in her freezer for something quick to have for dinner. After eating she loaded Maverik in the car and drove to the nearby park. Her idea of an early fall evening walk around the lake at the city park turned out to be a popular one. There were couples strolling and people like her, out walking their dogs, along with parents riding bikes with their children, and a few joggers.

Maverik behaved well on his lead, giving Lauren the chance to think about the trial testimony. She thought back to the very last thing Daniel said before stepping down from the witness stand. Mrs. Archer was getting ready to have a slice of pizza before he even left.

Over the course of the trial she had looked at the photographs of the pizza and the box enough times she had the images memorized. The pizza in the box was untouched.

Chapter Forty-Five

The Volvo screeched to a halt in the courthouse parking lot. Lauren turned to Maverik, "I'll be right back." She felt a little silly as she let herself in the building with the loaner badge. She took the stairs two at a time to the judge's chambers. She switched on the light in Zoe's office, went straight to the stack of exhibits and yanked out the photos. She stared at the one with the whole, untouched pizza. *If Daniel was telling the truth, how could that be?*

She pulled out the autopsy report, her eyes doing a quick scan of the document. She stopped at page eight. *Stomach Contents. Undigested sausage, pepperoni, green pepper, and onion.*

Daniel was telling the truth, Margaret ate pizza before she died.

She looked out the window. She could see across the street. A light shone in Eli's office.

Lauren made a copy of the autopsy report, turned off the light and hurried out of the quiet building.

She twisted in the driver's seat and said to Maverik, "Daniel's not guilty." A thought entered her mind. What if the jury already thinks he is and doesn't read the autopsy report? What if Eli has the same copy I had, the one with the missing page?

When Daniel stepped down from the witness stand yesterday, she had glanced at Eli. He looked confident but he was wearing his usual courtroom game face. He neither looked surprised nor excited. Did he realize the importance of his client's last comments? Should she tell him? Mind her own business?

Judge Brubaker's words rang in her ears from long ago. "Lauren, it's called a court of law, not a court of justice." But Daniel deserved justice. Margaret Archer deserved justice as well.

Chapter Forty-Six

$\mathcal{L}$auren pulled behind Eli's borrowed minivan which sat parked at the curb behind two other vehicles. Lights were on at the tattoo parlor next to his office and at Gentle Breeze Counseling. Busy place for a Saturday evening, thought Lauren. She lowered the passenger window a little and killed the engine. Maverik looked at Lauren, then curled up on the passenger seat. He knew the routine. If he could talk, he would surely say, "I know, Mom, you'll be right back."

Lauren trotted up the steps, autopsy report in hand, and rang the doorbell. She looked down the street, then back at the door. She was about to press the buzzer again when Eli opened the door. She rushed past him. "You have a minute? I need to talk to you."

"Sure. Come in – oh, wait, you're already in." He grinned. "I was just getting ready to take a break, grab myself a beer. Want one?"

"No, thanks."

"Have a seat. I'll be right back." He retreated to the rear of the house.

She took a seat meant for clients and looked out the large window. From where she sat she could see the rear of the courthouse and Zoe's office window.

"Nice view." He gestured with the Coors in his hand toward the window. "Can't get away from work." Eli sat at his desk and took a swig of his beer and wiped his mouth with the back of his hand. "Excuse my manners. Or lack of them, I should say. I still have to work on my closing argument for Monday." He spread his hands out across his desk emphasizing all the scattered papers. "It's been a long week, but you already knew that." He arched a thick eyebrow. "So tell me, what's so important that you showed up on my doorstep on a Saturday night?"

"Aren't you glad your client got up and testified?"

Eli gave her a questioning look. "Glad? That's not what comes to mind, no."

"Well, you should be."

"The state was able to bring up his past criminal history. If he hadn't gotten on the stand the jury would never have heard that. So I'm thinking, no."

"I was just at the courthouse reading the autopsy report." She placed it on his desk.

"Oh-kay. A little morbid of you but I'm listening."

"Eli, you read the autopsy report, didn't you?"

"I did a cursory review. I didn't read it line for line, just mostly to confirm the manner of death which as we know was a blow to the back of the head with a blunt instrument. Matches up with the evidence. Why do you ask?"

He wiped the bottom of the sweat from the beer bottle on his jeans, then set it on his desk.

"Read the stomach contents."

His brow creased as he read the page. Eli swiveled in his chair to face his laptop and opened up the electronic version of all the exhibits. He scrolled through the document. "There's no f'n mention of stomach contents in here. It goes from page seven to nine."

"The exhibit Martindale originally gave me was the same as yours. No page eight."

He shook his head. "I can't believe this."

"She ate pizza before she was killed. And your client said as much." Lauren leaned forward in the chair." Daniel said she was pulling a slice out he was leaving –"

"And there's a whole untouched pizza in the box."

Lauren nodded. "Exactly."

He stared at the document. "Danny and I went over everything that happened that night. But that's such a small detail. He probably didn't think it was worth mentioning."

"What about this scenario," says Lauren. "The killer comes over. He argues with Margaret. He hits her on the back of the head. Being elderly –"

"Or it's a pretty good blow."

"– it kills her. He panics."

"Unless it was planned." He looked at Lauren. "But I don't think it was. A blow to the back of the head doesn't seem like premeditation."

"That doesn't really matter to you, or Daniel. The question is how would the killer know she would be ordering pizza?"

304

"They didn't have to know. After they killed her they see the pizza there and use it to their advantage, pinning the murder on the poor delivery driver. And even though it can't be proven, they could have also removed her prescription meds to make it look like that's why she was killed. That would mean the killer knew some details of Margaret's life." Eli shakes his head slowly. "They happened to hit the jackpot with Danny. Between his background and drug use, they couldn't ask for a better fall guy."

Lauren cocked her head in thought. "Dallas Black knew she ordered pizza regularly, according to your client. You heard him describe the guy."

"He was describing Mr. Black." Eli thought a moment. He tossed the autopsy report on his desk. "I didn't read this thoroughly. Didn't catch that a page was missing. I almost screwed this case up." He shook his head.

"You would have caught it."

"When?" He pulled his fingers through his glossy black hair. "After the trial was over?" He sounded like a sulking teenager, not like a successful lawyer.

"Come on, that's not the point right now."

"I know you're just trying to help. And you have. This is great. Just wish I would have paid more attention and caught it. I've done a decent job so far defending Daniel. And I like the challenge. Madeline Hall – do you know her?"

"I know she's the head of the Wyoming Public Defender's Office, but I've never worked with her."

"I've been updating her on Daniel's case since I'm doing this on a contract basis for her."

"I thought that might be the case. I knew Daniel couldn't afford an attorney."

Eli nodded. "You already know a large part of my practice is domestic relations."

"Right. Divorce, custody. All the not-so-much-fun stuff."

"Exactly. But I also do quite a bit of criminal defense work, about fifty-fifty misdemeanor and felony. I've been wanting to expand that area of my practice. If I do a decent job defending Mr. Throgmorton, I'll get more work from the PD's office on their bigger cases. Maybe enough to cut back on the divorce work. I'm getting burnt out. Too many clients having emergencies and calling me in the middle of the night or on weekends."

Lauren's eyebrows went up. "You give your clients your personal cell number?"

"Not anymore. I learned my lesson about that pretty quick."

"I'll bet."

"But with you having to point out something I missed …" he exhaled deeply " … I feel like I'm back in law school. You've heard the expression, ineffectiveness of counsel." He poked his chest with his index finger. "Fits me to a tee right about now."

Lauren shook her head. "Whatever. Right now you should concentrate on how you're going to use the information. You can plan your pity party another time."

The corners of Eli's mouth turned up. "You're right. And you'll be the first one I invite." He reached for his beer but didn't pick it up, his mind still processing the new information.

"This has to help Daniel. A lot. Doesn't it?" Lauren tried to read Eli's thoughts, gauge his level of excitement.

Shadows of Doubt

Eli rocked forward in his chair and slapped the desk. "This is going to blow Martindale's case right out of the water."

"*Yes.*" Lauren smiled knowing this was good for Dominick's nephew.

"I've been trying to think who did kill her. I've thought about that ever since I got the case. Most of my clients profess their innocence, but Daniel's different. I've always believed him." He tapped the desk with his pen to a beat only he seemed to hear. "But I have also been very convincingly lied to."

"Did you ever come up with any possible suspects? We've both been listening to the same evidence in court, but you know a lot more than what's been testified to. And you know more about your client than I do."

"No. I haven't been able to come up with an alternative killer theory. But with this information I don't have to name a particular person. Other than to say, the real killer.

"I was thinking about throwing out Dallas Black's name in my closing arguments, but that's only because he found her."

"I thought about him too. Did you ever talk to John? John Whitmore?"

He nodded. "He couldn't tell me much."

"I think Mrs. Archer and Dallas had a falling out a few weeks before she died."

"Tell me about it."

"After listening to Mrs. Archer's testimony, at first I thought he was genuinely concerned about her." Lauren skooched to the edge of the chair, placing her arms on Eli's desk. "But what if he wasn't? What if it were an act?"

"Well, where there's money involved –"

"Lots of money."

"That's one of the three top motivations for murder. At least in my book. And anyone who's been in Crawford for any length of time knows Mrs. Archer had plenty of that," said Eli.

"Money. And love. And hate. And revenge."

Eli nodded. "Revenge is another good one. So maybe four top motives for killing someone."

"Except I don't know of a reason why anyone would kill Margaret out of revenge. I didn't know everything about her life from the couple of depos I took, but I didn't get the sense she had anything in her past that would make her a target for murder. At least not for revenge."

"In the end it doesn't matter – I mean it does matter. Nobody wants a killer loose on the streets of Crawford, but as far as Danny's concerned it doesn't matter. The jury's going to find reasonable doubt and won't convict him." Eli tipped his beer bottle in the air at Lauren. "Thanks to you."

Chapter Forty-Seven

"I'm back." Lauren bent her head toward the car window. "Have you been a good boy?"

Maverik let out a throaty growl. His warning came too late for Lauren. Her whole body tensed as a high-voltage electric shock set every muscle into one big spasm. She collapsed next to her car.

Hands grabbed her by the arms and shoulders, scraping her off the sidewalk.

Maverik snapped at the hand closest to the window.

"Ow." The hands released Lauren's shoulders. Unable to catch herself, the left side of her body once again met the sidewalk with a thud. Lauren tried to lift her head off the ground without success. She lay there, the coolness of the sidewalk sinking into her cheek, trying to make sense of what just happened.

Maverik snarled and growled.

A woman cussed. A familiar voice.

Lauren lay there a moment before placing her palms on the ground and pushing herself up on her hands and knees. She took a deep breath and waited. Waited to see if her muscles would support her.

A hand grabbed the back of her hoodie, along with some of her hair and yanked her upright.

"Open the goddamn door!"

Chief Newell. Lauren opened her mouth to cry out, but the sound came out as a croak.

Maverik snarled.

Lauren swayed, the ground beneath her feet unsteady.

The pair of hands now squeezed her upper arms tight, keeping her from sinking back to the ground.

Chapter Forty-Eight

*P*atricia Holland opened the front door.

The police chief lifted Lauren, half dragging, half carrying her up the front porch of Gentle Breeze Counseling. He deposited her inside the entryway, setting her down like she was a fifty-pound bag of dog food. Lauren used the wall as support to keep herself upright.

Trish closed the front door behind them.

Ray grabbed Lauren and propelled her into Patricia's office.

Lauren's thoughts swirled. She tried to focus on what was happening. *He tased me and now he's going to finish me off here where there will be no witnesses. Is Patricia going to let him do that? Or worse, help him?* Lauren's chest tightened. She tried to shake free of the man's grip, her attempt futile. Every muscle in her body ached as if she'd just ran a marathon race.

Patricia walked to her desk and opened a side drawer. "Why did you come to the office, Ray?"

"Never mind what I'm doing here. What the *hell* is going on?" Chief Newell's voice was low, tight."

His wife ignored his question, asking again, "What are you doing here? Why aren't you at home? Your shift ended hours ago."

"I *always* drive by your office when I know you're working late."

Trish looked at her husband, eyes wide. "You do?"

"Yes, Trish, I do."

Husband and wife held each other's gaze a long moment.

"And put that gun away," Ray hissed.

Lauren, still groggy, looked at her therapist and for the first time noticed the black barrel of a gun pointed in her direction.

Trish shook her head, tossing her hair back but otherwise her gaze remained fixed on her husband.

"I said, put that away." He released his grip on Lauren, who swayed and held on to the back of one of the chairs.

"She has something of mine. I need to get it back. Stay out of this, Ray." Trish's voice remained calm as she spoke.

"What? What does she have that you felt you had to tase her?" asked Ray.

Trish tased me?

"Just go home. This doesn't concern you," said Trish.

"This is crazy," said Ray.

Lauren caught the chief's expression of disbelief as they all stood in the small office.

He nodded to the gun in his wife's hand. "Put that away. *Now.*"

Trish ignored his words and looked at Lauren. "I want my earring."

"Your earring?" *What the heck did that tasing do to me? Earring?*

"Yes. I know you have it. Just give it back to me and I'll let you go." The therapist came around from behind the desk and in two strides stood next to Lauren. She brought the gun up close to Lauren's head.

"*Trish*," said Ray.

"I … I don't have your earring," Lauren exhaled trying to keep the tremor out of her voice. "I don't know anything about an earring."

"Don't play dumb. You have it. You were acting so strange at our last session. I know that's why."

Lauren didn't attempt to move other than to shake her head. "I have no idea –"

"You have it, and you somehow figured out it was mine." The therapist gestured with her head to three photographs in silver frames on the wall. The framed photograph on the left showed Ms. Holland smiling at the camera as she accepted some plaque from the mayor, hair swept back, diamond earrings twinkling. "Were you trying to decide whether you should blackmail me with it?"

"No. But is that what Mr. Bates was doing?" asked Lauren.

"He was nothing but a greedy son of a bitch," Trish spat the words out. "I'm not going to ask you again. Tell me where my earring is."

"Is this what you're looking for?" Ray opened his palm, revealing a diamond stud earring.

"Yes." Trish held out her free hand for the jewelry.

Ray's hand closed in a fist.

"You had it all this time? Where ... where did you find it?" asked Trish.

"Where you lost it. Next to Alden's body."

Trish's eyes widened with understanding at the same time the light in Ray's eyes seemed to extinguish, as if the earring had been his last lifeline, his last hope, that if it didn't belong to his wife, then he wasn't married to a cold-blooded killer.

"I can explain. Just give it to me and we can talk about it later," said Trish.

He shoved it back in his jacket pocket. "You tased her," he thrust a thumb at Lauren, "for nothing."

"Ray, it's not what you think. I can explain –"

The chief cut into her words. "*Don't*. Don't tell me some bullshit story how it wasn't you. I read your texts. I knew you were meeting him at the lake that day."

"What happened was an accident. I didn't mean to kill him. I had to. He –"

"*Had* to. Trish, are you freakin' crazy?"

"I did it for us." A crack appeared in Trish's calm veneer.

"Oh, for us. And I suppose you slept with him for *us?*" Ray's face grew scarlet, an angry vein pulsed at his temple.

"No, no. That was a mistake. I regretted it as soon as it happened. I was there at the lake to break it off with him once and for all." Trish straightened her shoulders and continued. "I told him it was over between us. He refused to listen. He became physical. Shoved me down. I was scared I'd never see you again. In that moment I realized how utterly stupid I'd been."

Alden and Trish had been having an affair. But she just used the word blackmail. Was that what Alden was doing?

Why would he be blackmailing her if he was sleeping with her? Lauren's mind tried to make sense of what Trish was saying.

"We struggled with the gun. It was an accident. I swear to you that's what happened."

Ray looked at the ceiling, then turned his gaze to his wife. "Hell, you're such a liar."

"No. I love you, Ray. You're —"

"*Enough!*" The police chief's shout filled the small space. "Enough with all the lies. I had a feeling you'd been sleeping with that piece of shit behind my back. I just don't know why you killed him."

While Ray and Trish argued, thoughts, like pieces of a puzzle, fell into place for Lauren.

"So, what, he threatened to tell me if you broke off the affair? Is that what it was all about?" asked Ray. "He was going to tell me, so you thought you had no way out but to shoot him?"

"I never meant to kill him."

"You didn't have to shoot him." Ray's voice shuddered, a mixture of anguish and resignation. "I would have forgiven you."

Lauren looked at Trish. Her explanation for killing Alden sounded weak. The chief knew about the affair and never did anything. And he knew his wife killed Alden. Until now he hadn't done anything about it. Had he been willing to just overlook it? Or did he not confront her because he was also a killer? Had he killed his own mother?

Would Ray let his wife shoot her, then bury her somewhere, and they would kiss and make up and live happily ever after? Lauren didn't know what to think. During the

315

past week she'd begun to believe the police chief killed Alden Bates. It turns out she was wrong about that. *What the heck is going on, Lauren? Think.*

Lauren remembered Margaret's deposition. She had fired Alden Bates as her accountant mere days before she was murdered. Lauren thought it was because she found out about Mr. Bates's embezzlement. But what if it was because she found out about the affair? And if Margaret knew of the affair, Trish would have the stronger motive to keep her quiet. To not lose her campaign funds. Was it a strong enough reason to kill Mrs. Archer?

"Mr. Bates couldn't go on with the lies any longer, could he?" said Lauren.

"What's she talking about?" asked Ray.

Trish waved her hand in a dismissive gesture. "Don't listen to her. She doesn't know what she's talking about."

The thought of Trish being the killer took purchase in Lauren's mind and before she could stop herself, she blurted, "You're not going to let your mother's murderer go free, are you?"

Ray's eyes widened in confusion. "My mother? What does this have to do with my mother?"

"Shut up." Trish jammed her heel into the side of Lauren's kneecap, causing her leg to buckle. She fell against the wall, gasping in pain.

The police chief stared at his wife. "What the hell is she talking about?"

Lauren steadied herself. She'd begun to sweat even though the room was cool. "You killed Margaret, didn't you?"

The chief looked from Lauren to his wife.

316

"Don't listen to her, Ray. She's trying to mess with your head. You know I could never hurt Margaret. I loved her like she was my own mother."

For the first time Lauren noticed the pistol in the chief's hand. *When did he pull that out?*

"She killed her because your mother found out about the affair and decided not to bankroll her campaign any longer." The theory came into focus as she spoke. "That's why you did it, isn't it?" She turned back to the chief. "And she killed your mother before she changed her will, the one she left your wife out of." Lauren looked at the chief. She could see he was trying to digest all the information.

"That's right. Your mother found out about the affair between your wife and Alden." Lauren looked at her therapist. "Is that why you went over to your mother-in-law's house that night? To talk Mrs. Archer out of telling her son? Or did it have to do with her no longer willing to bankroll your campaign, and if she pulled the plug on the money, there would be no way for you to continue?"

"*Shut up!*" shouted Patricia.

"You needed her money. Or maybe she found out Alden was embezzling all that money and thought you were in on it with him. Did she threaten calling the police?"

Trish pressed the barrel of the gun against Lauren's temple. The cold metal made Lauren flinch. Fear, sharp as a jagged piece of glass, cut into Lauren's chest, making it difficult to breathe.

"You need to put the gun down," said Ray. The chief was now in cop mode, trying to deescalate the situation.

Trish took a step back from Lauren but still aimed the gun at her head.

Lauren, determined to make Ray Newell see the truth before being silenced forever, plowed on. "You were at your mother's deposition. You heard the same thing I did. You heard her say she was going to see to it you didn't get control of anything. And when they were leaving the room, telling her attorney she was certain she was doing the right thing. She was going to change her will. Did you go home and tell your wife?"

The answer to Lauren's question was written on Ray's face. He had gone home and told his wife. Lauren remembered during one of her sessions Trish mentioning she had to drop something off – maybe a pan she'd borrowed – or return something that evening to Mrs. Archer, and that was why she had gone to the house. Whatever it was, it was more than likely an excuse to talk to her mother-in-law.

"Can't you see what she's doing?" Trish's words came out high and shrill. "She's trying to poison you with her lies."

"What I don't know is was Alden in on the killing or did he put two and two together after the fact and confront you? Or did you brag to him about it, that you took care of his problem?" Lauren's mind raced with ideas, throwing them out and hoping one of them made sense. Or at least were plausible. "Did you ask him to bring over a pizza? Then when he showed up you convinced him somehow to keep your secret?"

The look on Patricia's face told Lauren she was close to the truth.

"He was willing to keep your secret so long as he got some benefit. Your money for his silence. Is that what he wanted? Or did he want to tag along to D.C. and enjoy some of your perks as a congresswoman?" Again, was she even close to the truth? It sounded believable. It would explain why Trish thought she had to kill him.

"Is that when you realized Alden didn't love you? He was all about the money?" Lauren added. "Just like you."

Lauren felt the butt of the gun slam into the side of her head. Tears sprang from her eyes.

"She's crazy. She's been having these delusional thoughts in therapy. That's what I've been counseling her about. You can't believe what she says." Trish looked at her husband. "We both know it was that drug addict Daniel Throgmorton who killed your mother. I would *never* hurt Margaret. You have to let me take care of her, Ray. For both our sakes."

I'm the delusional one?

The chief looked at his wife, eyes wide with sudden comprehension.

"If she shoots me, what do you think's going to happen?" Lauren didn't wait for him to answer. "She's going to have to shoot you too. Then she's going to make it look like we fought and shot each other." Lauren looked at Trish for confirmation. "That's your new plan, isn't it? You —"

The cocking of the hammer cut off her words.

Chapter Forty-Nine

*I*n one quick movement Chief Newell shoved Lauren to the floor and lunged at his wife. He grabbed her wrist but not before she pulled the trigger.

An explosion reverberated in Lauren's ears. The office was suddenly quiet. She watched, almost as if in slow motion, as the window shattered, glass silently raining down.

Sam filled the doorway, firearm drawn. "Drop the gun! Now! Drop it now!"

Lauren could see Sam's lips moving but couldn't hear his words. She watched Patricia release the grip she had on the gun and place it in her husband's hand. Ray set it on the desk, then put his hands on his wife's shoulders and had her step away.

*   *   *

The flashing lights from three squad cars illuminated the front lawn of the therapist's office. Sam stood close to Lauren on the small porch of Gentle Breeze Counseling. They both watched Patricia Holland, head held high, being handcuffed by a sheriff's deputy. He escorted her to his squad car, placing her in the back seat.

"Come on, move over here. You're stepping on all that glass. You might get hurt."

Sam's voice sounded muffled, but Lauren let him take her by the elbow and guide her down the few short steps. They joined Crawford's police chief.

The shot being fired had temporarily deafened Lauren, but her hearing had slowly begun to return.

Chief Newell ran a hand down his face, revealing an older man all in the span of mere seconds. The lights from the police cruisers made the lines on his face deeper, the lines between his eyebrows more like crevasses, giving him a menacing expression.

"What the hell are you looking at?" demanded Ray.

His voice sounded far away but Lauren saw the scowl on his face clearly. "Nothing. Uh, thank you for saving my life."

The police chief turned away from Lauren.

After what just transpired she didn't expect to hear such an agitated tone in his voice. Thought he would be more … more what? Apologetic? Thankful? Humble? Whatever she thought, she didn't think he would be his usual unpleasant self. In a circuitous way she had saved his life. Or at the very least saved him from being accused of her murder. If not for speaking up when she did … she didn't want to think about what the outcome would have been.

When a life-altering event happens and your true personality is exposed, maybe you are what you always were, thought Lauren. In Ray Newell's case, an ass.

"Lauren, you'll need to give a statement, but you need to get checked out first." Sam physically stepped between her and the chief.

"Huh? What did you say?" asked Lauren.

"I said, you need to go to the police station and give a statement, but you should go to the ER first. I'm calling an ambulance."

"No, I don't need an ambulance. I'm just shaken up is all." She hugged herself, winced, then let her arms fall to her side.

"No, you need to go to the hospital."

"Okay, but no ambulance. I'll drive myself."

"I have a few more things I have to do here but after that I can drive you," said Sam.

"Thanks, but I have to get Maverik home."

"You're in no condition to drive."

Eli emerged from the shadows and walked over to the three people standing in the light that poured out the office window. He looked from Sam to Ray to Lauren, a puzzled expression on his face.

"Who's in the car?" Eli nodded at the police cruiser that just turned the corner.

Sam spoke. "Trish. Chief's wife. Listen, Lauren needs to go to the hospital but she doesn't want me to call an ambulance. Will you give her a ride?"

"I think I'm okay. I'll drop Maverik off –"

"Just *go*." Ray's shout surprised them all.

"Take it easy, Chief," said Sam.

"She needs to be gone." The chief glared at Lauren. "I can't stand to look at her. Just get the hell out of here!"

Eli and Sam raised their eyebrows in unison.

Lauren surprised herself by nudging Sam aside and standing in front of the police chief. She raised her head. "I'm not going anywhere. Get used to it."

She didn't know what the future held, if Patricia would be facing charges of murder for the deaths of Margaret Archer and Alden Bates, but what she did know was she was done. She was done with staying silent when he looked at her the way he did. Done with letting him intimidate her. Done with letting him instill fear in her.

Sam put his hands on her shoulders. "Come on now, Lauren. Let's all calm down."

"I don't need to calm down. He needs to leave me alone." Ignoring the pain, Lauren brushed away Sam's hands.

Sam looked at Ray. "What is she talking about, Chief?"

"I have no idea. She's probably batshit crazy." He sneered. "Just like her mother."

Lauren stepped in closer to him. The strong odor of sweat filled her nostrils, making her want to retreat, but she forced herself to stand her ground. "Whatever happened in the past with my mother has nothing to do with me. So you can quit giving me dirty looks when no one is watching. And save your snide remarks about my mother because I don't want to hear them. And you can quit stalking me."

The chief's cheeks bloomed a bright red.

"Yeah, I know that was you parked outside my house in the middle of the night." Lauren didn't know that for sure but thought it was a good possibility. She turned away and spoke under her breath, "I don't blame your wife for cheating on you."

Ray grabbed her by the hoodie, spun her back around and shook her. "You little bitch –"

Sam reached in his belt. "Let her go! *Now!*"

The chief of police looked at the Taser in Sam's hand. He opened his fists and released his grip. Lauren's leg buckled. She stumbled, landing against Sam.

Sam grabbed her.

She steadied herself. "Thanks."

Sam holstered the Taser. "I don't know what all is going on but, Eli, can you please escort Lauren out of here?"

"Sure thing," Eli gently put his arm around Lauren's shoulder. "Come on, let's go." He shot the chief a look that said, *Out. Of. My. Way.*

With her head pounding and her knee pulsing, Lauren let Eli lead her away, hobbling alongside of him.

She leaned against the Volvo while Eli went to his office and retrieved her dog. Maverik bounded over to her, sniffing her jeans, whimpering with excitement.

"It's okay. It's okay." She scratched him behind his ears.

They stood under the light of the streetlamp. "What just happened back there?" Eli gestured toward Trish's office.

Lauren pulled on the car door handle and shook her head. "Good question."

"You look pretty bad. Why don't you let me drop Maverik at your house, then I'll run you over to the ER."

Fatigue, exhaustion and suddenly feeling weepy combined into one potent cocktail. She looked up into her friend's face, his dark eyes pools of concern. She didn't trust herself to speak for fear of crying, and so merely nodded her head.

After a little bit of coaxing, Maverik climbed into the minivan.

On the ride to her house, Lauren told Eli what happened after she left his office.

Chapter Fifty

Lauren jiggled the doorknob of her front door, confirming she locked it. She walked slowly to the minivan and slid into the front seat. She fumbled with the seatbelt until Eli reached over and secured it in place.

"Thanks again, Eli." She leaned her head against the headrest. "I don't understand how Sam got to Patricia's so quick but I'm glad he did."

"I called him. I heard a dog barking nonstop, which never happens. When I went outside I saw your vehicle and saw Maverik ... cute name by the way."

"That's where I found him one day, at the Maverik gas station."

Eli continued. "Anyway, when Sam showed up, I explained you had been in my office and had left about five minutes ago so I didn't know why your car was still there, or where you could have gone. And I mentioned I didn't want to call the police just in case his boss showed up."

"What did Sam say about that?"

"Not much. I told him I wasn't his biggest fan. Sam was worried about you and let it go."

Lauren nodded her understanding.

"I went back to my office to get something to open your car door with. When I returned, he was picking your phone up off the sidewalk. He knew ... we both knew for certain something wasn't right." Eli flipped his turn signal on. "He asked why you were in my office. On a Saturday evening. I told him you came to share some information about the trial." He snorted. "I think he thought you and I were, you know, more than friends." Eli rolled his eyes. "If we were, I don't think we'd be hanging out at my office. I have a little more class than that."

Lauren started to laugh but the pain in her face made her stop.

The minivan turned into the hospital parking lot, and Eli drove to the emergency room entrance. "And that's how your knight in shining armor showed up in the nick of time."

"I'd say you were as much of a knight as Sam."

"No, I was just an irritated lawyer, trying to get some work done. I couldn't concentrate with the dog ... with Maverik's constant barking."

"I'll have to thank Maverik when I get home."

Her friend put the vehicle in park.

"Thanks for everything, Eli. For calling Sam. For taking care of Maverik. And for the ride." Lauren opened the car door. Her whole body ached and she didn't know if she could manage the short walk to the ER doors.

"Text me when you're done. I'll come back and give you a ride to your car."

"No. That's okay. I'll just call …" Lauren was about to say, *I'll call my aunt*, but didn't want to upset her. "I'll get a ride home."

"If you're sure."

"I am. Besides, it's late. You need to get some rest so you can work on your closing argument for tomorrow." The corners of her mouth turned up. "The one that's going to blow the state's case out of the water on Monday."

She gingerly got out of the seat. Eli put the minivan in drive. Lauren saw relief on his face at not having to wait in the emergency room for her. She couldn't blame him. No one likes sitting and waiting in such a sterile place, surrounded by sick people, people injured from accidents, domestic batteries or worse.

Lauren knew she might wind up at the bottom of a pile of what medical personnel considered an emergency, though when she caught a glimpse of herself in the side mirror of the minivan moments ago, the face looking back had shocked her. The whole left side where it met the sidewalk had swelled to the point her eye was a mere slit, and the skin on her cheek felt like it would split open any moment.

She ran her fingers through her hair and smoothed her bangs. Her knee hurt and her head still pounded. She hobbled toward the emergency room doors.

Chapter Fifty-One

" *L*auren, oh my dear, what on earth has happened to you?" Susan spoke so loud it brought Tony rushing out of his office.

"Good morning, everyone." Lauren tried to sound chipper.

"Geez, Lauren. What the hell happened to you?" Tony looked her up and down, concern in his blue eyes.

"I'm okay. I look worse than I feel." Lauren had contacted a couple of court reporters in Cheyenne on Sunday to see if anyone was available to report the final day of trial. Since it was a last-minute request, it hadn't surprised her when no one could help cover for her.

Other than a still-bruised face that could scare little children, a sprained knee and overall aches and pains, she would be able to report the proceedings. The extra thick layer of makeup she applied to cover her cheek and eye area achieved minimal success, but she told herself it would have to do.

Tony looked at her skeptically.

"It's a long story. You heard about what happened over the weekend with Chief Newell's wife?"

Tony nodded. "I spoke with Sheriff Wolfenden earlier this morning. They've charged her with the murder of Mr. Bates."

"But not with Mrs. Archer's murder?" asked Lauren.

"No. Wolfenden said they've opened an investigation into the matter."

"That explains why the trial is still on," said Lauren.

"Yes," Tony said. "Though I'd consider a motion for mistrial from Mr. Dresser. You look awful. Are you sure you should even be here?"

"I can make it through closings. That shouldn't take too long. I have a headache but I've already taken something for it." Lauren knew Tony would see past the half-hearted attempt of cheerfulness in her voice, but with court starting in about five minutes, there wasn't much he could do.

Chapter Fifty-Two

*S*everal jurors openly stared at Lauren, no doubt seeing right through the thick foundation.

Ms. Martindale, dressed in a black suit over a white
linen top and black pumps approached the podium. It was
times like these that Lauren was glad to fade into the background while the attorneys took center stage to argue their
case in front of the jury.

The prosecutor spent the next forty-five minutes
touching on all the reasons why Daniel Throgmorton was
a killer and should be found guilty of murder beyond a
reasonable doubt.

Lauren had never heard this prosecutor give a closing
argument before. Her remarks were lackluster, her words
not holding much conviction. Lauren couldn't help but
wonder if that had anything to do with the events that
transpired over the weekend or whether Ms. Martindale

was incapable of giving an impassioned argument on behalf of any victim.

The prosecutor hadn't even taken her seat before Mr. Dresser shot out of his, addressing the jury even before he reached the podium. He spoke with such passion and enthusiasm it became infectious. And when he pointed out to the jury the whole pizza being in contradiction to his client's testimony, and that they should read the autopsy report in detail because it backed up what Daniel said, the jurors were nodding their heads in understanding.

Chapter Fifty-Three

*I*t took the jury less than an hour to return a verdict of not guilty. When they did, the quiet courtroom erupted with sound. With jurors talking and laughing amongst themselves, people conversing with one another as they made their way out of the courtroom, and briefcases being clicked shut, Lauren's headache worsened, turning into a migraine, threatening to make her vomit right there on the courtroom floor.

She had excused herself, telling Tony she would return for her writer and computer the next day. He offered to drop them off at her house, but she declined.

* * *

Lauren stepped out into the sunshine, reached in her bag and put on her sunglasses to ease the pounding behind her eyes and the pain she felt when squinting with her puffy eye. She took the courthouse steps, one by one, like a child learning to walk down stairs, and made her way toward the Volvo, welcoming the warm air after being in the air-conditioned courtroom.

She slowed her already cautious pace when she noticed a man leaning casually against her car. She walked a few more feet then recognized him.

Sam leaned up against the Volvo like he owned it.

Memories of her botched kiss with him surfaced. She felt something catch in her throat.

He hadn't spotted her yet and she considered turning around and going back inside until he left. *Don't be stupid.* If the recent events taught her anything, it was that life is short. And her life, if it weren't for the chief doing the right thing, might have ended Saturday night.

Whatever Sam's reason for being at her car – he probably needed to ask her something about the other night – she wouldn't know until she spoke with him.

She lifted her head high, her brown bangs sweeping away from her face. *I am done avoiding people, situations, and things that make me uncomfortable. Let's get this over with.*

She tried to look casual as she walked to her car, ignoring her sore muscles and the pain behind her left eye. The sooner she spoke with Sam, the sooner she'd be home, in her most comfortable pair of sweats, curled up on the sofa with Maverik by her side.

"Hey. Got a minute? We need to talk." Sam's body blocked the driver's door.

"Sure. But can you please move." Lauren motioned to the locked door.

"I'll move but I have something to say first." He unfolded his arms, tucked his hands in the pockets of his chinos and looked at her. "I need to explain my reaction to you that day when you kissed me. You know, by the trailhead parking lot."

Like I could ever forget. "So you're not here to ask me about what happened the other night?"

"No. I knew you'd be in court this morning. I wanted to catch up with you before you went home since you haven't replied to any of my texts." He lifted his sunglasses and peered closer at her face. "How are you feeling?"

"Okay. After I left the ER I went straight home. Deputy Rodriguez was nice enough to come to my house yesterday to take my statement. After that, I slept the rest of the day. The hospital sent me home with some very powerful painkillers." *Why am I explaining any of this to him? I need to go home.*

"I understand. You were probably out of it."

"I was. Deputy Rodriguez wouldn't tell me anything when I asked though. Has Patricia confessed to killing her mother-in-law yet? Or Mr. Bates?"

"No. She's hired a lawyer."

"What's happening with the chief?"

"It's still being sorted out. He hasn't been charged with anything. Yet. Department of Criminal Investigation is handling it." Sam took stock of her face. "Are you going to press charges?"

"For what – oh, for him grabbing me? I hadn't given it any thought." Lauren considered his question. "Probably not. He did grab me but he also saved my life."

Sam shrugged. "Like I said I'm not here to talk about

any of that. I need to explain why I reacted to you the way I did. It's important you understand."

Her face flushed with renewed embarrassment and was glad for the thick foundation that clung to her skin. She refused to meet his gaze. Maybe she wasn't ready to face *everything*. Until now she had been successful at avoiding this awkward conversation. "There's nothing to explain. Really." *And Someday I'll have a new car and I'll chirp it unlocked and be on my way.*

"You don't understand –"

"Sam, I think I do." She spoke, her voice resigned, matter of fact. "You're not interested in me … that way." Lauren made a vague gesture with her hand. "You made that perfectly clear. I get it. Trust me, I do. Besides, it was … I was just upset from what had happened otherwise I would have never … you know." Again, she gestured with a weak wave of her hand.

"And now," she motioned with her head for him to move, "if you don't mind."

"I'll make it quick, then I'll leave you alone. I promise." He turned, stood in front of her and looked at her.

She met his gaze. "Okay. But I really don't feel good so please make it quick." *Before your shoes are covered in vomit.* Lauren had thought back to that afternoon. Replayed his reaction, his backing up abruptly over and over in her mind until she had said out loud, "Quit it." But her embarrassment refused to fade.

And the signals he had given her, if there were any, she had read them all wrong.

"I like you."

"Yes, I know. Like a friend."

"No." He blew out a deep breath. "You just took me by surprise. That's all." He kicked at the blacktop with his boot. "It's really hard to explain."

"Then I'll explain it for you. You don't like me that way. And I'm sorry I ever..." *Don't you dare cry.* She swallowed and continued. "I'm sorry because I've ruined it, for us to be friends. It'll always be awkward." She looked at her feet. "If you haven't noticed, I don't have a lot of those." *Why did I just share that? What did that fall do to my head?*

"Eli's your friend," Sam offered.

"Yes, well – wait. What?"

"Never mind. Listen –"

"In case you haven't noticed," she nodded at her knee brace, "I'm not supposed to be on my feet." The pounding in her head intensified. "Besides there is nothing more –"

He reached out, cupped her face and pressed his lips to hers, swallowing the rest of her words.

Lauren stood motionless, the sounds of midday traffic drowned out by the beating of her heart in her ears.

Sam straightened. "I'm not leaving until you hear me out. And you need to quit interrupting me. I'm not ready for any kind of relationship yet. I have ..." He cleared his throat. "I have feelings I still need to work out. It has nothing –"

"You're still in love with your ex-wife. I get it." She'd found her voice but it sounded shaky to her own ears.

"No, you *don't* get it. And you really *don't* know how to be quiet and listen, do you?" He dragged a hand through his wavy dark hair and exhaled sharply.

"It's hard to listen when I'm not being paid to." Her attempt to joke fell flat. "Sorry. Go ahead."

Sam looked at her and shook his head. "I'm not over my late wife."

Lauren stared at him. "Your late wife?"

He nodded. "Abby."

"I didn't know you were married before Ashley."

"Yes. And that day, it was Abby's birthday. She had been on my mind all day. Your kiss, it just felt like, like I was cheating on her." He lifted his shoulders. "Prit-tee lame, right?"

She shook her head. "No, it's not." A soft breeze lifted her bangs. "I just wish I knew. I had *no* idea you were married before, and that she passed away."

"Like I said, I do like you. I just need to take things slow so I don't end up hurting you. Like I did with Ashley. Her and I, we should never have gotten married. It was way too soon. I just didn't know it at the time."

Lauren shifted onto her good leg. "How come you never told me about Abby before?"

Sam looked out across the parking lot, eyes unfocused. "I don't like to talk about it."

"But friends talk about stuff like that. I thought that's what we were."

"We are. I just hate telling people I'm a widower. As soon as I do, I can see the pity in their eyes. I don't need pity. From anyone."

"Technically you're not a widower anymore. You're a divorcee."

An almost imperceptible smile tugged at the corners of his mouth. "You're right. And ever since my divorce from Ashley, I've been trying to deal with the loss of Abby. Something I should have done before marrying her."

They stood side by side, the late morning traffic the only sound between them.

Sam turned and faced her. "I've been attending a grief support group for a while now."

"That's good. It's not run by Patricia, is it?"

"No, Cheyenne. The drive gives me a chance to think about stuff." He gave a small laugh. "I'm so glad I never went to see Trish. That would have turned out to be one heck of a cluster ..." He stopped himself from saying more. "But I was sucked into her campaign. She wanted to fight the big drug companies, make it harder to prescribe narcotics, make doctors and pharmaceutical companies more accountable, for people like Abby. People whose only crime was driving down the road at the same time some drug addict was high and driving out of control."

Lauren let his words sink in. His late wife must have been senselessly killed because of someone else's careless actions. "Are you forgetting you're the one who recommended her to me? Not a very nice thing to do to a friend." She smiled to let him know she was making a joke.

"I am sorry for that."

"I'm just kidding. You couldn't have known what she was capable of." Lauren was quiet while she thought about her therapy sessions. "And you know, she actually did help with my nightmares. She was a good therapist. Maybe she would have made good on her campaign promises."

"Maybe. So you can be a cold-blooded killer and a good therapist." He shook his head. "I don't get it. I take that back. Whatever your profession, it doesn't automatically exclude you from being capable of murder."

Lauren nodded her agreement. "So has the support

group been helping you?"

"It has."

"That's good."

"Just wish I'd done it sooner."

"At least you're doing it now."

He nodded, then moved away from the driver's door of the Volvo.

She unlocked the car and spoke. "What's going to happen with Chief Newell?"

"For now he's on administrative leave. I had a chance to read your statement. He's got a lot of explaining to do. At least when it comes to Mr. Bates."

"Ray knew his wife shot Bates after he found her earring lying next to his body. When I saw him that day, and he was reaching his hand out, I thought he was moving the gun closer to Alden's hand but he must have been picking up the earring."

"It will all get sorted out."

Lauren slid into the driver's seat. She threw her messenger bag on the passenger seat and winced from the movement. With a turn of the key, the old car rumbled to life.

Sam knocked on the window and waited for her to roll it down. "So are we okay?"

Lauren thought a moment. "Yeah, we're okay."

He smiled at her. "Then we'll meet up for coffee. Or lunch."

"As soon as I'm feeling better." She added, "And a little less scary looking."

"And we can go for a hike." He saw her expression. "Somewhere besides Horseshoe Lake, I promise. Sorry. We can —"

"Coffee is good. And soon. I'll text you." Lauren rolled her window up and backed out of the parking space. Sam's revelation left her with mixed feelings. On the one hand she was relieved to know she wasn't the reason for his reaction, but at the same time wondered why he never told her about being a widower. She had thought of him as a friend. Real friends share the good and the bad. She'd told him about seeing a counselor. He could have used that as an opportunity to open up about his own life, yet he chose not to. Maybe it was a guy thing, keeping feelings stuffed deep down inside.

His failed marriage with Ashley, he said it was his fault. Did that mean he would always be in love with his first wife? If so, she and Sam were destined to just be friends. She didn't think she could compete with the memory of someone who surely would grow more perfect with the passage of time, whose flaws would diminish with each passing year. But then again, he also said he had been working on his feelings.

Lauren glanced in the rearview mirror. Sam was walking toward the police department. She pressed her fingers to her lips, remembering his kiss.

Chapter Fifty-Four

Click-click-click. Lauren slapped the legs of the tripod closed. The sound echoed in the empty courtroom. She placed her gray carrying case on the chair and slid the tripod into its designated spot. She looked up when she heard the large doors to the courtroom open.

Eli strode in. He stood in the entrance and raised his arms up, fists high in the air Rocky Balboa style, which caused the edge of the briefcase he carried to hit him in the cheek.

Lauren started to laugh but laughing still made her face hurt so she stopped. He approached her, set the briefcase down and perched on the corner of the court reporter's table, the small space no longer hers since the trial ended. She was only here to gather her belongings and leave.

A smile spread on Eli's face, softening his naturally serious expression.

He raised his hand in a high-five and Lauren did the same. "Good job, Counselor."

"Thanks. I was in the clerk's office and saw you in here. Are you working today?"

"No, just came to get my writer. I went home right after the verdict."

"I have to say I was surprised when I saw you here yesterday."

"Are you kidding, I didn't want to miss your closing argument."

"Of course you didn't."

"That, and I couldn't find anyone to cover for me. I'm glad you're here. I have to ask, how come you didn't bring up Patricia Holland in your closing as a possible ... more like *the* killer?"

"I thought about it. The public is going to know about that whole mess with her soon enough. But I wanted the jury to come to the conclusion on their own, that not only was Danny not guilty but that he was innocent. All they needed was to be directed to the autopsy report, and it was a done deal." He glanced at the prosecution table. "I spoke to Ms. Martindale yesterday. She denies she left out page eight on purpose. Swears it was an honest mistake."

"Do you believe her?"

"No. I have my own theory about why she did it."

"Because she's a condescending jerk?"

"I was going to say she may have seen that page late in the game, well after Danny was charged. Maybe even right when the trial started. Too late for her to drop the charges."

Lauren rolled her eyes. "Right. You know it's never too late."

He shrugged. "There's no way to prove she did it on purpose. I'll just have to remember to watch my back if we ever have a case together again." He stopped talking, leaned in toward Lauren, examining her face. "Are you okay?"

"Um-hum."

Eli raised an eyebrow, questioning her reply.

"When you saw me yesterday I was wearing a *ton* of makeup. That's why I look worse today."

He nodded.

"But I do have a chipped zygomatic bone."

"A chipped zygo ... what?"

"That's what I said when the doctor told me. It's your cheekbone. Chipped it when I slammed into the sidewalk." She gently brushed her fingertip across the bruise.

She pointed to her knee. "And I have to wear this brace for a while. When Tony saw me yesterday, he almost told me to go home." Lauren chuckled. "But then realized there would be no one to make a record. So he decided to *let* me stay."

"You are an important part of the process."

"I knew there was a reason I liked you so much." She grinned. "But seriously, you get it, how important a court reporter's job is to the legal process." Lauren looked into his eyes, into the face of someone she'd grown close to over the past couple of weeks.

"What? Did I miss a spot shaving?"

"No. I'm just glad that we're, you know, friends. I don't have enough of those in my life." Lauren blinked back a tear. "Sorry. The fall the other night has left me a little ... emotional."

344

"Don't apologize. You've been through a lot."

Lauren pressed a finger to the edge of her eye. "How's Daniel doing?"

"He's a happy guy. I think he'll be okay. Dominick met him when he was released yesterday. I think for now Daniel's going to stay with him. I'm not sure what his long-term plans are, if he's going to stay in town or return to New York. Whatever he does, I hope he stays clean."

Lauren nodded.

"Daniel is not the only happy guy around. I can actually say I'm ecstatic." He cocked his head to the side as if in thought. "Don't get to use that word much."

"Have you ever?"

He shrugged. "No. But what's even better, justice prevailed."

"It would have been nice if justice prevailed from the beginning."

"Yeah, well, it's certainly not a perfect system."

"And knowing Dominick, he'll be forever in your debt, which will equate to free food and coffee for life."

"Whoa. Free food?" He stroked his chin as if in deep thought. "This day just gets better and better."

Lauren placed her writer in its gray bag, grabbed a zipper on each end and closed them in the middle.

"Are you happy the trial is over and you'll be out of here?" Eli nodded at the judge's bench.

Lauren surveyed the room. She was glad the trial was over, that much she knew. But something changed inside her these last few weeks, making the idea of spending her working life here in the confines of this space less appealing than it used to be. The drab, neutral-colored walls looked more drab than usual. Even the large windows couldn't lessen the feeling. To her it felt like the courtroom was letting out a long overdue sigh, that after all the years of hearing nothing but negative things, people's anger, grief and pain laid bare, the room could no longer take it in, no longer contain it, and began leaching decades of built-up sorrow. Lauren thought if she did stay she might begin to absorb the room's atmosphere, leaving her with her own aura of sadness.

Lauren shook her head slowly. "You know, after that first day of the trial, it was like I'd never left. And I thought it would be hard to leave once it was over. I mean, it was so easy to fall back into a routine. Part of me will miss that," she took one more look around the room, "but right now I'm happy to be out of here."

He nodded, then pointed at her bruised face. "When you're feeling better, text me. We'll get together for that cup of coffee."

"Sounds good. Coffee. And lunch. After all, I helped you crack the case." Lauren grinned to let him know she was joking.

"I owe at least a dozen lunches for that. And if you ever need some free legal advice," he cocked his head in an exaggerated come-hither look, "just call me."

"Will do." Lauren added quickly, "But I hope I don't ever have to."

His voice grew somber. "Lauren, I don't know how I can ever thank you. You picked out the missing needle in the proverbial haystack."

She shook her head. "I wouldn't go that far. I know you would have figured it out."

He stood. "You have my gratitude."

"Yeah, yeah, yeah." She waved her hand, swatting away his remarks. "But you know what, we're going to have to have that lunch pretty soon. Once word gets out that you can get acquittals on 'slam-dunk,'" Lauren did air quotes, "murder cases, you're going to be in high demand. Your secretary will be scheduling your lunch appointments for you."

He shook his head. "No way."

Lauren nodded slowly. "Yes, it's true. People from all over the state are going to be calling you. You'll have so much work that you'll have to hire an associate."

"Hey, you just might be right about that." His smile reached all the way to his deep-set dark eyes, the lines around them deepening. "What a problem to have."

"I know, right?"

"Text me." He grabbed his briefcase off the table and did a slow, exaggerated swagger toward the door.

Lauren smiled. "I will." She went to the jury box and as she straightened each chair thought about his question and the answer she gave. Was she happy to be leaving?

Chapter Fifty-Five

Susan sat at her desk looking at her cell phone and laughing. She looked up as Lauren walked by. "It was so nice working with you again. I'm going to miss, Lauren."

"I feel the same way. I'm going to miss you too." *I can match you lie for lie.* "I'm just going to organize the exhibits, then I'm out of here."

"I'll need your security badge back." Susan held out her hand, palm up. "I forgot to get it from you yesterday. My bad."

Lauren patted the side of her bag, reached in, pulled out the rectangular laminated badge and slapped it into Susan's palm. "Here you go."

"And please make sure there's nothing of yours left in the refrigerator. Or the break room."

Lauren tidied up daily. There wouldn't be anything of

hers left behind. "Oh-kay, Mother. I'll make sure I clean up after myself."

Susan huffed. "There's no need for sarcasm." She looked at the clock on the wall. "Well, I'm off. I have an appointment." She fluffed the back of her hair with the palm of her hand. "And then lunch." She reached into her desk drawer, pulling out an oversized handbag, and stood. She did a little finger wave as she passed. "Bye, Lauren."

"Bye." She parroted Susan's finger wave, then flapped her hand to shoo away the secretary's lingering perfume.

Lauren pulled a sheet of paper out of her bag that she'd printed at home. It contained the caption of the case, *State of Wyoming vs. Daniel Throgmorton.* Lauren taped the piece of paper to an accordion file and then placed all the admitted exhibits in the case inside.

"Lauren, good, you haven't left yet." Tony stood in the doorway.

"Just making sure all the exhibits are together so Zoe can put them in the evidence room when she returns."

"I enjoyed seeing you, working with you."

"At first I wasn't sure subbing for Zoe was a good idea, but it turns out it wasn't as horrible an experience as I thought it was going to be."

"I will miss that biting humor of yours." He shook his head. "Does this mean you'll be willing to help us out again when Zoe needs a substitute?"

"Sure."

"Good to know. Don't forget to send us your bill."

"Oh, I won't forget."

"You heading home?"

"Yes. I'm going to go home and relax."

Tony looked at her as if he had more to say, but instead patted the doorjamb with his palm and turned. Over his shoulder he said, "Bye, Lauren."

Chapter Fifty-Six

October

*L*auren pulled to the curb, waited for a car to pass by, opened her car door and walked around to the sidewalk. "Sorry I'm late."

Sam waved away the apology. "That's okay."

"I thought for sure the deposition would be over at noon." Lauren stood at the outdoor table where Sam had made himself comfortable. "I should know better by now than to try to meet up for lunch when I'm working. Whenever I think a depo should be short and sweet, turns out not to be."

He stood, opened the door to the bakery and gestured for Lauren to enter. He followed her inside.

Lauren inhaled and smiled. "Smells so good in here." She looked around the room spotting a couple of empty tables. They went to the counter, studied the specials on the chalkboard menu and placed their orders with Hector.

He gave her a friendly nod as he took Sam's credit card.

"I thought I heard my favorite customa." Dominick appeared from the kitchen. "How you doin' these days? Haven't seen you lately."

"I'm working again so that's good."

He wiped his hands on his apron. "I see that's where you must have been this morning, all dressed up business-like."

"Yes. I'm done for the day though. How are you?"

"I'm great." Dominick turned his attention to Sam. "How are things with you, Detective?"

"No complaints. Staying busy."

Dominick laughed. "As usual I'm sure."

Lauren looked past the baker into the kitchen. Since there were no customers behind them, she asked, "How's Daniel doing?

"He's gone back home. Said he wanted a fresh start. He's got himself a job lined up delivering auto parts to different dealerships."

"That's good," said Lauren. She looked at Dominick and smiled to herself. He was his usual upbeat self.

"With everything that's happened to him here, I think he's ready to stay clean." Dominick pulled a towel out of his waistband. "I think he will."

Lauren nodded.

"Eli Dresser was in here a week or so ago. He told me about how you helped him win the case."

"No, he was exaggerating. He's a good attorney," said Lauren.

"I don't know, young lady. I think you're just too modest to admit it."

Lauren shrugged.

Dominick looked at Sam. "I saw you sitting outside. I figured you were waiting for someone. She's worth waiting for, this one is."

"I agree," replied Sam.

Lauren bent to look at the selection of pastries in the case, hiding her embarrassment at his remark.

The baker reached into the pie case and took out a large cinnamon roll, plated it and set two plastic forks on the plate. "My compliments."

Lauren straightened and looked at Sam. "Thanks," they said in unison.

"Should we eat inside or outside? Your choice," said Sam.

Dominick answered for them. "It's beautiful out. You two enjoy the weather while you can."

With a vanilla latte for Lauren, a black coffee for Sam, a white sack and an oversized cinnamon roll, they went out into the sunshine.

"Now you see why I can't lose any weight." Lauren pointed at the dessert.

"You look great ... I mean you don't need to lose any weight."

"Sorry, I don't usually say stuff like that." *I do think it though.* "I wasn't trying to force a compliment out of you."

"Are you sure you weren't?" He arched an eyebrow.

She smiled, appreciating his making light of the comment.

In between bites they talked. First about the weather, then about the case Sam was working on, the vandalism at the quarry. They'd arrested an ex-employee.

When the conversation slowed, Lauren asked the question she had on her mind since the night Patricia Holland tried to kill her. "What's happening with Chief Newell?"

"That's another reason I wanted to meet you for lunch. Ray turned in his resignation. Effective immediately."

"That is good news. There wasn't any way he could have stayed on as the police chief. Not with everything that happened."

"I know." Sam took a sip of his coffee. "But this way he saves a little face. No hard feelings."

"But he could also go to another town and become a cop there. Work his way up. There's nothing to stop him from doing that, is there?"

"He's in the process of making a plea bargain. He can't talk about the details with me, but I think his days in law enforcement are over. For good."

Lauren stopped mid-chew and waited for Sam to explain.

"He's willing to testify against his wife if she goes to trial for Mr. Bates's death. In exchange the county attorney ... special prosecuting attorney, excuse me –"

"It's not Martindale, is it?"

"No, no. This one is from Cheyenne. He's going to drop the one charge they had on him, the aiding and abetting after-the-fact."

The two stopped talking while a mother and her two children walked into the bakery. Once they stepped inside, Sam continued. "And the same prosecuting attorney – I can't remember their name – and Trish's lawyer are pretty close to working out a deal. They've offered to lower the charge from murder to manslaughter in Mrs. Archer's death if Trish pleads guilty to first-degree murder in Mr. Bates's death."

"A deal?"

"It's in the early stages."

"Sounds like she's getting away with murder. You don't hit an elderly person in the back of the head with an iron skillet and expect them to live."

"It's possible. And how did you know what the weapon was?"

"Eli told me. Sean Abram, he's an attorney who shares office space with Eli, is representing Patricia." She wiped her mouth with a napkin. "He told Eli it was found during a search of her home."

"Can't keep any information quiet in this town for long."

"But Eli didn't tell me about any plea deal."

"Like I said, it's in the early stages. But in a way it makes sense. You've also probably heard from Eli, that she's putting a lot of this on Alden. She claims he persuaded her not to call the police that night. It was his idea to order a new pizza, put it in the box, make it look like Margaret hadn't eaten it, implying that Throgmorton was likely involved. And –"

"And since Alden's dead it's her word against … it's just her word. Clever. Yes, Eli did mention it."

"The state is smart to make the deal. Might be hard to prove otherwise." He leaned forward in the chair and eyed the cinnamon roll. "You have room for dessert?"

Lauren thought about lying, saying she couldn't eat another bite. Instead she said, "Always." Then laughed. She stuck her fork into the end with the most frosting and took a bite.

After that they took turns digging into the pastry.

"Has the mayor decided on a new police chief yet?"

With his mouth full, Sam shook his head.

"Do you think he'll ask you?"

He swallowed. "No. I already told him I wasn't interested in the position."

Lauren's face lit up. "Does that mean he did ask you?"

"Just asked if I would be interested in applying." He put his fork down. "I'm not ready for that."

"Are you sure? I think you'd make a good chief of police."

"I'm good at what I do. Investigation. I don't know if I could be a good leader or if I would even want to be in charge. I think I'll let someone else deal with all the headaches it comes with. At least for now."

She scraped the last bit of frosting off the plate with her fork.

"I'm pretty sure that was the best cinnamon roll I ever had." Sam patted his stomach.

"I totally agree." Sitting here with Sam, the sun warm on her back, Lauren thought the afternoon just about perfect. She hadn't felt this relaxed in a long time.

They both were quiet for a long moment, each in their own thoughts. Sam finally stood and put his empty cup in the paper bag. He held it open. Lauren crumpled her sandwich wrapper and let it drop inside.

They walked to Lauren's car. She unlocked the door and Sam opened it for her. "Thanks for lunch."

He smiled at her. "You're welcome. This bakery is beginning to grow on me."

"Another fan. I knew once you tried some of his desserts you'd be hooked."

"I wouldn't go that far. It's partly the company."

Lauren felt her cheeks grow warm.

Sam cocked his head to the side. "I've been thinking. You know what we should do?"

"What?"

"We should take a drive into the mountains on Saturday. We can check out the fall colors. Then stop someplace on the way back and have dinner. That is, if you're not busy."

Lauren's hazel eyes brightened. "Yes – no, I'm not busy Saturday. And yes, that sounds like fun."

"Pick you up around eleven then?"

"Sure. Eleven works."

"Great. Then it's a date."

She slid in behind the wheel and he shut the car door for her. He gave a tiny salute.

Lauren tugged the seatbelt, buckled it and watched Sam stroll down the sidewalk, hands shoved in his jeans pockets.

It's a date. It's a date?

Acknowledgements

I'd like to thank the members of Nite Writers of Cheyenne. Their input in my writing process has been so helpful on many levels. Belonging to this critique group has helped me grow and improve as a writer.

I wish to thank Dean Jackson for sharing his expertise on police procedure in Wyoming, making my storytelling more accurate.

My editor, Chris Rhatigan, also deserves a thank you. His suggestions and feedback were invaluable.

To my brothers Chris and Butch, thank you for the extra set of eyes, helping to ensure the final manuscript shines.

About the Author

Merissa Racine was born in the Bronx, and grew up on Long Island, New York. When she was a teenager her family moved to Florida, where she lived for several years. Missing the change of seasons, she left the Sunshine state and settled in an even sunnier place, Cheyenne, Wyoming, where she grew to love the open spaces the High Plains offers, including views of the Rocky Mountains.

She became a court reporter while living in Miami and continues to be a court stenographer in Cheyenne. Merissa's career in the legal profession provides the authentic flavor to the Crawford Mystery series.

When not working or writing, she loves spending time with her grandchildren, baking and trying new recipes, gardening, hanging out with her two dogs, Roz and Maya, and her cat, Zelda.

Dear Reader: If you enjoyed my book, please consider leaving a review on Amazon or Goodreads or Barnes & Noble.

YOU CAN CONNECT WITH ME AT:
www.merissaracine.com
www.facebook.com/authormerissaracine
Twitter: @merissaracine
Instagram: #racine55

Made in the USA
Coppell, TX
14 December 2021

68602156R00203